Katie MacAlister

DRAGON STORM

A Dragon Fall Novel

HODDER

First published in Great Britain in 2015 by Hodder & Stoughton
An Hachette UK company

1

A CIP catalogue record for this title is available from the British Library

Paperback ISBN 978 1 473 61118 4
Ebook ISBN 978 1 473 61119 1

Typeset in Times

Printed and bound by Clays Ltd, St Ives plc

Hodder & Stoughton policy is to use papers that are natural, renewable and recyclable
products and made from wood grown in sustainable forests. The logging and manufacturing
processes are expected to conform to the environmental regulations of the country of origin.

Hodder & Stoughton Ltd
Carmelite House
50 Victoria Embankment
London EC4Y 0DZ

www.hodder.co.uk

... nal romance novels:

'An instant classic!' *RT Book Reviews*

'Buffy...pleasingly crossed with Bridget Jones' *Telegraph*

'Katie MacAlister has an easy voice that brims with wit and fun' *Everything Romantic*

'[MacAlister's] world-building is excellent' *USA Today*

'Wild [and] zany' *The Best Reviews*

'The paranormal romance equivalent of soul food' *Errant Dreams Reviews*

'A humorous take on the dark and demonic' *USA Today*

'Smart, sexy and funny – Katie delivers!' Christine Feehan, *New York Times* bestselling author

'With its superb characterization and writing that manages to be both sexy and humorous, this contempary paranormal love story is an absolute delight' *Booklist*

'A book rich with humour, loaded with sexual tension, and packed with interesting, if sometimes slightly off-beat, characters' *Romance Reviews*

'Readers who delight in satiric romances will want to learn the rules of *A Girl's Guide to Vampires*' Midwest Book Review

About the author

Award-winning *New York Times* bestselling author Katie MacAlister has a passion for mystery, a fascination with alpha males, and a deep love of history that qualifies her perfectly for the fiction she writes. She lives with her husband and dogs in the USA.

www.katiemacalister.com

Also by Katie MacAlister and available from Hodder:

Love in the Time of Dragons

The Silver Dragons
Playing with Fire
Up in Smoke
Me and My Shadow

The Dark Ones
A Girl's Guide to Vampires
Sex and the Single Vampire
Sex, Lies and Vampires

Dragon Fall
Dragon Fall

Way back in 2003 when Aisling and Drake first hit the ground running, my then editor Laura Cifelli always had my back with the dragons. Although she's no longer working in the publishing industry, Laura has been of great help to me by running her eyes over my current dragon books, and for that, I'm dedicating to her all of Constantine...er...all of Dragon Storm.
Baltic is still mine, though, Laura.

Acknowledgments

I'd like to thank the following members of my awesome street team for working so hard for global domination... er... spreading the word about my books. And for being so patient with my many demands. You guys rock!

Amanda Whitbeck, Amy Lochmann, Andrea, April Parmelee, Barbara Bass, Bridget McElroy, Cadra Hebert, Candice Allen, Cathy Brown, Cely Havens, Chantal Clem, Charlene Fraley, Cheryl Ann Moore, Chickermunker Brown, Christine Brooks, Dawn Addleman, Dawn Henry, Dawn Oliver, Deana Peterson, Erin Havey, Gabrielle Lee, Heather Mottel, Heather Savio-Wolf, Holly Adamson, Iris Pross, Jennifer A. Rollins, Jennifer M. Albert, Jennifer Quirke Clavell, Jennifer S. Markowski, Julia Hovermale, Julie Atagi, Kala Bartic, Kat Thomas, Kate Williamson, Kathryn Chasteen, Kathryn Reid, Katie Fortenbacher, Katie Wall-Gomez, Kayla Lindberg, Kimberlee Gardner, Kristina Spargo, Kylie Hicks, LaJean Rodewald, Laura, Laura Hondl, Laura Weber, Leona Merrow, Linda Townsend, Lisa Boyce, Lisa Partridge, Lori Moreno, Lynne Kinniburgh, Mandy Snyder-Johnson, Marcie Damiano Kimura, Mary McCormick, Melissa Deen, Michelle Biller, Michelle

Meinhold, Misty Snell, Nettie Wray, Nikki Harris, Nikki Lhota, Pat Conroy, Peg E. Olkonen, Rebecca McElravy, Rebecca Taylor, Rebecca Vargas, Sabrina Ford, Samantha R. Lemaster, Sandra Masche, Sandy Musil, Sharleen Wells, Shiloh Gibson, sopranosmolder, Stacey S. Lewis, Stacey Schleisman, Stacia Ahlfeld, Summer Steelman, Susan Giddinge, Susanna Jolicoeur, Susanne Adamson, Tammy Gahagan, Teresita Reynolds, Teri Robinson, Theresa McFarland, Tina Suntheimer, Tiphney Waldon, Toni Cameron, Tonia Wert, Tonya Clenney, Tori, Tracy Goll, and Veronica Godinez-Woltman.

DRAGON
STORM

DRAGON
STORM

One

"Baaaaa."

Constantine of Norka, once the famed warrior leader of the sept of the silver dragons, jerked upright from where he had been dozing in the weak morning sun. The air in the small sitting room was still and quiet, the gas fireplace gently blowing warmth into the room, leaving him with a sense of being frozen in an endless moment of time. He cocked his head and held his breath, wondering if his mind had been playing tricks on him.

"Baaaaaghhh." The distant noise started out in a thin, mechanical approximation of a sheep's bleat, but ended in what sounded like the cough of an asthmatic toad. One with a heavy smoking habit.

"Constantine!" The bellow that followed the horrible noise all but shook the stone walls of Dauva, permeating even the farthest point of the castle. The gas jet sputtered as if in sympathy with the noise.

With a martyred sigh, Constantine got to his feet, taking a corporeal form despite the desire to fade into the spirit world where no one could see him.

"Is it too much to ask you to keep your deviant sexual aids from my son?"

Constantine pursed his lips, crossed his arms, and leaned against the wall as the dark-haired, dark-eyed man strode toward him, clutching in one hand a fast-deflating blow-up sheep clad in fishnet stockings.

"What makes you think that belongs to me?" Constantine asked, taking a conversational tone. He'd found through centuries of experience—not including the time while he had been inconveniently dead—that doing so had the tendency to enrage Baltic even more. And there was nothing Constantine liked better than to push Baltic's emotional buttons. It was payback, he felt, for all that he had suffered at the hands of his once friend, later mortal enemy, and, finally, reluctant housemate. "That guard of yours—what is his name? Pablo? Pachelbel? You know who I mean, the one who enjoys both sexes—he has many such things. You do me wrong to accuse me when it likely belongs to him."

"His name is Pavel, as you well know," Baltic said, breathing heavily through his nose.

Constantine gave himself two points for the loud nose-breathing. He wondered if he could get Baltic to grind his teeth—that was a worth a full five points, and getting that would push his daily Aggravating Baltic score over twenty. It would be a new high, and one that he had long sought. "Pavel? Are you sure?" Constantine rubbed his jaw as if he was considering the fact. "Doesn't sound very likely to me. You've probably gotten it wrong. Such things happen when you get old, you know."

Baltic's jaw tightened, but Constantine didn't see any sign of teeth grinding. "I'm younger than you, a fact you like to forget."

"Well, strictly speaking, you *were* younger than me. But my beloved Ysolde had my spirit form summoned just a short two years ago. That makes you older."

Baltic took a deep breath. "I don't know why I bother conversing with you. You never have anything of intelligence to say and simply use up air."

"You talk to me for the same reason you begged me to join your sept—you know I am the superior wyvern."

"You are deceased," Baltic said, enunciating with deliberation. "You are a former dragon. You no longer exist. You are, in effect, a nonentity, and the only reason I went against my better judgment to include you in the sept of the light dragons is because Ysolde—*my* Ysolde—pleaded with me to keep you from being without a sept."

Constantine sniffed. He disliked the way the conversation was going and said the one thing he was sure would derail it. "Perhaps Ysolde got that sheep with the charming garters and stockings to distract your lusty attentions. Perhaps she is tired of you, but is too kind to tell you. Perhaps she desires another. Say, for instance, me..."

"Out!" Baltic bellowed, pointing dramatically at the door. The sheep gave a feeble "Baaagh" before the last of the air slid out of it with a rude noise.

"Out?" Constantine brushed his fingernails along one arm, and lazily examined the results.

"Out of my castle! Out of my sept, and my hair, and most of all, out of my life!" Baltic yelled, glaring at the sheep when it uttered one last rude noise before falling limp in his hand. He flung it to Constantine's feet.

"My beloved Ysolde wouldn't allow you to kick me out," Constantine said, buffing his fingernails again. Should he give himself a point for the wisp of smoke that emerged from one of Baltic's nostrils? No, he decided after a moment's thought. All dragons tended to such things when under the grip of strong emotions. Even he had the tendency to get smoky about the nostrils when he was riled.

"She is *not* your beloved!" Baltic snarled. "She is my mate! She always has been, and she always will be. Stop referring to her in that obscene fashion."

"It's not obscene. I love her."

"You do not. You simply desire her because you know she prefers me to you." A little smile curled the edges of Baltic's lips. "She is *my* mate, not yours."

Constantine sadly deducted three points for that blow. Dammit, how was he to reach his goal of twenty irritation points if Baltic made zingers like that? "I gave my life so that she might live. If that does not show eternal dedication and love, then I do not know what would. Besides, my beloved Ysolde enjoys having me about the castle. She told me so just the other day."

"Then she is in the grip of brain fever, and I will have her doctored as soon as possible." Baltic pointed to the deflated plastic sheep lying in a heap on the floor. "See that you keep your sex toys from my son."

"I can't help it if Alduin favors my beloved Ysolde with his shared fascination of all things...unique...," Constantine said with a little smile of his own. He figured mentioning Baltic's eighteen-month-old child would push his former foe over the edge, but, alas, Baltic had a better grasp on his temper than Constantine liked.

"Ysolde has many tastes, all of them unique, but she

does not try to corrupt our son with them. See that you do the same." Baltic strode off before Constantine could goad him further.

"Fourteen points," Constantine said with morose pleasure, idly looking through the window to the wilderness beyond. Dauva, the home of Baltic and Ysolde, and all the rest of the light dragons (whose numbers totaled six, including Constantine), was situated outside of a remote town in Russia. Constantine had been born and raised in a region that was now Poland, but he much preferred the south of France and its balmier climate.

"Only fourteen points, and I used my best weapons. What has gone wrong with my life that I find myself here, at this time of year, cold even when it's sunny? I am unwanted, undesired, and alone," he said aloud. No one answered him, which was exactly what he expected. All too frequently he'd found himself on the outside of the family that was made up of Baltic and Ysolde, and their two children. Even Pavel, Baltic's right-hand man, was a part of the family, whereas he, Baltic's oldest friend and once (for about two minutes) mate to the lovely Ysolde, existed on the fringes of their attention. He'd never felt so ghostlike and insubstantial as he had the last few months. Lately, there were days when he didn't even bother to slip into his corporeal state.

A woman with long blond hair bustled into the room, speaking as she did so. "...told him that we do too have to worry about it, but will he listen to me? No, he won't." Ysolde de Bouvier stopped in front of Constantine, a toddler perched on her hip. "Honestly, there are times when I could just whomp him on the head with the nearest blunt object."

"If you're speaking of Baltic, I would be happy to be of service. Bashing him over the head is always high on my list of things to do," Constantine said, rising and making a formal bow before chucking the child under his chin. Constantine had a love of babies that led him to making secret forays into the child Alduin's chambers, bringing toys that he thought would amuse.

Alduin said, "Uncle Connie!" and held out his arms for Constantine.

"Lovey, Uncle Constantine doesn't want to hold you, not after you've been helping Uncle Pavel make baklava. You are one sticky little boy, and are going to have a bath just as soon as I'm done here." Ysolde set the boy down and gave him a look of mock regret before turning a smile onto Constantine. "Good morning. Why do you look so sad?"

Constantine affected a martyred look. "Baltic was here belittling me."

"Pfft," Ysolde said dismissively, whapping him lightly on the arm as she did so. "Since when do you let that upset you?"

"No one wants me," he found himself saying. Part of him cringed at the words, but the other was a bit relieved he had finally spoken of the darkness that had claimed him of late. "No one even likes me except you."

"Of course people like you. You're smart, and you have a good sense of humor, and you're handsome as all get-out. Just look at you! You're all broad shoulders, and pretty browny-gold eyes, and your manly stubble could make any woman swoon."

"Does it make you swoon?" he asked without hope.

"No, but I'm madly in love with Baltic, so I don't

count." She glanced down at his feet. "Wallowing in self-pity never did anyone good. Do you have a moment, or are you busy planning something with your blow-up doll? If so, please let me have a little talk with you first. It's really most important. No, lovey, leave the sheep alone. Uncle Constantine doesn't want to have to clean honey out of that faux sheepskin before he uses his toy."

"It's not mine," Constantine started to say, but stopped because he made it a point never to lie to the woman who had claimed his heart so many centuries before... and then stomped all over it in her mad dash to fling herself into Baltic's arms.

"Of course it's yours. I was in the sex toy shop with you when you bought it. But that's of no real matter. I want to talk to you about this curse."

Constantine frowned. "The one afflicting the dragons, or is there a new curse?"

"No, that's the one."

Alduin clasped the deflated sheep to him with a cry of delight. Both Ysolde and Constantine ignored the sheep's plaintive baa. "We've had a message from Aisling Grey—she's mated to Drake Vireo—that they have a Charmer planning to break the dragon curse by using Asmodeus's ring."

"Did they find the ring, then?"

"I gather so, or they wouldn't have a Charmer lined up to break the curse. Now they're looking for something that belongs to Asmodeus to use to help break it... a talisman of some sort."

Constantine scratched his chest, wondering if he should make his daily declaration of love to Ysolde now, or if it would be better to wait until Baltic was around. He decided on the latter—it was usually worth an irritation point or two. "What has this to do with us?"

"I told Aisling that you'd get the talisman."

He gawked at her, outright gawked, something he never did. "Ysolde—"

"Now, hear me out," Ysolde interrupted before he could express his displeasure at the idea of her volunteering him for any such act. He was a wyvern...or at least he had been. He once led the famed silver dragon sept, with well over five hundred members! He was no mere flunky to be sent after a trifling artifact, and he told her that.

"It's not trifling. It's hugely important."

"I do have some standards, after all," he said stiffly. "Just because I don't actually lead a sept anymore doesn't mean I don't have important demands on my time."

Ysolde pursed her lips and raised an eyebrow at the deflated sheep.

Constantine sniffed again and looked away.

"I know you have lots of important things to do," Ysolde said soothingly. "But don't you see just how ideal you are for the job? For one, you think well on your feet."

He had opened his mouth to protest, but at the words of praise, hesitated. "This is true. But—"

"And you can blink in and out of the physical world, which no other dragon can do."

"Yes, but—"

"Not to mention the fact that you are clever enough to get in and out with the artifact before anyone even knew you had been there."

"Again, you speak the truth, but I must point out—"

"And you would be saving all dragonkin," Ysolde ended triumphantly. "You would be a hero!"

"I'm already a hero," he protested. "I am the wyvern of the silver dragons! I fought the dread wyvern Baltic—"

"Whom I love."

"And defeated him at the gates of Dauva—"

"Which he rebuilt."

"And gave my life for yours," he finished with a dramatic sweep of his arm. "That act alone makes me a hero."

"Constantine," Ysolde said in a distinctly chiding tone of voice. Constantine did not care for it at all. "I can't believe you'd be such a coward."

"Coward?" he asked on a gasp of disbelief. "Me?"

Ysolde brushed a bit of lint from her sleeve. "Well, what else am I to think when you, a brave and heroic dragon who has sworn himself to my eternal service, won't even do this one simple little task for me?"

"If you think such ridiculous statements are going to bait me into jumping to your command, you are mistaken," Constantine said dryly, but despite that, he began to seriously consider her request. He didn't want to do it for a number of reasons, but he had to admit that when he reached the state where the high point of his day was irritating Baltic, he should reassess his life plan. Perhaps a little adventure would be just what he needed to shake himself of the sense of gloom that pervaded him of late. "You say this talisman belongs to Asmodeus?"

"Yes. He's the head of Abaddon, isn't he?"

"So I've heard." He thought about that for a few moments. "Asmodeus is sure to be in Abaddon."

"I assume so."

"I don't like going to Abaddon," he said slowly, still considering the idea.

"Really?" Ysolde looked mildly curious as she picked

up Alduin. "I've never been there, myself. Baltic always said that the demons of hell—sorry, Abaddon—don't like to mess with dragonkin, so I didn't think we had much to worry about. Other than the curse, of course."

"It's not for that reason—" Constantine stopped himself from continuing. It would do little good to explain his preferences to her. "All I would need to do is find this object, a talisman? Is there one in particular, or will any item do?"

Ysolde pulled a strand of her blond hair from her child's sticky grip. "I think it's safe to say you can get anything that suits the bill."

"Which means any object of a personal nature to the being in question." Constantine thought about this. He added, more speaking aloud to himself than to her, "I suppose I could get in Asmodeus's palace and find an object quickly enough. I wouldn't have to spend any time in Abaddon, not that—" He remembered he wasn't alone, and once again bit down on his words. With a brief nod at Ysolde, he added, "Very well. I will undertake this quest for you, my beloved former mate. But only because I live for you."

"Oh, you do not. One day you'll meet a lovely woman who will make you forget all about me."

"Never will the sun set on a day in which I do not spend my time devoted to your welfare," he said, suitably dramatically. He thought of striking a noble yet humble pose, but she was watching her child at that moment, and he hated to waste a good pose.

"Uh huh." She rolled her eyes briefly. "I'd think that bringing about the end of the curse would be reward enough without the dramatic declarations. Just the thought of having the world be a normal place with all the septs able to talk to each other again, and no one at war, would be heaven compared to how things are now."

Slowly, so Ysolde would not notice, Constantine nudged the deflated sheep behind him. "I will pack my things. Where must I go to accomplish this burdensome task?"

"Pack?" Ysolde looked amused and curious at the same time. "I didn't know ghosts had luggage."

"Of course we do." He waited until she was looking at Alduin before snatching up the sheep, and holding it behind his back. "We have need of things just the same as you do. I wear clothing, do I not? I must shave, and bathe, or I would be unpleasant to be around."

"Yes, but you're a spirit. You can wear the same thing every day if you like, and I doubt if you'd stink if you didn't take a bath."

He pulled himself up to his full height, and shook his finger at her. Unfortunately, it was the hand holding the sheep, which baaed forlornly before he jerked his arm behind his back again. "Just because I'm a spirit does not mean I wish to appear unfashionable or be unclean!"

Ysolde giggled. "I'm sorry. I didn't mean to offend you. Of course you must pack your clothes and…" She glanced at his arm. "…accessories if it makes you feel better."

"You did not answer the question of where I must go in order to accomplish this mission."

"You are the cutest sticky child in the world," Ysolde said to her son when he started to sing in a high, singsong voice. "Hmm? Oh, the Charmer is evidently in Paris, so it's probably best if you get into Asmodeus's palace by one of the European entrances."

"Evidently?" Constantine picked out a word that made
him frown. "Do you not know for certain where the
Charmer is?"

"I don't know the Charmer personally—this is just
what was passed on to me." She dropped a kiss on her
son's head and started toward the door. "Thank you so
much for doing this, Constantine. I would tell you how
much I appreciate it, but it's so much more than just my
wishes that're at stake here. You'll free all the dragons,
and be a hero forever. All right, my darling, it's the bath-
tub for you..."

Constantine's frown grew darker as he absently watched
the love of his life leave the room, his thoughts, for once,
not on his own grievances, but instead reaching back in
time to his youth. "I wouldn't do it if Bael were not safely
confined in the Akashic Plain," he said softly to himself.
"But as he is, and has no way to get out, then I will act the
hero. I will save the dragonkin. I will take my place in
the annals of modern dragon history. I will do this for the
glory of the silver dragons."

With a little nod at his noble intentions, he took the
sheep to his bedroom, already planning the items he
would need on the trip. It didn't occur to him until later
that he never once thought of undertaking the job for
Ysolde's sake alone.

Two

The spirit world version of Seville looked almost identical to the real world version, if you discounted the fact that there was a slight sepia haze over everything, and all the angles were a degree or two off from what they should be. Constantine never could figure out why the spirit world wasn't filled with broken, straggly headstones, willow trees draped with long creepers that moved eerily in the breeze, and odd little spots where fog seemed to cling to the ground, obscuring the vision, but giving flashes of movement that disappeared as soon as one looked at them.

"In other words," Constantine said aloud as he examined the dark red door before him, "it should look properly spooky. This just looks like something out of an old film."

No one answered him, which was right and proper, since the mortals couldn't see or hear anyone who was in the spirit world, even though it occupied the same space as the mortal world. Unfortunately, that also meant that while Constantine could bear items into and out of the spirit world, he couldn't use anything that had its origins in the mortal world, which meant the notes he'd taken regarding accessing Asmodeus's palace could only be read if he summoned the energy to switch to a corporeal form.

"As if getting to Spain just to enter the blasted palace wasn't enough of a drain of my corporeal energy," he grumbled to himself, moving around the side of the sepia-stained stone walls of the building to what he judged was a relatively concealed position. "Now I have to use up precious energy just to read the notes."

He stepped into the real world, an act that he always thought of as walking through a slightly translucent curtain, glancing around quickly to make sure no one saw him suddenly appear. Since he was in a small side yard containing trash bins and tall, spiky wrought-iron fence rails with nary a person in sight, he relaxed and pulled out the paper with his notes.

He strolled to the street and compared house numbers. "This is the right location, but it doesn't look very 'entrance to hell' to me. Hmm." He glanced up and down at the passersby, but none of them looked particularly demonic. "Well, I'll just have to risk that I wrote down the correct number."

Getting into the house via the spirit world was easy enough—he simply entered through a slightly ajar window at the back of the house. But once inside, he ceased to be in what was the spirit world version of reality and instead found himself in Abaddon, that hell-like place where demon lords ruled and sorrow abounded.

"What an uncomfortable place. I can't imagine why anyone would wish to stay here," he told himself as he wandered down a hallway, noticing that the angles in the Abaddon version of the spirit world were even more askew than in other locations. "Which is why I need to just find the damned talisman and get out as quickly as possible."

He turned a corner and saw two people standing together, a man and a tall, whiplike, slender woman.

Demons. He froze, waiting to see if they had the ability to see him in the spirit world.

The one facing him glanced briefly in his direction, but gave him no more attention than if he'd been a whisper on the wind.

That didn't stop Constantine from tiptoeing past them, a fact that made him angry with himself. He was a wyvern, dammit! He was a man who'd battled in countless wars, protected his beloved sept of silver dragons, and fought desperately to save those who were weaker. Wyverns did *not* tiptoe. And yet when it came to the point where he was brushing by the pair in the narrow hallway, he held his breath.

The demons didn't stop talking. Constantine let out an inaudible sigh of relief and hurried past them down the hall, then turned into an open space that contained a cluster of doors, each bearing spiked metal bars. Clearly, this was the dungeon area, the last place he wanted to be.

He hurried past the first door, trying hard not to look at the occupant while at the same time deciding where Asmodeus was likely to have his private quarters. Upstairs, definitely upstairs.

Just as he passed the last door, there was a rush of air,

and a woman appeared at the bars, yelling at the top of her lungs. "I demand to be released! You, you can tell your boss that he's going to incur the wrath of not only the dragons, but the Charmer's League, as well as the officials in the Otherworld. They don't take the imprisonment of their members light— Hey."

Constantine, who froze when the woman started shouting, turned slowly to look at her. She was gazing at him with a curious look on her face, part annoyance, part astonishment. She pointed at him. "Hey, you're not a demon."

With a glance up and down the hall (thankfully empty), he shifted out of the spirit world and into his corporeal form. "You could see me? How is this possible? No one can see me when I'm in that state. No one but another spirit, and you—" He studied her closely for a moment. "You are not a spirit. Did you say Charmer's League?"

"That's right, I'm a Charmer. You're a ghost? What are you doing in Abaddon? You look like a dragon, but dragons don't get resurrected."

"They do if they are exceptional specimens," he said smugly. "I am Constantine Norka, wyvern of the silver dragons." He made a formal bow.

Her eyes widened, then narrowed into little slits of glittering blue. "Did Kostya send you after me? He did, didn't he? I told him that I would be perfectly fine getting the talisman, but he kept insisting that he'd send someone else in to get it. Honestly, you dragons are the stubbornest beings I've ever encountered."

Constantine eyed the woman, then pointedly looked at the bars.

"Pfft," the woman said, waving a dismissive hand at them. "I know what you're thinking."

"I doubt that," Constantine said with a wry little smile.

"You're thinking that I was hasty in trying to get the talisman myself, rather than waiting for whoever Kostya came up with to do the job, but that's unfair. It was just the merest coincidence that those stupid guards were upstairs when I came through the tear."

"The tear in what?" he asked, wondering if there had been a less arduous way to enter the palace.

"Space, of course. I hired a demon to tear open space so I could sneak in and out without anyone noticing me. And it would have worked, too, if those guards hadn't chosen that moment to walk into the room." She sighed. "Oh well, it's a moot point now. If you're the man Kostya hired to help steal the talisman, then you can let me out and I can get it and be on my way."

Constantine thought quickly while absently taking in her appearance. She wasn't overly tall, but had dark red hair that seemed to move around her as if it had a life of its own. Her eyes were a clear, warm blue that reminded him of the Aegean Sea. She had freckles on skin the color of very milky coffee. He couldn't make a judgment on her breasts, since the sweater she wore concealed them, but he was willing to bet she had a nice ass.

It was at that point he realized he was ogling her hips in an attempt to qualify that guess, and with an effort, snapped his gaze up to her face.

She was glaring at him. "Had a nice gander, did you? Need a little longer? Maybe you'd rather take pictures so you can look at them later?"

"Er...no. That's not necessary." He thought for a moment. "Unless you really wouldn't mind, that is. Just a few informal shots would suffice."

She grabbed the bars, yelped, and released them, but stood as close as she could, her nostrils flaring in a manner that he found wholly enticing.

Ysolde never flared her nostrils in just such a way. He froze at that thought, immediately filled with an odd sort of guilt. How could he even compare this woman, this Charmer of curses, with his beloved Ysolde?

"Look, I don't know who you are—"

"I told you: I am Constantine Norka. It used to be Constantine of Norka, but I am now very much with the times. I have a mobile phone. I listen to podcasts. I twat."

The woman's eyes rounded in utter surprise. "You... *what*?"

"I write twats. Not often, and only Ysolde and her oldest son follow me, but I frequently use my mobile phone to post pictures. Ysolde always has nice things to say about them. What is your name? I keep thinking of you as 'unnamed woman' and it's getting annoying."

She stared at him a moment longer, then blinked, taking a deep breath before answering, "My name is Bee Dakar. And the word you were looking for, but horribly mangled, is *twit*. You post tweets on Twitter, not that other word, which in case you didn't know, is sexually objectifying and demeaning. So don't use it again."

"Is it? No, you are incorrect. I'm sure it's Twatter."

"Trust me, I know what I'm talking about. *I* have more than five hundred followers on Twitter."

He pursed his lips a moment, then pulled out his mobile phone and touched a button. He held it up to the bars.

The woman named Bee looked. "I'll be damned. Twatter."

"I told you."

"It's clearly a rip-off of the original site. It's probably run by some horrible virus guys who are infecting your computer every time you use it. Now, will you get me out of here, please?" She carefully grabbed a section of the bars that wasn't spiked, and rattled it. "I'm not having a ball here, so I'd like to get the talisman and beat it before the next idiot guard runs into me."

"I don't think that would be wise," Constantine said with regret. He was a bit startled to find that he genuinely felt regret at the idea of leaving Bee trapped in Abaddon, but he prided himself on being a thoughtful man, one considerate of the feelings of others, especially those who were weaker or more vulnerable. He informed Bee of this fact.

"What do you mean, you're only thinking of what's best for me?" She rattled the bars again, her eyes all but spitting little slivers of blue at him. "Okay, one, I didn't ask you to protect me. Two, how is leaving me to rot in Abaddon going to benefit me? And while we're on that subject, what's this crap about me being weak and vulnerable? I'll have you know that I'm a damned good Charmer, so good that people who know me don't even try to slap a curse on someone because they know I'll simply un-work it."

"You are not immortal," Constantine pointed out.

She all but bristled at him. "So?"

"I am. If I am caught by the guards who saw you the first time, I can simply slip into the spirit world and they will not be able to touch me. But if you are with me under the same circumstances, then you would be left alone to face their wrath."

"We're not going to be caught—" she started to say, but Constantine interrupted.

"I'm already dead. They can't kill me again. They can't even destroy my spirit—the most they can do is banish me to the Akasha and demon lords do not have that ability without some outside assistance. But you . . ." He shook his head. "I would not risk your life in such a manner. You are safer here, where you are not incurring the wrath of demons or their lord."

"Are you freakin' nuts? How on earth can you tell me that I'm safe when I'm trapped in a cell in freakin' hell!"

"Abaddon is not hell," he felt obliged to point out. "It is what mortals frequently think of as hell, but the two things are not the same—"

"Argh!" she screamed, shaking the bars more vigorously.

Constantine nervously glanced up and down the hallway. Much though he had enjoyed the interlude with the woman named Bee, he was using up far too much of his precious energy by standing there in a corporeal state. Not to mention risking discovery by the very same guards who found Bee.

"I can't believe you're being so pigheaded about this! Wait, you're a dragon, I guess I *can* believe it."

"Madam," Constantine said formally, giving her a look down his nose. "I understand you are in a less than desirable situation, but there is no need to fling about insults."

"If you don't let me out of here, so help me goddess, I'll make sure you are the saddest dragon who ever lived," she threatened, breathing heavily.

"Once I have the talisman safely outside, then I will inform Kostya of your whereabouts. I'm sure he will send an armed group to free you, one that will be able to protect you against any retribution for your escape."

"Who knows how long that will be!" Bee wailed. "I

can't wait around for you to round up a posse to rescue me! I don't need a posse—I just need you to get this door open."

"I'm sorry. It just wouldn't be prudent."

"Prudence be damned! If you're going to send dragons to break me out later, you might as well do the job now and save everyone trouble."

"I cannot protect you should we be caught," he repeated. He felt sorry for her, and wished the situation were otherwise, but he was a man who protected those who were weaker, and he wasn't about to put Bee in danger if he could help it. "A group of dragons who are well armed and able to keep you safe is a different matter. Cease trying to grab me, woman. I'm not going to allow you to drag me up against those spikes."

"Gah!" Bee, who had indeed been trying to reach through the spiked bars to grab him, slapped her hands on the wall instead. "I don't understand why you won't listen to me! I swear to you that I won't get caught again, so you don't have to worry about what happens—no! God damn it, Constantine Norka! Don't you fade away on me!"

Her voice took on that slightly muffled, distant sound that voices did when heard from the spirit world.

"Don't you think I can't see you, because I can! Oh! You're smiling at me? You bastard! You rat bastard! How dare you leave me trapped in here."

Her voice took on a strident quality that he felt was unbecoming, and gave the impression that she was a shrew. He strode quickly down the hallway, making a mental note to warn her about that at a future time.

"Constantine! Come back here, you coward! I'll get you for this, see if I don't! I'll make you suffer like no one has made—"

Her threats were cut off when he slipped through a doorway, closing the door softly behind him. Idly, he wondered why she was able see him when no one else could, but decided that was a puzzle that would have to remain for another day.

It took about half an hour for him to locate Asmodeus's private chambers. They were empty of all but a small birdcage hanging next to a magnificent canopied bed. Constantine hesitantly approached the cage, not seeing a bird in it. At the bottom was an oddly shaped lump, one that stirred a certain amount of dread in his belly. He wouldn't put it past Asmodeus to have something hideous caged next to his bed, something vile and repulsive.

He stepped closer, and the lump rolled over. "Hi!" it said brightly.

Constantine stared in mingled horror and disbelief. The lump had turned out to be a head, a human head, a disembodied human head.

"How ya doin'? I'm Gary. It's Gareth, really, although everyone calls me Gary, so I gave up trying to correct them. Demons!" The head laughed. "Awful with names, aren't they? It's like they just can't keep them straight. I suggested mnemonics to try to remember my name, but you know how they are—testy, very testy. Don't like to be corrected, either."

"Er..." Constantine cleared his throat. Although he wouldn't put it past Asmodeus to keep the head of his latest victim as some sort of a grisly prize, he hadn't expected it would be so...chipper. And friendly. Not to mention animated. "Hello. Are you...forgive me, but I was not expecting to find anyone in here. Is there just your...head? Nothing more?"

"Nopers, just a head. Used to have a body, but one day I was sitting by a creek doing a little fishing, and suddenly my pole jerked. I thought I must have caught a whopper of a catfish, and was playing him out when *whoosh!* Up rose a leviathan that chomped me right in two. Talk about inconvenient!"

"I can imagine so." Constantine glanced around, but there didn't seem to be anyone else in the room. It had to be the head talking to him, not to mention the fact that it was looking at him with bright gray eyes, and a smile on its lips. "Most people die when they are consumed in such a manner."

"I know, right? Luckily, I'm not mortal. I'm a knocker, see?" The head rolled over to the side of the cage and rapped its forehead against it a couple of times.

"Do you mean like a door knocker?"

"No, no, knockers are best known as being spirits that live in mines, and warn the miners when a collapse is imminent. We knock on the walls to warn them. Knockers. Get it?"

"Ah, just so."

"Nowadays," Gary continued sociably, "we tend to watch over industrial outfits, and let the locals know when their safety is being compromised. Most of us work in some form of environmental regulatory agencies, you see. So when a local power plant is about to explode, or a dam burst, or fracking is creating sinkholes, we warn people about the damage before it happens. Of course, most of the mortals don't pay us any attention, but eh." Constantine imagined that if the head could shrug, he would do so now. "We do what we can."

"I can't imagine why a demon lord would be interested in that unless he was causing the damage."

"Well, that's an interesting story on its own. When the leviathan started gobbling me down, I knew I'd be okay so long as there was one part of me it didn't get. And luckily, he was the precursor to a horde of demons coming out of a portal at the bottom of the creek. One of them picked up me up as a tribute to his master, and that's all she wrote." Gary leaned back against the bars, a contemplative look on his face. "It's not a bad life, really. Asmodeus is a big ole grumpy-pants, but he mostly leaves me alone. I get fed—although Asmodeus doesn't understand why I need feeding since I don't have a body, but a head can't survive on nothing, you know—and there are plenty of demons to talk to. They tend to be a bit shouty and a bunch of Negative Nellies, but there you go. It's Abaddon, after all. So who are you? You're not a demon, are you?"

"I am a dragon," Constantine said, squaring his shoulders. "I am Constantine, wyvern of the silver dragons."

"Coolio! I've never seen a dragon before. Although the way you kind of shimmered into being gave me the impression you were some other sort of being. You know, like poltergeist, or one of those creepy Japanese ghosts with black eyes and long, streaming hair that suddenly appear out of nowhere." Gary blinked for a moment, then did a little head bobble. "Oh, wait, that's from a movie, isn't it? Sometimes I get creepy beings mixed up. What's a dragon doing in Abaddon?"

"Looking for something." Deciding that the head posed no immediate threat to either him or his mission, Constantine turned to scan the room. The likeliest offering was a large onyx bowl sitting on top of a narrow bookcase that was inexplicably filled with bones.

"Oooh, is it a scavenger hunt? I *love* scavenger hunts!

We used to have the best ones at the Knockers Local Forty-two annual parties. We'd have to go hunting for days for this item and that, really obscure stuff, you know? Graphite moderators, and core cooling pumps, and oh yes, there was that time in the Ukraine where we had a party that lasted a week, a whole week. My team was close to winning the scavenger hunt—all I needed was a separator drum—and wouldn't you know it, the whole thing exploded." Gary gave a little shake of his head. "That was one hell of a party until it got out of hand. What items are you supposed to find?"

"A talisman of some sort." The words slipped out before Constantine thought better of it, but after a few seconds' thought, he decided that it most likely would not be a problem if a disembodied head knew what he was after. "Something personal."

"Gotcha. Something personal. Hmm." Gary squinted, and looked around the room while Constantine examined the contents of the large bowl. It held a collection ranging from engraved idols to figurines bearing ominous rust-colored stains, to several sharp scalpels. The last were also stained, a fact that had Constantine hurriedly moving past the bowl.

"I know! I have just the thing!" Gary rolled over to the other side of the cage and pointed his nose toward a small tufted footstool. "See that? If you lift the lid, there's a small wooden chest inside. I saw one of the demons snooping around in there one day when he thought I was napping."

Constantine set down the book he had picked up, and moved over to the object in question. The cushioned top of the footstool lifted to reveal a recess, which did indeed contain a small chest. He pulled it out and opened it just as Gary added, "It has a finger in it."

Constantine twitched as he gazed down at the unsightly digit. It was small and dark and withered, as if it had been mummified.

"I think it's Asmodeus's finger. At least, I know he is missing a pinky, and I assume that's his." Gary watched with interest as Constantine tucked the chest away in his shirt. "What else are you looking for? Like I said, I'm a whiz at scavenger hunts. I can help you find some other stuff, if you like."

"That won't be necessary," Constantine told the chatty head. He inclined his own in thanks. "This will suffice. Good-bye."

"Aw, you're leaving?"

Constantine slipped back into the spirit world, Gary's words trailing eerily after him. "I was hoping you could stay to lunch. It's been forever since I had someone to talk to who didn't want to go into details of the latest flesh rending going on downstairs…"

Three

The path out of the palace wasn't particularly fraught with danger, but Constantine, aware of the shriveled finger stashed away on his person, took the precaution of pausing whenever he came to a room or hallway that was occupied. Most times, the demons were passing through on some errand or other, but it wasn't until he had almost reached the exit that something ruffled his equanimity.

"—don't think you have the authority to give me orders," one demon was saying to another when Constantine rounded a corner. Beyond the demons, the doorway to the mortal world was in sight. His spirits rose; he was almost out of Abaddon, away from the risk of discovery, and better yet, about to become the savior of the dragon world.

"I am a demon third class," the second demon protested. He poked the first demon in the chest as he spoke. "While you are only fourth class. By the laws of Asmodeus, you must attend to my bidding."

Constantine edged around the pair, realizing they were the same two demons he'd seen when he first entered Abaddon.

The first demon gave the second a shove, almost sending the latter reeling into Constantine. He danced to the side and hurried past the two demons, heading straight for the door to Seville.

"You'll go on report for that," the second demon said, pulling out a notepad and writing something down. "As well as for refusing to kill the mortal. Let me see, your name is Vian?"

"Don't report me!" the first demon shrieked. His demeanor had changed in a blink of an eye. Constantine had a moment of sympathy for him—punishment in Abaddon for an infraction of any sort was bound to be arduous, to say the least. But it was the demon's next words that had him pausing at the threshold of the door. "I'll do it, I'll do it. But...the mortal is a Charmer. What if she does something to me before I can kill her?"

Constantine spun around to stare at the two demons, his body suddenly tense with the fight instinct. Were the demons talking about Bee? No, they couldn't be. Why would Asmodeus imprison her if he simply wanted her dead?

"She has few powers here," the second demon was telling the first. "You worry for nothing. Besides, the order came from Lord Asmodeus himself. He has no time to deal with her, and wants to be rid of any potential trouble."

"But she could do things to me. *Unnatural* things," Vian the demon whined. "You could kill her quite easily. You're bigger than me, and a demon third class."

"Which is why you'll do what I tell you to do, and I tell you to go kill the mortal."

Constantine was past the pair and halfway to Bee's cell before he was out of earshot of the arguing demons. Damnation, he hated feeling like he had been backed into a corner, but there was nothing for it—Bee was too important to the salvation of the dragons to allow Asmodeus to kill her, not to mention the fact that he had always prided himself on being a sensitive dragon, one who understood emotions better than most. True, no one else seemed to see that side to his personality, but he was confident that someday he would be known for his sensitivity. He knew he'd never be able to live with himself if he allowed the unprotected Bee to be slaughtered when he could prevent such an atrocity.

Bee was sulking in the back of her cell when he approached the door. Although he could no longer hear the demons, he knew it was merely a matter of seconds before one of them came to fulfill his horrible plan. Constantine stepped out of the spirit world just as Bee looked up and made an exclamation.

"Oh, it's you. Come to taunt me some more, have you?" she asked with an injured sniff.

"Unfortunately, no."

"Unfortunately?" she asked on a gasp. "You really are a bastard, aren't you? I mean, I know you dragons are cold-hearted, and think only of yourselves, and never do anything without being paid for it first, but—"

"Be quiet, woman!" Constantine said loudly, and before she could recover, added, "Get to the back of the room."

She put her hands on her hips, and stuck her chin out in

a stubborn manner. "I like that. You think you can tell me what to do? Well, I have news for you—"

"If you don't get out of the way, you'll be burned," Constantine snarled.

Bee blinked at him for a couple of seconds, her mouth opening and closing, but evidently she thought better of continuing, and scurried to the back of the cell.

Constantine, with a quick look up and down the hall, took a deep breath, summoned as much of his energy as he dared risk, and blew dragon fire onto the bars.

The bars turned gold, then white, shimmered for a moment, then crumbled into gray, ashy dust.

"Well, why didn't you do that in the first place?" Bee asked, running forward.

"Because it takes a tremendous amount of energy." Constantine held out a hand for her, his fingers closing around her narrow wrist as he turned and took off down the hallway at run. "We don't have much time, and we're going to have to fight our way out past two demons, but at least I can distract them while you get through the door."

"What on earth are you talking abou—"

They rounded a corner and skidded to a halt. Rather than the two arguing demons, which Constantine was fairly confident he could handle, or at worst, occupy long enough for Bee to escape, the hall was filled with at least a dozen demons who appeared in all shapes and sizes of human form.

"Bloody hell," Bee said at the same time Constantine swore, "Sins of the saints!"

"I thought you said there were two?" Bee smacked Constantine on the arm before gesturing toward the packed hallway. "There's got to be at least ten demons there."

"There *were* only two," he said tersely, his mind racing with a way to get out of the situation. "And for the record, this is exactly the situation I discussed with you earlier. You remember it: it was the reason why I said I couldn't release you."

"And yet you did," Bee said with thinned lips. "Thanks a lot, dragon."

"Bite me, Charmer," he said without thinking.

Bee turned a shocked face to him that almost made the situation worthwhile. But before he could grab her and run in the opposite direction, the mass of demons parted as if by magic, and one giant of a man lumbered toward them. He stared first at Bee, then at Constantine, and, after a moment's thought, said in a deep voice that seemed to come from the very bowels of the earth itself, "Lord Asmodeus wishes to see you."

Constantine was about to respond when the giant gestured in the air and spoke a few words in an ugly, grating language.

It was as if someone had thrown over him an invisible net weighted down by anvils. He moved a step back, holding out his left arm to see if he could even lift the limb. The movement was slow and reluctant. "What have you done?" he demanded to know, looking from his arm to the demon. "What spell have you cast upon us?"

"Not spell, bête noire," the giant said, and with one massive pawlike hand on Bee's shoulder, and the other on Constantine's, he marched them up the hallway.

"A bête noire? That means black beast, doesn't it?" Bee struggled against the paw, trying to peer around him to look at Constantine. "Are you going to turn into the Hound of the Baskervilles or something?"

"Hardly. I am a dragon." Constantine tried to remember what a bête noire was in the immortal world. He had a vague feeling it had to do with being ostracized from something, but couldn't figure out why this demon would cast such a thing.

"Hey, I don't suppose you're open to bribery, are you? Because I have almost unlimited wealth at my disposal via my clients, and I'm sure they would be happy to reward you very generously indeed were you to let me go." Bee tried to smile up at their captor. "What you do with the dragon is none of my business."

The demon rumbled in a negative manner. Constantine glared across the giant's chest at her. "It's like that, is it?"

"You're a ghost. They can't hurt you." Her lips narrowed. "Besides, your objection to rescuing me was based on concerns about my safety. I'm simply trying to relieve you of that burden so that you have only yourself to take care of. Leave off, you big oaf! You're hurting my shoulder."

"You'll notice I'm not complaining," Constantine said righteously, even though his shoulder was beginning to ache under the steely grip.

"I notice you're not doing anything to free us, either," she said quickly, and twisted around to land a punch on the demon's crotch.

It didn't bother the giant in the least. He kept marching onward, dragging them down a maze of corridors.

"I didn't become one of the most well-respected wyverns of my time by fighting against a situation I cannot win," Constantine answered irritably.

"You could escape into you-know-where," Bee said with a sidelong look at the demon.

"I already told you that I would not leave you behind in that manner. I dislike having to repeat myself."

The demon stopped before a pair of massive wooden double doors bound in iron, and dropped Constantine in order to throw open both doors, then more or less tossed them both inside the room.

Constantine staggered forward, but managed to keep from falling onto the floor. Until the demon flung Bee in after him. She slammed smack-dab into Constantine, sending him toppling backward, their foreheads hitting each other with an unpleasant *thunk*.

"Ow!" Bee said, vigorously rubbing her forehead. "Crap on a shingle, Constantine! Your head is as hard as a block of cement."

Constantine rubbed his own forehead before getting to his feet, and was in the act of extending his hand to help Bee up when a voice echoed down the large, high-ceilinged room.

"Con man!"

"What the—" Bee started to say, turning around to look behind him. Her face went through a series of expressions, from disbelief to fear to outright horror.

Instinctively, Constantine spun around and put himself between Bee and whatever it was that was threatening them.

A man strolled toward them. He was of middling height, had dark hair and eyes, and a complexion that would normally be called swarthy when it wasn't applied to what was, Constantine assumed, the premier prince of all the demon lords. He carried a small brass birdcage, in which resided a grinning Gary.

"Long time no see!" the head called to him, the lines around his eyes crinkling with delight. "I was just telling

Asmodeus what a nice chat we had, and he said that since
I enjoyed it so much, he'd see that we could do it again.
And here you are! Hi, I'm Gary. Are you with Connie?"
The last was spoken to Bee.

Constantine swore to himself for his mistake in leaving Gary where he could spill everything. Either he'd done
it deliberately, taking in Constantine and leading him to
believe the former knocker was a friendly, harmless being,
or Constantine had the worst luck in the world in the form
of befriending a monumentally clueless, overly chatty head.
Either way, they were in a very serious situation, one out
of which Constantine didn't see an immediate way. Especially not with Bee to consider.

"What . . . on . . . earth . . ." Bee's face was a mask of confusion and terror as Asmodeus stopped before them. Her
gaze was locked on the birdcage, and Constantine had a
suspicion she was a hair's breadth away from screaming.

"That is Gary," he said with resignation at the situation, gesturing toward the head.

"Gareth, really, but no one calls me that. Hi!"

"And I believe this is Asmodeus." Constantine, whose
mother raised him to respect his elders, even if they did
head up a bunch of demons, bowed formally. "I am Constantine, wyvern of the silver dragons."

Asmodeus, whose eyes were as black as what remained
of his soul, glanced briefly at him. Constantine felt the
look as a whip of pain through his being. "Former wyvern,
surely."

Constantine inclined his head. "Unfortunately, that is
so. I have yet to convince the current wyvern to return
the position to me. I would like to take this opportunity to
object to the bête noire that your minion has placed upon

me. As you pointed out, I am a spirit, and as such, I do not have a part of the war between you and the dragonkin."

Bee stopped staring at the head in order to look in frank astonishment at him. He couldn't warn her against speaking, but trusted she had enough wits about her to keep from letting Asmodeus know he was bluffing.

Asmodeus's eyes closed halfway. Power crackled around him in tiny little black whips that occasionally reached out and snapped painfully against Constantine. "You presume much, spirit. You will return to me what you stole from my chamber."

Annoyed, Constantine looked at Gary.

The head made a little apologetic bobble. "Sorry, Connie."

"My *name* is Constantine."

"My lord!" A demon burst into the room began bowing and groveling. "My lord, there is word of your rival— Oh. Er. I have news of which you would be interested."

Asmodeus sighed, and set down the head before striding over to the demon. The two spoke together in low tones.

Gary gave Constantine an apologetic moue. "The thing about the finger just kind of slipped out. I mean, I wasn't going to tell Asmodeus why you were there, but we got to chatting, and you know how it is—one thing led to another and I happened to mention you were at the chest, and . . . well, I am sorry, truly I am. I hope this won't affect our friendship."

"There is no friendship," Constantine said acidly.

Gary looked horrorstruck. His mouth hung open slightly until his lower lip began to quiver. To Constantine's surprise, tears filled the knocker's eyes. What was worse (Constantine hated tears from any anyone—man, woman, or disembodied head) Bee seemed to have a sudden change of character, for instead of gawking at the head as she had been ever since she clapped eyes on it, she rounded on him.

"Well, now look at what you've done, you great big ghostly baboon! You've made Gary cry."

"It's all right," Gary said nobly, his voice thick as he turned away. "I deserve his scorn. What sort of a friend grasses on his buddy? A horrible sort, that's what. I am not worthy of his friendship."

Bee punched Constantine in the arm, gesturing at the head, who was now quietly sobbing against the bars of the cage. "Well?"

"What is it you want, woman?" he asked irritably. He was watching the demon and Asmodeus closely, trying to lip-read the former, although he'd never really mastered the skill.

"Apologize to him!"

"To Asmodeus?" Constantine shook his head. "It will serve no purpose. It has all come to pass as I feared, and all because I stopped to save your life. It is your fault we are in this situation."

"My fault? I like that! You're the one who said you could disappear where no one could get you. Well, I don't see you doing it."

"Because you're here," he snapped. "If you hadn't allowed yourself to be captured in the first place—"

"I was trying to do my job and help you dragons, not that you deserve it—"

"I am a spirit. Your foolish trip here could not help my cause at all."

Bee took a deep breath and whomped him on the chest. "Stop being pedantic and apologize to Gary."

"For what?" He didn't look at the head. Ever since he had been a small boy child, he had been overly affected by tears.

"For hurting his feelings. I'm sure he didn't mean to tell Asmodeus what you did."

"No, I didn't. I truly didn't!" Gary wailed from where he sat on the floor. "The last thing I wanted was to endanger our friendship."

"Five minutes' acquaintance does not make a friendship," Constantine tried to point out, but he knew in his heart that it was useless. Bee had clearly taken Gary's side and would no longer see reason.

"Not if you're a pigheaded asshat, no," Bee said, glaring.

For some insane reason, Constantine wanted to laugh. He wondered at that fact, since it had been a long time since anyone but Ysolde had had the power to tickle his sense of humor, and yet, the irate woman next to him had done just that.

It wouldn't do to let her see that, though. "Wyverns do not apologize," he said stiffly, and turned his back on the still sobbing Gary.

Behind him, he heard the soft murmurings of a woman who was attempting to soothe the hurt feelings of a disembodied head. That lasted for half a minute before Asmodeus snarled something to his minion that had the demon prostrate on the floor, begging for mercy.

Asmodeus stalked away from him, heading straight to Constantine. He held out his hand. "Return to me what you have taken."

Constantine hesitated.

"If you were thinking of escaping into the spirit world," Asmodeus said in a deceptively mild voice, "you should dismiss the thought. The bête noire placed on you has the effect of limiting you to a corporeal form only. Permanently. There will be no escape for you."

Constantine frowned and, without looking at Bee, tried to step into the spirit world.

Nothing happened. The leaden weights he'd felt cast upon him kept his form as solid as any living being.

In a rush of irony considering how long Constantine had railed against being a slave to the energy needed to maintain a physical form, he wished he was back to the way he had been before the demons had found him. There was something peaceful about lounging around the spirit world rebuilding his energy.

Asmodeus's hand did not waver, but his voice sharpened. "Return the object now."

Slowly, wondering just how much Gary had told the demon lord, he reached into the inner pocket of his shirt and deftly manipulated the small box, sliding the desiccated finger from it. He dropped the finger onto Asmodeus's outstretched hand.

Asmodeus looked at the finger, and lazily considered Constantine and Bee. "You risked much to seek a strange object, one that apparently has no importance to anyone but me."

"We're quirky that way," Bee said, and once again, Constantine had to fight the urge to smile.

"One would almost think that it was the type of object that held meaning to you, rather than the object itself," Asmodeus continued, his eyelids dropping until he was once again watching Constantine through half-closed eyes. The tendrils of power snapped and danced around him, leaving the air charged with static.

Asmodeus's presence seemed to leach the heat not only from the room, but from Constantine himself.

There was a rustle of movement behind him, and a hand suddenly slid into his, cold fingers making him start. Constantine kept his face from expressing surprise that Bee would be driven by fear into taking comfort from physical contact with him. The last thing he wanted Asmodeus focusing on was her. He shifted slightly to the side, so as to better block the demon lord's view of her. "You may think what you wish, naturally, but I will repeat that I have no parcel in your war with the dragons. Your desire to parlay with me will be of no use."

"Parlay," Asmodeus said softly, and gave a little smile.

Constantine braced himself against the effect of the smile.

"An odd choice of word and one that is meaningless here. What does have meaning is a former dragon seeking an object of a personal nature to me, and the presence of a Charmer who was caught sneaking around, presumably on a task of a similar nature."

Bee's fingers tightened around his. He squeezed hers in a silent warning against speaking. He wanted all of Asmodeus's attention on himself. "The Charmer is mortal. She does not know the ways of the Otherworld."

Bee gave a little gasp, but thankfully, kept silent.

"That much is obvious," Asmodeus agreed. His gaze flickered over Constantine. "Just as it's clear to me that dragons would not seek such an object unless there was a need for it. For instance, in the use of the breaking of a curse."

"Oooh," Gary said, clearly over his crying fit. "Is that what you were—"

Asmodeus shot a look at the head, who promptly swallowed what he was going to say.

"Perhaps," Constantine said with studied nonchalance. If he could have pulled off the act of buffing his fingernails as he had with Baltic, he would have, but he knew there was no way he could face down Asmodeus in the same manner. Instead, he rallied the arrogance natural to all wyverns, and wrapped it around himself. "If that is the case, there will be others seeking the same."

To his amazement, Asmodeus smiled a second time. It was just as painful as the first. "And they would be just as unsuccessful as you find yourself, spirit."

Constantine was formulating a suitably vague threat as a response when Asmodeus snapped his fingers, and two wrath demons, part of the elite group that headed up all of the minor demons, burst into being, and stood attentively beside him.

"Shackle them," he said, gesturing toward Constantine and Bee. "I do not have time to get the information I need from them until I deal with this latest situation."

"I do not think—" Constantine started to say, but the breath was knocked out of him when the two wrath demons lunged forward, a long length of chain suddenly manifesting itself in one of their hands. He thought briefly of attacking them, grabbing Bee, and making a dash for the door that led to the mortal world, but Asmodeus, who now stood at the door watching, quelled that idea.

And so it was that two minutes later he found himself attached to Bee by means of a leg shackle, being walked (slowly, due to the chains) down a flight of stairs to Asmodeus's dungeon.

"I am so not happy about this," Bee muttered to him, kicking her foot so the black metal chain rattled ominously.

"Well, *I* think it's a good look for you both," said Gary, happily beaming at them from the cage that Bee still held. "You are a very nice looking couple to begin with—wait, dragons have something different than a girlfriend, don't they. It's a…it's a…mate, that's it! So you're Connie's mate? How long have you been together?"

"About three minutes," Bee said, looking at her watch.

"She is *not* my mate. She is mortal. And a Charmer. Neither of which are qualities I seek in a mate, even if I was seeking one, and I'm not, because I had one and she opted to tear out my heart and stomp on it while rushing to the arms of another."

"And then there's the fact that you're a dead dragon," Bee said with annoying candor. "I mean, yes, I'm not getting any younger, and to be honest, I wouldn't mind having a steady relationship with a man who wasn't so self-centered that he couldn't see beyond the end of his nose, but that doesn't mean I'm willing to consider that sort of a relationship with a dragon. Especially not a spirit one. That's just…weird."

Constantine looked at her with dislike, marveling to himself that one woman could stir so many emotions. "I'm sorry that my presence disgusts you."

"Aww," Gary said, giving Constantine a sympathetic look. "I don't think that's very nice of you, Bee. Connie is very handsome in a rugged, dangerous sort of way. Sure, he's a spirit, but he's a very corporeal spirit. It's almost like he's not a spirit at all, really. I'd certainly be happy to be his mate." A wistful expression drifted over his face. "I don't suppose you'd consider a male mate?"

"I'd consider it," Constantine said, noting that they were now on the floor that contained the door that led out of the palace. Their guards turned them in the opposite direction, however. "But I am not seeking a mate. As I said, my heart has been broken by the glorious Ysolde, and it will never recover. For the love of the saints, woman, will you stop kicking your feet around?" He stopped with an aggravated and exaggerated *tsk*.

"What?" The look Bee shot him was confused. "I'm not kicking you."

He turned to face her, grabbing her by the upper arms, and gently shaking her. "I've taken all the abuse from you that I will tolerate!" he said loudly, before adding in a much softer voice, "When I disable the guards, be prepared to turn and run."

"Oooh! Are you breaking out?" Gary asked excitedly, then immediately looked contrite.

Constantine allowed himself a second to sigh, then snatched the birdcage out of Bee's hand, and swinging it wide, slammed it upside the head of the first wrath demon.

"Whee!" shouted Gary.

The demon, caught off guard, windmilled into the second one, whom Constantine nailed on the side of the face with a backswing.

Gary, hooting triumphantly as he rolled around the cage, clamped his teeth down on the guard's ear, and yelled mostly unintelligibly, "You guyth run! I'll handle theeth two."

"Don't leave Gary—they'll torture him!" Bee shrieked when Constantine slammed the cage a second time into the first guard. The demon howled and clutched his head. Evidently Gary hadn't let go of his ear when Constantine swung the cage a third time.

It wasn't easy to try to match his stride with Bee's as

the pair of them ran shackled together down the hall-way, the screeches of the downed demons following after them, and in the end Constantine shoved Gary's cage at Bee, and hoisted her over his hip, the position an awkward one, but allowing him to run with relative ease.

"What the hell do you think you are doing?" Bee yelled, her voice thick and breathless, no doubt due to being bumped around on his shoulder. "Mother of pearl, I can't breathe! Let me down!"

"Mmfrrmph!" Gary mumbled from behind Constantine, and made a wet, unpleasant noise that sounded suspiciously like someone spitting out the ear of a particularly unlucky demon. "They're up! They're coming after us! Run, Connie, run!"

"My name"—Constantine gritted his teeth against the pain of Gary's cage whacking against his legs with every stride—"is Constantine."

"I'm seeing spots," Bee gasped, her voice somewhat strangled. "Everything is going black. I need air!"

"They're about ten yards and closing," Gary yelled.

Constantine made a heroic effort, and leaped forward to the door that led outside the palace, almost ripping it off the hinges in his desperation to get out of Abaddon.

The late afternoon sun of Seville blinded him momen-tarily, but he had enough sense to keep moving forward even though he couldn't see.

Which is why he stumbled over a trash can, and sent himself, Bee, and Gary crashing forward into a black wrought-iron fence.

Four

"Ow," came a pathetic moan from the birdcage. "I think I chipped a tooth. Wow, was that exciting! I was all 'oh noes, we're gonna die' and then whammo! Connie sprang into action and was super dragon dude! That was the most exciting thing that's ever happened to me, and that includes having the behemoth eat my body!"

Constantine, dazed for a moment when he hit his head on the grill, got groggily to his feet, prepared to fight off the demons if they had followed them out to the mortal world. He glared down at the shackles that still bound him to Bee, wondering idly how he was to protect her if he couldn't order her away.

"Bloody hell," Bee moaned from where she sprawled on top of a trash can, her legs hanging from the side. She pulled herself up to a sitting position, and promptly rolled off the can and onto Gary's cage, jerking Constantine's leg as she fell. "Bloody buggery hell."

"Oh dear, fashion malfunction," Gary said, rolling over onto the back of his head to stare up into where Bee's chest was pressed against the cage. "A couple of buttons are undone, dear, and evidently you've ... popped out, for lack of a better phrase ... of your unmentionables. Which are a lovely shade of mauve, I do have to say. Aren't they nice, Connie? The lingerie, not the parts that are popped out of it, because really, once you've seen one breast, you've seen them all."

Constantine, being a male, and having natural instincts and urges common to those of his gender, couldn't help looking, but he realized almost instantly that congratulating Bee on her nice breast wouldn't be appreciated, and instead pretended not to watch when she swore and wrestled herself into what was admittedly a very feminine bra. "I don't think we're likely to be set upon by the demons who confined us, but we should move from this spot."

"Because they can't enter the mortal world, you mean?" Bee asked, taking his hand when he offered it. He helped her up, and plucked off bits of banana skin and leaves of lettuce from where they clung to her back. "I know some demons can, but don't you usually have to summon them?"

"Wrath demons are different," Constantine answered. He frowned down at where Gary had righted himself in his cage, and was looking around with interest. "We should put him back, but I hesitate to open the door again."

"I don't want to go back!" Gary protested. "Asmodeus will just stuff me back in his bedroom, and that's no fun. He hardly ever talks to me, and he doesn't even like to watch movies together. Can't I stay with you guys?"

"We are shackled together, have a demon lord and who

knows how many demons after us, and have to get from Seville to Paris without being captured again," Constantine said, putting the birdcage on top of a garbage can. "We have no need of a disembodied head to add to our concerns."

"You can't just throw him away," Bee said, standing still when Constantine tried to walk away.

Gary's lower lip trembled again.

"Why not?" Constantine asked, averting his eyes.

"Because he's a person, not a piece of trash you can just dispose of because it's not convenient to carry him around."

"I don't want to be a burden," Gary said with a moist sniff. "I don't want to stay if I'm not wanted."

Bee nudged Constantine with her foot. "Tell him he's wanted."

Constantine considered her for a moment. "You can't expect me to believe that you've formed a bond with a disembodied head after seeing it for a just a few minutes."

"I can and I have," she answered, tipping her chin up in a defiant move.

"And I don't have time for a debate on the subject," Constantine said, thrusting the cage at her. "Let's leave before we regret standing here arguing about whether a head is worth all this trouble."

"He is," Bee said at the same time that Gary said happily, "I knew you wouldn't leave me! We're like best buds."

"We are nothing of the sort." Constantine tried to lessen his stride so that he and Bee weren't walking at odds, but their rhythm was off until he took her hand in his.

"Bros. We are bros together," Gary said, nodding. "Bros in solidarity."

"Stop that!" Bee said, jerking back as if Constantine had struck her, and pulling her hand from his. "I don't like being touched by strange men."

"Dudebros. Is that a word? It should be. We are dude-bros together against the world."

"Do you favor women, then?" Constantine couldn't keep from asking.

"Not in the sense you mean," Bee said, trying to pull her hand back when he took it again. "I just don't like people who I don't know pawing me. Especially men like you."

"I am not a men like me," Constantine said indignantly, throwing grammar to the wind. "When I paw a woman, she enjoys it."

"Ha! I bet that's what women tell you, but no woman likes to be treated like something paw-worthy. Let go of me!"

"What's not paw-worthy?" Gary asked. "I mean, people like to be touched. Men like to be touched. Women like to be touched. Knockers who are just heads like to be touched. Especially by men who have nice hands with long fingers, and sensitive, caring-looking knuckles."

Constantine and Bee both stopped to look at the head, who bore a faraway look.

"Well, I don't like to be touched," Bee said, walking forward purposely until she reached the limit of the chain. "Not by women, disembodied knockers, or even dragons with dreamy knuckles."

"My knuckles are not dreamy," Constantine said quickly, and waited for her to turn back to him before he moved forward, once again taking her hand. "They are simply hands, nothing more. Functional in a manly sort of way, but just hands. They are certainly not worth commenting about."

"For pity's sake, will you stop trying to paw me!" Bee stopped and whirled around to face Constantine, banging the birdcage against his hand in an attempt to loosen the grip. "I'm not interested in you, okay? Talk about arrogance—will you get it through your thick head that just because you're handsome, and have eyes that are the color of an old piece of amber, and hair that you think at first glance is just brown, but then you realize is shot through with dark honey, doesn't mean that I'm going to swoon at your feet just because you keep touching me."

"Do you dislike men?" Constantine asked.

"No! At least, not in the sense you mean." She tugged down her shirt in an irritated manner. "I just don't like being manhandled, okay? Not even by handsome dragons. Especially by handsome dragons."

"You say the word *dragon* like we are some sort of beast. We are not human, but we are an ancient race, and have adopted human mores. We are polite, we are considerate—when it behooves us to be—and we have very nice manners."

"Ha! I knew a dragon once, and he was anything but nice. He was always grabbing me, and teasing me with his fire, which hurt like the dickens if you want to know the truth."

"You don't like dragons?" Constantine couldn't believe his ears. He'd met women who hadn't desired him personally, but never one who was prepared to damn all of the dragonkin.

"Let's just say that given past experience, I don't seek out your company."

Constantine stared at her in confusion, then did the only thing he could think of. He kissed her.

She started when his mouth claimed hers, but despite his guess that she'd push him away, or slap him for such a brash move, her mouth opened under his and welcomed him into her sweetness.

For about five seconds—but at the moment his tongue touched hers, she was suddenly a hellcat, one intent on getting as far away from him as possible.

"What...mother pus-bucket!" She wiped at her mouth, her eyes blazing at him. "What do you think you're doing? Who gave you permission to molest me?"

"You enjoyed it," he said by way of a non-answer.

"I did no such thing," she said, clearly aghast.

"You didn't slap me for kissing you," he pointed out. "That's what women in books always do."

"Of course I didn't slap you. I'm not the slapping sort of woman." Her gaze dropped to his mouth for a few seconds and seemed to be unable to move on. "I can assure you that outside of gothic romances, women don't need to resort to something so cliché as a slap to the face to get the point across that a man's attentions are not welcome. Mace and pepper spray are more the modern woman's way to deal with that."

"I love kissing!" Gary piped up, apropos of nothing.

"I do not read gothic romances," Constantine said with dignity. "Well, not often. Only when I can't get a Georgette Heyer."

Bee stared at him, her face expressing disbelief.

"What?" Constantine asked, feeling defensive. "You don't care for books dealing with the manners and mores of mortals engaged in romantic escapades?"

"Not particularly, no. Manners and mores?" Her eyes narrowed a little. "You're not using the books as a source of information, are you?"

Constantine, well aware that he'd picked up the books in an attempt to understand how society had changed during the centuries he had been deceased, maintained an injured silence.

"Really?" Bee asked, giving him a little shake of her head. "I've never met anyone who is such an odd mixture of arrogance and naïveté."

"If you have finished abusing me simply because I have an inquiring mind—"

"I'm abusing you because you kissed me without my permission," Bee interrupted, poking him in the chest. "Don't do it again."

"I've never had to ask permission to kiss a female before," he said, a little outraged at the idea.

"Well, you'd better get used to doing so, because if you try playing sucky-face on anyone else without first asking, you'll find yourself on the receiving end of a foot to the crotch. Or worse."

"I do not care for rough sex play," Constantine said, adding as an afterthought, "with the exception of the use of restraints. Those can be quite titillating if they are used correctly."

"Oooh, yes," Gary agreed. "Silk scarves! Fur handcuffs! Those stretchy cords that people use to fling themselves off the sides of bridges!"

Bee shook her head again. "I don't believe this day. The whole thing, from this morning right on down to the point where you locked your lips on mine. It's all just a dream, isn't it?"

"So romantic," Gary said with a happy sigh.

"Perhaps I kissed you harder than I knew," Constantine said, looking closely at Bee. "You seem to be a bit rattled."

"I'm not rattled," she said with an exasperated sigh. "I just don't want you to go any further!"

He looked down the alley. "It would not be wise to stay here."

"No, I mean this." She lifted their joined hands. "Did you not hear me mention that I wasn't looking for a dragon lover?"

"Yes. I also heard you state that you were interested in finding a man."

"Look, my romantic life, or lack thereof, is not of any importance. I'm simply saying I don't want you trying to seduce me."

"Oooh," Gary said. "Seduction with manly hands."

"One kiss does not a seduction make," Constantine said abruptly, and assuming she had recovered from their enjoyable—if unexpected—kiss, he pulled her forward down the alley. "I'm simply holding your hand because it makes coordinating our movement easier if I can feel when you are about to start and stop."

"Fine." They walked for the count of twenty before Bee added, "Just so you don't get any ideas about kissing me again."

"I can't help the bad opinion you have of dragons." He paused at the end of the alley to glance up and down the street before continuing. "But I feel obligated to point out that I don't need to force myself where I am not wanted. Now, if you are finished suspecting me of base motives—"

"I like base motives," Gary said softly. "They can be oodles of fun."

"—then I'd like to discuss what steps we should take next."

Bee shot Constantine a look of disbelief. "I don't know why you're even asking what we should do, because the answer is pretty obvious to me. We need to get these shackles off, and then one of us has to go back into Abaddon to get that blasted talisman back."

"I have the talisman," Constantine said, taking in the population of the street with a couple of quick, assessing glances. There were a handful of people strolling the street, but since it was approaching the heat of the afternoon, many people were inside in air-conditioned comfort. But he saw no signs of demons.

"You do?" Bee shook her head. "I saw you give that… that thing back to Asmodeus."

"It was a finger, not a thing," Gary said. "You see, one day Asmodeus had a battle. I don't know who with, although the demons said something about it being vampires, but I think they were just trying to scare me. Anyway, there was this battle, and his finger got lopped off—"

"You saw me give the finger to Asmodeus, but that wasn't the only thing I took," Constantine said, ignoring Gary.

Bee stopped dead in the middle of the sidewalk, gawking at him. "You have a talisman?"

"Yes."

"Where? What is it? Show me."

"Not here. We are too close to the entrance of the palace, and although the demons won't come after us here, it would be best to not flaunt the possession."

They started walking again, pausing when a passerby, an elderly lady in black, smiled gently at them both, then happened to glance at the birdcage.

"Good afternoon," Gary said politely, and made a bob of the head that made Constantine believe that the knocker would have lifted his hat in polite greeting had he the requisite arm and hat.

The old woman shrieked, clutched a nearby light post, and began screaming in unintelligible Spanish.

Bee *tsk*ed, and peeled off her cotton sweater, which she threw over the cage with an apology to Gary. "Sorry, kid, we can't have you attracting undue attention."

"It's okay," Gary's voice came from the cage, now slightly muffled. He sounded unusually subdued. "I know I'm a pariah. Unwanted by mortals. Unloved. Ill-kempt to look at..."

Constantine would have rolled his eyes at the dramatic statements issuing from the cage, but he prided himself on never having been an eye roller when he was formerly alive, and wasn't about to start it now. "Do you know Seville at all?" he asked.

"Me? No, not a bit. I entered the palace in Paris. I don't know how we got to Spain," Bee said, glancing around with curiosity.

"There's a Paris entrance?" Constantine stopped at a corner. "I wish I'd known that. I was only told about this entrance." He glanced back toward the house that was the mortal world manifestation of the palace, hesitating for a few seconds. "I wonder if we shouldn't go back."

"Are you kidding?" Bee worked her hand free, and took a handful of Constantine's shirt, tugging him after her as she hurried around the corner. "You've got the talisman! Why should we go back in and risk capture again?"

"For a number of reasons. For one, it would be easier to get to Paris via a door in the palace than having to attempt to fly there while shackled together."

"Pfft," Bee said, waving the thought away. "We don't have to fly. We can take a portal."

"Oooh, a portal," came the muffled voice of Gary. This was followed by a pause, then, "What's a portal?"

"Hush. We'll tell you when we get there," Bee said loudly, ignoring the hoots of two male youths who just noticed their shackles. "I bet there's a portal shop somewhere in this town. It looks big enough. Drat. My phone is back in my cell. Let's find an Internet café, and we can look up local portal facilities."

"I have a smart phone," Constantine said somewhat proudly.

Bee shot him a considering look. "I always thought dragons had an aversion to technology."

"Most do not care for it, but there are some who appreciate it. I am one. I enjoy much of the new technologies. The episode with Twatter aside, of course."

Bee mouthed the word *Twatter* before shaking her head and halted when she reached a café with small metal tables painted white infringing on the sidewalk. "I really don't want to know where you found that site. Right, we can sit here and have a big glass of ice-cold lemonade, and you can locate the nearest portal place, and then we'll get ourselves to Paris, and have the shackles taken off, and I can Charm the curse. Sound like a plan?" She plopped down in one of the chairs and tucked Gary under the table.

"Would it be possible to get a glass of ice water? With

lemon?" the latter asked as Bee hailed a waiter. "I'm parched, and your sweater is making it a bit stuffy in here."

"Hush while we're around mortals who could hear you," Bee said, gesturing to a waiter before slanting a glance up at where Constantine still stood. "You can sit down, you know. It would allow my leg to be a bit more comfortable if you did so. I don't know why Asmodeus had them attached to us anyway, since he put the kibosh on you slipping into the spirit world. What point did the shackles make after that?"

"Asmodeus likes to throw people off balance. He says it helps make them vulnerable," Gary offered from under the table. "But honestly, I think he's just a big ole meany-pants, and he gets his jollies from messing with people."

"Hush," Bee reminded the head before tugging at the chain.

Constantine sat, but slowly. "Your plan does not have merit. Or rather, the part concerning a portal company does not. We will go to Paris, yes, but first we must remove these shackles. They make it difficult to walk, and I cannot imagine fighting while being so hindered."

"Fighting who? Demons?" Bee's voice dropped when a waiter delivered a tray of beverages to a nearby table. "Look, I want the shackles off just as much as you, but unless I'm very much mistaken, it's not going to be a matter of simply finding someone with some bolt cutters. Or a locksmith. These are a demon lord's shackles. They aren't normal."

The waiter finally gave them his attention. Constantine absently ordered lemonade for Bee, and a pitcher of ice water. "I know what they are, which is why I want them removed immediately."

Bee looked insulted. "It's not a barrel of monkeys being strapped to you, either."

Constantine was about to point out that he simply wanted to be able to protect them should they need that ability, but was distracted. "Why would you put monkeys in a barrel? Is it an odd sexual kink that I've not heard of?"

"Why would you even go there?" Bee asked, squinting at him. "How do you get from barrel of monkeys to sexual kinks? Wait—you aren't one of those freaky guys who gets off on things like animals and bondage and... well, I guess barrels—are you?"

"I am not freaky," Constantine said with much dignity. "There is no sense of freaky in exploring those items and apparatuses meant to enhance sexual pleasure. It is an entirely normal and natural thing."

Bee stared at him for a second before shaking her head, and saying softly, "No. Not going to ask."

"I will," came Gary's muffled voice. "What sort of apparatuses?"

Constantine ignored the head, instead pulling out his phone. "I see there are a number of locksmiths within walking distance. We will try them, and while they are working on the shackles, I will find us a flight to Paris."

"Flight?" Bee waited a minute for their drinks to be placed on the table before continuing. "Why bother when there's bound to be a portal office here?"

"I don't wish to use the portal." Constantine got lost in a search for flights from Seville to Paris, and shook the phone in an attempt to reset it. "We will fly."

"Don't be ridiculous. It will cost more to fly, not to mention take a lot longer. Plus, it'll be easier to get you-know-who to Paris."

"Are you talking about me?" Gary asked. "You are, aren't you? I can tell you are."

"Then he can stay here," Constantine said.

"I don't want to stay in Seville! Bee, don't let him leave me here. I dehydrate easily!"

"Constantine," Bee said severely, evidently about to read him the riot act, then her expression softened. She reached across the table and gave his hand a quick pat, an act that shocked him almost as much as it gave him a little spurt of pleasure. How long had it been since a woman had initiated physical contact with him? "Okay, what gives? What do you have against portals? It's obvious you don't want to use one, but I don't understand why."

"Dragonkin do not like portals," he said, stretching his hand to stroke hers in return. He half expected her to recoil from the touch, but she just looked puzzled.

Whereas he felt as if his hand was alight.

"In what way?" she asked.

He shrugged, both at the question and the fact that someone other than the glorious Ysolde could give him a tiny morsel of pleasure. "We do not travel well through them. It is something to do with our physical properties and the act of portaling through space. We come out...rumpled."

"No one is going to judge you on whether you're suitable to go on the cover of *GQ*," she chided, and he could have sworn he heard her mutter under her breath, "which you are."

"Regardless, we will take a plane."

"It'll cost more. Come on, you can't tell me that a big brave dragon like you is afraid of one little portal?"

"I will pay. I have some money that Ysolde forced Baltic to give me until I can make my own."

"And it will take longer. Surely you want the dragon curse broken pronto."

"A few hours will not matter."

"The longer we hang around here, the more in danger we are of Asmodeus's demons seeing us," she argued. "And if I can put up with being chained to a dragon, then you can just suck it up and go through the portal."

He raised one eyebrow at that. "You can't really imagine that they don't know exactly where we are right now, can you?"

"Of course I can." She frowned. "Why shouldn't I?"

"We were allowed to escape," he said simply.

Bee looked like she wanted to protest that idea. "But— you knocked the demons down so that we could get past them and go through the door."

"Yes, and when is the last time you saw a dragon take down two wrath demons with one blow to each?"

She opened her mouth, closed it, and opened it again a couple more times before answering. "Well . . . they were . . . you took them by surprise . . . you *are* pretty buff . . ."

Constantine shook his head. "We were allowed to escape, Bee. Asmodeus is no fool—he clearly understood the importance of you and I both trying to get a talisman from him. He knows that his ring must be in the possession of dragons, and thus he intends to use us to find it. That is why we have nothing to fear from demons while we are in Seville. It would be folly for them to attack us before we've led them to the ring."

"Ugh. That wouldn't be good." Bee thought for a few minutes, then tapped him on the wrist when he straightened up after giving Gary a glass of water. "But it does give us even more reason to take a portal. The company won't transport demons—they never have, and I can't see why they'd suddenly start now. This is our chance to get away. We can get the jump on them and make it to Paris before they even know we're out of town."

"A plane is fast," Constantine said stubbornly, but he feared he was losing the battle.

"Also, there's a chance it can break the shackles."

"How so?" He looked down at the metal around his ankle. "It is forged by a demon lord. It will not be easy to remove."

"You melted the bars of the cell I was in," Bee said, looking thoughtfully at the chain. "Do you think you could break this that way?"

"I can try, but I doubt it would work." He studied the chain for a moment. "The bars were not forged by Asmodeus. The links in this chain have runes on them, which means that a demon lord most likely made it."

"It's worth a try, isn't it?"

Constantine agreed, and bent down until his head was under the short white-and-blue-checked tablecloth, whereupon he blew fire on the chain held between his hands.

"It is as I thought," he said, sitting up in his chair again.

"Dammit." Bee bit her lower lip for a few seconds before saying, "The portal is going to be our best bet. No, hear me out: portals displace time and space, so using one might well knock the shackles right off our legs. Plus, there's the added bonus that most portalling places refuse to cater to demons, and thus anything demonic like the chain formed in Abaddon wouldn't be transported."

"Which might also result in our legs being left behind as well," Constantine pointed out. "Flying poses no such risk."

"Look, I'm not some brave superhero woman out to save the world. I'm a simple Charmer, one who came into the trade wholly by accident. I do what I can to help people because that's what my parents raised me to do—although they had no idea I'd end up unmaking curses, and hanging around people who could be found in a medieval bestiary. All that aside, I'm willing to take the chance with the portal," Bee said, her chin raised in challenge. "So get with the program, and let's get this done so that I can do the job I'm being paid to do."

A muscle twitched in his jaw. He liked his legs, dammit. Both of them. He didn't want to lose one, but on the other hand, he did wish to be rid of the shackles, and if there was no time to find someone locally who had the ability to do so, then he had little choice. He felt that the potential loss of a leg in addition to the trauma of traveling through a portal qualified him for sainthood.

And that is why, less than an hour later, when he leaped through the swirling oval of nothingness that was confined in a back room of the small portal shop deep in the heart of Seville, he resigned himself to feeling as if his atoms had been smashed flat against an anvil, then exploded into a million bits.

"Anvils," he groaned when he hit the landing mats on the receiving office in Paris. He rolled to his side, his head spinning, and feeling as if he were covered in barbed wire. "Definitely lots of anvils."

"What on earth are you babbling about?" Bee suddenly loomed over him looking tidy and not the least bit in disarray, whereas he felt as if he'd been turned inside out and back again. She also appeared to have both of her legs, and no shackles.

He tried to raise himself to see if he did as well.

"Hrn," he told her and fell back when the room spun and dipped perilously.

Just as he got to his knees, a strange keening noise seemed to come from nowhere, then resolved itself into a joyous "Wheeee!" that resulted with the metal bird-cage bursting free of the portal, and smacking him in the kidneys.

"Are you all right?" Bee asked, pausing in the act of helping Constantine to his feet. Both of them, he was relieved to note.

Gary rolled around his cage whooping with laughter. "All right? That was a blast! Can we do it again? What a trip! It was like *wham, bang, zippee*!"

"Did you notice the shackle is gone, Constantine? I'm so relieved we don't have to fight with that any longer. Now we can go find the ring and get this job done. No, Gary, you can't go through the portal again."

Constantine got to his feet at last. He was missing a shoe, his shirt had turned around so that it was on backward, his hair felt like it was standing on end, and his one bare foot was on fire. He cast a look at where Gary lolled around on the back of his head giggling. "I hate you," he muttered to the head before jerking his arm from Bee's grasp, and limped with as much dignity as he could manage from the room, trailing fire with every step.

Five

I assumed that even a spirit dragon would be familiar with the most famous nightclub in all of Europe—at least so far as denizens of the Otherworld went—but I was sadly mistaken.

"What are we doing here?" Constantine silently read the curved text over the door. "Goety and Theurgy."

"G&T is a club, yes. It's *the* club for the Otherworld, and is the home ground of the Venediger—the woman who more or less polices all immortal activity in this area of the world—and is the most neutral meeting place in Europe. All of that is why we are here."

Constantine glanced around, sending piercing looks up and down the street. It seemed that he didn't like what he saw because he left me to stroll a few yards down the road to where he subjected an intersection to further scrutiny. This section of Paris had few mortal visitors, despite its appearing to be nothing more than a slightly eccentric neighborhood.

I tried not to notice how the slight breeze rippled Constantine's shirt against his chest, or how the little hairs on his arms gleamed golden in the late afternoon sun, and how the same gold threads glittered in his shoulder-length mane of hair.

Worse yet, I could still remember the feel of that kiss he had planted on me in Seville. I badly wanted to believe that he had taken me by surprise, and that's why I'd allowed it to go on as long as it had, but my father had made sure that both Aoife and I knew how to protect ourselves from unwanted advances and, unfortunately, the thought of self-protection hadn't even entered my mind when Constantine had kissed me.

All I could think about was how hot his mouth was, and how much hotter I wanted him to make me feel. I shook that thought away, and tried to focus on the here and now.

I spent a few minutes trying hard to not watch him, since he wasn't a man, but a dragon, the most arrogant, alpha, and annoying of all the races. "And I should know," I said softly, refusing to let myself dwell on the way his jeans fit (sinfully tight). "It took me three years to wash Ben Fong out of my hair."

"Who's Ben Fong?"

I turned at the whisper behind me, and peeked into the cage that I'd set next to the door. "Oh, hello, Gary. I didn't realize you were awake."

"I just took a little catnap while you got Constantine set to rights after going through the portal. Are we where we're supposed to be?" He tried to look past me, but just in case there were any mortals on the street, I dropped the edge of my sweater, which I'd wrapped around his cage.

"Yes, but I'd appreciate it if you'd keep quiet until we're inside."

"So, who's Ben Fong?" he repeated.

I sighed, and with my eyes measuring the width of Constantine's shoulders, answered dismissively, "Just an old boyfriend."

"A dragon boyfriend?"

"Yes."

"Did he kiss you like Constantine did?"

"For heaven's sake, Gary! That's none of your business."

"Maybe not, but I was right there when you and Constantine went at it, and it looked like it was a really good one. You were moaning and squirming against him, so I figured it must have been awfully nice."

"I did not squirm!"

"Okay, wiggled. Your derriere definitely wiggled with happiness."

"For the love of—look, it was just a kiss, okay? Unexpected, but nothing more than a little peck."

Gary heaved a sigh of pure longing. "If Constantine kissed me like he did you, I would have yelled about it from the highest mountain."

I peered into the cage just long enough to give him a good glare. "I repeat: none of your business. Now pipe down until I uncover you."

Constantine turned back toward me, a half-frown pulling his golden brown eyebrows together. Just as I refused to notice how nice his butt looked in his jeans, now I told myself that it didn't matter in the least that the man was built like an Adonis and had the lips of an angel. A sexy angel.

Dragons were trouble, pure and simple.

"I see no demons, but that doesn't mean they have not followed us here."

"Yes, but G&T is the one place in Europe where it doesn't matter if they do know exactly where we are." I opened the door and stepped into the cool darkness, a handful of memories of my time with Ben threatening to swamp my brain. I refused to let them, just as I refused to acknowledge that Constantine might be just as irritating and arrogant and intolerable as the next dragon, but he was also chivalrous. And honorable. And maddeningly interesting.

Dammit, I was perilously close to going against my no-dragons rule of boyfriends.

"Why do you say that?" he asked, and for a moment, I thought he had read my mind.

"Say what?" I cast my mind back a few seconds. "Oh, that G&T is the one safe spot? Because demons can only enter the premises if they are summoned by someone. And that someone would be under the control of the Venediger while in the club. It's something to do with the original magic used centuries ago. I'm not quite sure what the original mage who built the place did to it, but it sure works. Hello?" The last word was called out into the darkness. My voice echoed unpleasantly.

"I was told the club had been destroyed," Constantine said, moving Gary to a stack of wooden packing crates. He glanced around, clearly unimpressed with the interior. "I see that information was accurate."

"It's in the process of being rebuilt. Hello? Jovana?" I made my way through a maze of packing crates, chairs wrapped in plastic, and a several pieces of new bar-related equipment stacked against one wall. Overhead, lights dangled by electrical cords, obviously awaiting further installation. The room had a naked, unsettling ambiance heightened by the fact that apparently no one else was present. "I can't imagine that she'd leave the place unattended. Oh, hello."

A nondescript middle-aged man hurried from the area that used to hold the back offices of the club. In his hand he held a clipboard, while a cell phone was clamped between his ear and shoulder. "—paid to have the lights properly installed, not just hooked up and dangling, dangling they are from the ceiling. No, you'll finish them today. I don't care if you have other work—" The man stopped when he saw us, his eyes widening when Constantine, who had been peeling my sweater off of Gary's cage, stepped forward. "Dragons! Oh dear, the Venediger won't be happy about that, no she won't, she won't be happy about that at all. What? No, next week will not suffice. You will finish installing the lights today, or a blight will descend upon your testes. Do you hear me? It will descend with all due vengeance. Good day."

Constantine stood with his hands on his hips, eyeing the other man. "Who is this?"

"Jovana's assistant. Um…Willem?" I said, trying to remember the name. I'd seen him around, but never had occasion to speak with him.

"Guillaume," the man corrected, shooting little worried looks toward Constantine. It wasn't that the latter was so much bigger or more physically intimidating that clearly concerned Guillaume; I suspected it was an almost indescribable sense of coiled power that seemed as natural to Constantine as breathing. "Mistress Jovana will not be pleased to know that you have brought a dragon to the premises without her permission."

"It's the only place we could go. Constantine—oh, let me introduce you. This is Constantine Norka. He used to be a member of—"

"Wyvern," Constantine interrupted. "Wyvern of the silver dragons. Until I died. Now another is wyvern in my place. Unless I decide otherwise."

Wisely, Guillaume chose not to reply. Instead, he gestured toward me with the clipboard. "Indeed. I see, indeed I do see. You must be here for the item. It was left in the mistress's safe only this morning, very early in the morning, far too early in the morning for our happiness, but that is the way of some people, is it not? As it is, we were told that we'd be notified before it was called for."

"Item?" I rubbed my forehead where a slight headache was forming. "What item is that?"

"The ring, of course." Guillaume gave Constantine one last look, then turned and started back the way he'd come. "What could it be but the ring? I ask you, could it be anything else? If you will accompany me to the safe, I'll have you sign the register, and you may then take the item away."

"You have the ring here? Aoife gave it to you?" I shook my head, not understanding what was going on. "She wouldn't do that. She swore up and down she'd only release the ring to me when it was time to break the curse, and not a moment before."

Constantine spun around on his heel, and marched over to the door. There he began hefting wooden crates and setting them down smack-dab in front of the door.

"Nonetheless, it was she who brought the item to be

placed in the safe. They said it was the safest spot since their location had been compromised as you were no doubt tortured while being imprisoned in Abaddon." Guillaume's pale hazel eyes were dispassionate, leaving me with the impression of a man who was not at all interested in us or our plan. "It must have been unpleasant to be tortured while imprisoned in Abaddon, so one could not blame you for saying all that you knew about the item, one could not blame you in the least. I, myself, have a low tolerance to pain. What is the dragon doing?"

I glanced over my shoulder at where Constantine was making a pyramid of crates. "Looks like he's blocking the door, which is understandable given what you have in your safe, although not in the least bit necessary due to the enchantments wrapped around the club itself."

Guillaume was clearly unimpressed. "If you will come this way, I will give the item to you, and we will have fulfilled our obligation to the dragons. The Venediger will be most happy, exceptionally happy. We are not overly fond of dragonkin."

"Ah, but I'm not a dragon," I pointed out, and handed Gary's cage to Constantine when he had finished moving the last crates into place.

"Woot!" Gary said, obviously excited when Constantine put him at the apex of the stack. "I'll be your guard, okay? I can yell out if the door is forced open. And I'll bite anyone who tries to get past me, just see if I don't."

Constantine made a noncommittal noise, pausing when Gary asked, "Hey, do you have any tunes?"

"Tunes?"

"You know, music? Guard duty gets kind of boring when there's nothing to do but stare at a door."

"There is music on my phone," Constantine said, and set his phone up so that it leaned against the cage, turning on a curated music program before returning to my side. "The door has been made fast. Let us conduct the ceremony quickly, before the demons realize that the ring is here." He took my elbow, and hustled me past Guillaume toward the door leading to the back part of the building.

"Wait just a minute!" I tried to stop, but Constantine was like a rolling stone, and had no intention of giving me a little time to assess the situation. "Who says we're going to charm the curse right now? It's not a simple matter of saying a few words, and hey, presto, it's gone. A curse is a physical manifestation of magic. I have to unravel it to break it and, depending on how intricate it is, that will take some time. I'll want to study the curse for a while to see how best to tackle it. Here's how I see this going down: I'll do some research on other dragons who were cursed, and how they broke it, and then we'll get Kostya and my sister Aoife, and the other dragons who are around, and once I've studied the curse's physical form, then we'll have the formal ceremony where I—"

"We will do it now. It will work. You are a famous Charmer," Constantine said matter-of-factly, pushing me through the door. "I am confident that you will break the curse without the slightest trouble."

"You can't possibly know that," I protested, trying to appeal to him, but he ignored me, and just kept pushing me along a dark hallway until Guillaume called out that the safe was in the room to the left.

"I know you are a competent Charmer," Constantine said calmly, his amber-brown eyes so bright they almost seemed to glow with an inner light.

Dragon fire, I said to myself, shivering slightly. I'd only seen dragon fire once, when the dragon I'd been dating became aroused, and the experience had not been a positive one. Absently, I rubbed my hand, which still bore the scar of a burn. "I appreciate that you're so confident, but I just don't think—"

"Do not *think* about what you will be doing," Constantine said, opening the door to the left and with a hand on my back, escorted me inside. "Just *do* it."

"You sound like a horrible mutation of Yoda," I grumbled, but my gaze went instantly to the massive black metal safe lurking in a corner of the office. "And you're misguided if you think I'm going to be able to Charm a curse without first getting a good look at it."

Guillaume hurried forward, attempting to block the safe by inserting his body between us and it. "One moment, please! The Venediger said nothing about you attempting to break the curse while you are on the grounds of Goety and Theurgy, nothing at all. No indeed, she did not."

"What harm can it do?" I said, about to point out that breaking a curse didn't affect the environment. Before I could do so, Constantine took my hand and strolled forward until he had Guillaume pinned against the safe.

"Bee assures me that the ring will be secure so long as it is within the confines of this club. Therefore, she will use it here. Open the safe."

"The Venediger has rules, many rules, very strict rules about magic being performed at G&T—" Guillaume squeaked, squishing himself tighter against the safe.

"Open the safe." Constantine's eyes lit brighter. I jerked to the side when I noticed the ring of fire around his feet, fire that spread outward, licking the tips of Guillaume's toes.

The little man shrieked and tried to stamp it out.

"I dislike repeating myself," Constantine said, his eyes now shining like sunlight through amber. "Open it or suffer my wrath."

"The Venediger—"

"OPEN IT!" Constantine roared, making both Guillaume and me jump.

He opened it. He complained the entire time that he was going to have to report us to the Venediger, and then we'd know what real trouble was, but neither Constantine nor I paid him much attention. Constantine was staring intently at the safe, and I... well, I was staring at Constantine. I knew from previous experience just how bossy and dominant dragons could be, but Constantine was different from the other dragons I'd met. He was forceful, but it was a comforting sort of forceful. Protective, almost.

In a fanciful sort of way, it made me feel cherished. And *definitely* aware of him as a man.

I shook away the sudden smutty thoughts that followed that revelation, and focused on the situation in front of me. Inside the safe was a collection of small boxes, the usual legal-looking documents, a pale metal sword, two long gold chains, a couple of pretty crystals, and a small green-stone statue that bore a strong resemblance to a fertility figure.

"That is it?" Constantine asked when Guillaume handed me a small onyx box. I opened it to reveal a ring of pale sand-colored horn chased in gold. "It is... uninspiring."

"I admit it's a bit anticlimactic," I agreed, putting the

ring on the palm of my hand. "But appearances are often deceiving, and all that. I'm still surprised that Aoife let me have the ring after making such a big deal about it."

"The dragon mate said that the ring may not let you use it, indeed, it may not, and if it does not, then I am to return the ring to the safe, so you will let me know what transpires. The onus of its preservation is upon you, indeed it is, and thus I wash my hands of it."

Constantine's nose twitched, and I remembered from my time with the dragon boyfriend how gold had struck him like a powerful aphrodisiac.

"The gold is of a good quality. Very pure and pleasant." Constantine plucked the ring off my palm, squinted at it for a few seconds, and then before I could warn him, stuck it on his index finger.

"Wait!" I cried, grabbing at his hand at the same time that Guillaume, with a moan, dropped to his knees and covered his head. "Don't do that!"

"Why not?" Constantine waggled his fingers at me. "Did you fear I would become all powerful and destroy you? If so, I remind you that I risked not just the success of this mission but my own personal well-being by returning to save you from Asmodeus."

I held out my hand for the ring, nervous about it being out of my protection. "I should hope you wouldn't become a raving lunatic with it."

"Please," Guillaume moaned, peeking through his fingers at us. "Take it from here. The Venediger will have my head if anything more happens to the club."

We both ignored him. "The ring itself isn't evil," I continued, addressing Constantine. "But it can heighten existing or even latent powers."

"I am a dragon. I do not need my power heightened," he said simply, plucking the ring off and dropping it back onto my waiting hand. "Such things seldom have an effect on dragonkin."

"That was a fascinating peek into the makeup of dragons, but not really pertinent at the moment." I closed my fingers around the ring. "Now, if you don't mind me examining you, I can get a better idea of just how the curse is made."

Guillaume moaned again, and clutched his head, making his hair stand out in spiky clumps. "I'm a dead man, I am indeed, dead as dead can be when the Venediger discovers that I've allowed you to perform your ceremony here. I will be a former Guillaume, nothing but a memory of Guilluame."

"Do not be such a drama llama," Constantine told him, and was about to leave the office when I stopped him with a puzzled look.

"What?" he asked.

"Drama llama? I think you mean drama queen."

"The phrase as I spoke it is correct," he said loftily. It was then that I noticed his eyes weren't truly amber, but were more amber with brown, gold, and black flecks dashed around the irises. His lashes were darker and thicker than he had any right to, the sort of lashes most women would kill for. But it was the tiny spray of lines radiating from the outer edges of his eyes that made a little ball of warmth glow deep in my belly.

I'd never seen a dragon with laugh lines before. It was strangely appealing, and very sexy. "I think you'll find I'm right, and the phrase is drama queen."

"Just because you are mortal and raised in this time

does not mean I am completely clueless," he argued. "I am quite conversant with Internet memes and social phrases. I Twatter. I read the Wikipodium. I am as hip as they come."

"All right, Guillaume, we'll leave your mistress's precious office, so you can stop wringing your hands and moaning."

"Just like a drama llama," Constantine added without looking at me, heading for the door.

I *tsk*ed and shook my head at his back, but said nothing until we reentered the main room of the club.

Six

"Now you will break the curse," Constantine announced. "Do you need anything special for it? Do you need to inscribe a circle? Draw wards? Call the quarters?"

"No, all I need to do is hold the ring, the talisman that you stole, and unmake the curse. But I do need to examine it first."

"How long will that take?" he asked, frowning slightly.

I gave a one-shouldered shrug. "As long as it needs. Normally I'd like a few days, but since you're being Rushy McRusherton about the whole thing, I'll try to pick out the best unmaking path as I go along." I glanced around, then took him by the wrist and pulled him away from the windows, into the darkest part of the room. I gestured to the floor, and sat on my knees, my hands on my thighs, as I tried to clear my mind.

"Why are you taking me here?" he asked, sitting down with his feet flat on the floor, and knees bent. Beside us, the dark mahogany wood of the bar, shaped like a U, hid us from the sunlight streaming in from the bank of windows.

"Because the bar blocks the light."

"Wouldn't it be better to be where you can see?"

"Not in this case." I shook out my hands, closing my eyes for a few seconds while I attuned myself with the part of my brain that was so very good at unraveling knots and mazes. "Since the curse is bound to all dragons, the pattern of it will be visible on your body. Faint, but visible, and oddly enough, the darker our surroundings, the easier it'll be for me to see. Okay, I think I'm ready."

He watched with interest as I opened my eyes and leaned forward onto my hands, my gaze focused on his shirt. "What is it you seek to find?"

"A curse," I said absently, my eyes narrowing to try to catch the glimmer of the curse that I knew must show on him if I looked at it just right, "can take many shapes, but they all resemble Celtic knots, some more intricate than others, but that's what they remind me of. Drat."

I sat back, rubbing my lower lip as I thought.

"What is drat?" He looked down at himself. "I do not see any stains or other markings, although the wrinkles are due to you forcing me into the portal—"

"I'm not dratting your shirt. I'm dratting the fact that I can't see the curse shining through the material. Um. This is going to sound a bit crazy—"

"I will take it off," he said quickly, pulling his shirt off over his head, a suitably wicked glint to his eyes.

I blinked for a moment at the sight of his chest, all glorious with soft, golden hair, swells of pectorals that suddenly made my mouth feel dry, on down to the thick layers of muscles that lay just beneath soft, satiny skin.

"Can you see it now?"

"Hrm?"

"Perhaps you need to be closer to see." His voice was almost a purr.

I shivered a little, and swallowed a couple of times, telling myself to stop being so silly. I'd seen bare-chested men before, even handsome bare-chested men. There was no reason to find my mind wandering down a path where I got to touch all that chest with my fingers and lips and even my own naked chest... "What?"

"You'll be able to see better if you are closer," he repeated, and this time I got caught up in the heat simmering in the depths of his eyes. That and his voice, which hummed inside me, making me feel warm and needy.

And then I realized that I was guilty of ogling the man, outright ogling him (accompanied by the almost overwhelming desire to lick and touch and taste), and I had to remind myself that I was a professional Charmer, and he was a cursed man, and just because he was so sexy he could drive a saint to distraction, it didn't mean I had to give in.

"Sorry, was just, uh, communing with my inner self. That's what we Charmers do when we see a chest. Er... curse. Yes, curse. So. Let's take a look at yours."

"I thought that's what you were already doing," he said, his golden brown eyebrows arching in a way that I found highly seductive. "Where is this curse? I cannot see anything."

"Not everyone can." I gave myself another mental reprimand at finding eyebrows alluring, and leaned forward again to try to find the pattern of the curse on his torso. At first I saw nothing but his delectable chest, but out of the corner of my eye, a little black curve flashed into being for a moment before fading away. I scooted forward, and squinted again. "I thought I saw one of the twisted edges...no, it's gone now."

Constantine rubbed a hand down his chest, and at first I thought he was deliberately attempting to arouse me, but his eyes had lost their simmering heat look, and were now filled with genuine curiosity. "What does the curse look like? Why can't I see it if I am one of the dragons cursed by it?"

"Like I said, not everyone can see curses, not even those affected by it." I clicked my tongue against my teeth in frustration. Every time I thought I had a glimpse of the curse, it faded to nothing. "I hate to ask this—I assure you that I do so in the strictest professional sense—but would you mind if I got closer?"

The corners of his mouth curled in a way that sent a little zing of pleasure through me. "I invited you to do so twice."

"You did?"

"Yes. Just a few minutes ago." The heat was back in his eyes, making me feel like I was sitting in the full sun on the middle of the equator. At noon.

"Oh. I...uh...must have missed that." I cleared my throat, which was strangely tight. "My interest is purely professional, I assure you."

His smile grew and he moved his legs so they formed a V, then gestured at his chest. "Many women have sought to touch me and tease me, but none have ever done so *professionally*." He thought for a moment. "Well, there was a harlot in Alsace, but that was in the year 1430, and she refused remuneration the following morning."

"No one likes a braggart," I said, a bit breathless despite the fact that I had sternly told myself to ignore the lovely, warm, slightly spicy scent that seemed to drift up from his bare chest. Nor would I look at his eyes. Or his shoulders. Or even, heaven help me, the thighs on either side. Feeling as if my clothing was suddenly several sizes too small, I knee-walked forward until I was between his legs, my nose now a scant inch away from his gloriously naked upper parts.

"I do not need to brag. My past speaks for itself." He took a deep breath, causing his chest to rise and bump against my nose. For a second, I thought seriously of turning my head slightly and licking the pert little nipple that resided in the soft golden-brown hair. Instead, I tipped my head back and glared at him. "Stop that. And don't deny you did it on purpose, because I know you did. Just sit there and let me try to find this curse."

"Where does it start?" he asked, his breath ruffling my hair.

I ordered myself to stop thinking of him as a desirable (if annoying as hell) male, and to focus on the curse. "I'm not sure. The start isn't as important as the end. I have to unravel it, you see. Ah. There it is."

"Where?"

I placed a finger on his right side, below his last rib. "That's where it curls over onto itself, completing the pattern. If I trace it back to the origin point, then I will have a good idea of how it's made, and how I can best unmake it."

"Interesting. I've never been cursed before. Damned, yes. Accused of many crimes, absolutely. Suffered untold torments, of course. But never cursed."

I tried to follow the ethereal black pattern as it danced

in and out of my view, but it was impossible without some way of marking where I was. "I'm sorry, I'm going to have to touch you." I gave him a long, cool look. "It is purely in the interests of identifying the curse, and not because you hold an intense sexual attraction that no woman can refuse, as I see you are about to suggest."

"You see incorrectly," he said simply, watching with interest as I placed my fingertip back on the end of the curse. "I was going to suggest that you get naked so that we both could enjoy ourselves."

I pinched the skin on his side. "Not going to happen, dragon boy."

"Dragon *man*."

"Just remember I'm a professional, and don't get any bright ideas. And stop doing that thing with your eyebrows. It's not affecting me in the least."

"What thing with my eyebrows?"

"Arching them in a way that makes me want to—never mind. Just stop it. Oh, where's the talisman you said you got out?"

He reached for his jacket and extracted a small onyx box, handing it to me.

"No, I can't touch it. Its power has to flow through the curse. Just set it on your stomach, so one corner is touching the curse."

He glanced down at himself, looked thoughtful for a moment, then laid back, his hands pillowing the back of his head, and the box covering his belly button. "You may proceed."

"I am not at all moved by you lying here in front of me," I said primly, and started at the end of the curse again. It swirled up and across his chest, forming an elaborate pattern of swoops and double-back loops, all of which I trailed with my finger. My fingertip grew warmer as I did so, but I assumed it was friction until the curse, tired of weaving back and forth on Constantine's chest, swung up to his collarbone, then curlicued along his neck.

I was deep in the curse, on the left side of his neck, my nose almost brushing his hair when my finger suddenly burst into flames.

I stared at it in horror for a moment before I realized that the fire wasn't burning my skin. It was warm, yes, but warm in a way that I'd never felt before, a heat that left me yearning for more. "Oh! I appear to be on fire. But it doesn't seem to be burning me."

One of his eyebrows rose. "It is dragon fire."

"It can't be. Dragon fire hurts when it touches you. Or rather, it hurts mortal beings like me."

"Mine doesn't."

My gaze met his, and instantly I felt as if I were about to fall into an amber pool. He took my hand and tipped my finger into his mouth, swirling his tongue around it in a way that should have been disgusting and gross, but in truth was the complete opposite.

"Stop it," I said, reluctantly pulling my finger from his mouth.

"I was merely showing you it was indeed dragon fire, and not of a mundane origin."

"Mundane as in mortal?" I shook my head. "I knew that much. I've never had my finger suddenly burst into normal everyday flames." Covertly, I rubbed my finger on my pants. It wasn't that I wanted to get rid of the sensation of it being in his mouth, but I felt like I had to regain control of the situation. "Regardless, I don't know how that happened, but I apologize. I was almost to the end of the curse, too."

He crossed one ankle over the other and watched me from half-closed eyes. "You will start over, then?"

I moved restlessly, irritated at myself for being so easily distracted from what was important. "I think since I was so close to the end, I'll just take a chance that the pattern doesn't do anything odd right before it gets to the starting point." I hesitated a moment, frowning at the small black box. "I really would like to have longer to examine the curse. I wouldn't want anything to . . . happen."

"Happen?" Guillaume must have entered the club proper just in time to hear the last word. He hurried over toward us, saying, "What sort of things do you expect to happen? You said nothing would happen to the club, nothing at all. You reassured me!" He stopped when he rounded the bar and caught sight of the bare-chested Constantine lounging on the floor, his eyes widening in shock. "Merciful Zeus! You are engaging in sexual shenanigans right there on the floor? You are, you cannot deny it, it's right there in front of me. The Venediger will be furious, furious, I tell you!"

"Oh, calm down, you big ole drama llama," I snapped, irritated both by the fact that he assumed Constantine and I were getting it on and that there was a part of my mind that wouldn't be opposed to that idea at all.

"Ha!" Constantine said.

I pinched his side again. "I said that merely to be ironic. As for you . . ." I sent a frown over to where Guillaume lurked. "Your precious club is safe. I meant what I said—no harm will come to it from Charming a curse. Unfortunately, the same can't be said for Constantine."

Constantine, whose feet were bopping in time to a

B-52s song that came from Gary's cage, suddenly stopped humming along and propped himself up on one elbow. "What cannot be said about me?"

"That's why I want a longer time to study the curse, really study it, so that I have all of its nuances down pat. If I get something wrong, or even slightly out of order, it could spell the end." I waited a minute before adding, "The end for both of us."

"Oh, well, if that's all…" Guillaume didn't finish his sentence, shuffling off to the back room again, evidently reassured that the club would be fine.

Constantine prodded my arm. "I heard Charmers were not affected by the curses they charm."

"We aren't, but… wait, you're not worried about yourself?"

"Not particularly. I died once before."

"Yeah, but you're physical now." I couldn't resist sliding an appraising glance at his chest. "If the Charming goes pear-shaped, then you could be harmed."

"It's not likely. I am a wyvern first, and a spirit second. Even bound to a physical form as I now am with the placing of the bête noire, I do not fear for my well-being. You, however…" He frowned. "We do not have time for you to study the curse in leisure, not with the demons of Asmodeus obviously on our trail. You must break the curse now, but do so without harming yourself."

He laid back, arranging the box in place.

I bit back the desire to tell him that I didn't appreciate the bossiness, but since he included my well-being in his list of concerns, I felt it was wiser to move past it.

"Very well. But if we both turn into bearded lizards named Bernie, then you have no one to blame but yourself."

He looked puzzled. "Why Bernie?"

"Why not?" I slipped the ring on my finger, immediately aware of heat that seemed to glow within it. "All right, let's give this a shot and hope we don't end up as lizards."

"Your obsession with lizards is confusing, and one I will wish for you to explain at a later date," Constantine said, lifting his head to watch as I placed a finger on his side just as I'd done before. This time, with the ring on my hand, the touch felt different. My finger felt heavier, as if the curse clung to it, and made it slow to move along the pattern that still flashed in and out of my vision.

"You don't say anything? There are no verses? No spells?" Constantine asked after a minute of watching me. I was wholly focused on the curse now, on forcing my (seemingly reluctant) finger to travel along the intricate twists and circles of its design. I was itchy and unusually warm, but disregarded those sensations for what was most important: keeping my finger on the right path. If I slipped up, it would at best mean starting over...at worst, it might cause the curse to lash out at Constantine or me.

"You draw no wards of protection first?"

"No, no, no, and no," I said, my face a scant inch from his chest as I forced my finger along the fleeting lines of the curse. The ring grew hot and tight on my finger, and my fingertip tingled when it moved, a little trail of fire following it before dissipating into nothing. It was as if the dragon fire burned off the curse, for the lines glowed first black, then gold, then dissolved into nothing. "Charming a curse is just a matter of unmaking the pattern that holds the power. Now be quiet so I can focus."

Constantine obliged by being silent, but the room was anything but quiet. Not only was Gary rocking out to Freebird at the other side of the bar, but in the distance I could hear Guillaume talking to someone, presumably to his boss on the phone. Faintly, over both of those distractions, the sound of Paris intruded on my little corner of the world.

And beneath my hands lay a man who was both irritating as hell and oddly intriguing.

"You stopped?" Constantine asked softly.

"Yes, sorry. I got distracted for a moment."

He glanced over at the door. "Should I tell the head to turn off the music?"

"No, it's okay, I listen a lot to music when I meditate. This is just another form of focus." I took a deep breath, pushed away my awareness of everything but the curse, and continued to move my hesitant finger through the design of the curse.

When I reached the beginning of the curse, the whole thing flared to life for a second, hanging black above Constantine's chest, then it faded to nothing.

"There we go," I said, sitting back on my feet. I felt drained, which was normal with a Charming, but at the same time, there was an emptiness inside me, a hollow feeling that something had gone not quite right.

I looked down at Constantine's chest, trying to see with my peripheral vision, but saw no sign of the curse. Mentally, I ran over the way I had Charmed the curse, but didn't see anything that I'd done wrong.

"Well?" he asked, sitting up. "Is it broken?"

"Yes," I said slowly, shaking my head over my odd feelings.

"You do not seem certain. And your finger is still on fire."

I looked down in surprise, shaking my hands to put out the little blob of dragon fire that burned merrily away on my forefinger. "I am sure. Pretty sure. It's just...I don't know, it's hard to describe exactly. It looks like the curse is gone, and everything went the way it should, only I didn't feel the curse break."

"Is that normal?" Constantine asked, reaching for his shirt. He slipped it on, but didn't button it.

"For the curses I've Charmed before?" I shook my head. "I've always felt them break, but this is a curse laid by a demon lord, the most powerful practitioner of curses there is. Maybe theirs don't dissipate like the others do."

"There is only one way to tell," Constantine said and, looking around, spied a phone that was connected to the wall, but sitting on the floor. He went to it and dialed a number. "I will call Kostya."

"I don't see what you expect to do by calling him," I told Constantine. "You can't talk to anyone outside your sept. He's in a different sept; therefore, you won't be able to understand him."

"Ah, but if he understands me, then we will know you succeeded in breaking the curse after all."

"Oh. That makes sense." I reviewed the Charming a second time, unable to shake the feeling that it hadn't been done correctly.

Could I have traced the pattern incorrectly? Gotten confused on one of the more detailed circles? Maybe I didn't touch every part of the curse...I looked at Constantine's chest with speculation while I considered the problem.

And that's how I saw the curse flare back into life a scant half-second before I heard Constantine's intake of breath prefatory to speaking, and I knew with a sudden flash of insight that the curse was going to strike back for the attempt at breaking it.

"No!" I screamed, and threw myself at Constantine to protect him just as his lips formed the words, "Hello? Kostya?"

A percussive blast followed, knocking me backward with a force that slammed me up against the bar counter. Glass tinkled down in a rain of sharp noise, and in the distance, I could hear the squeal of car brakes, and muffled voices shouting questions.

I lay slumped against the side of the bar for a few seconds, my mind reeling with the echoed percussion.

"Bee!"

The voice was close at hand, and yet sounded so far away. Idly, I wondered how that could be.

"Bee, are you harmed? Sins of the saints." A crash followed, one that was sufficiently loud as to cause me to open my eyes. Constantine flung off a heavy mirror that had been hanging on the wall, blood dripping down his chest and belly. To my horror, he got to his knees, clearly intending on making his way over to me.

"Don't move!" I spoke without being consciously aware of it, and likewise I suddenly found myself crawling over to Constantine, shoving bits of plaster and wood and glass out of my way. "Mother of mayhem, you're bleeding, don't move at all. That mirror must have sliced you to ribbons."

He looked down at himself, surprise flitting across his face before it turned to concern as, despite my order, he got to his feet and moved the few remaining yards to me. "Stop crawling through the glass. You'll cut yourself, you deranged woman."

That pulled me up short. I sat back on my heels and glared up at him. "Deranged woman? I like that! Here I was trying to save you from spilling your guts all over the room and you call me deranged? Hey." I frowned at his belly, then moved my gaze upward. There was blood on his chest and stomach all right, but it wasn't due to gashes. The blood followed the pattern of the curse. I reached up and gently touched the edge of one bloody curve. "That's the curse. It embedded itself in you. Oh, Constantine! I'm so sorry."

"You can't think you are responsible for this?" He lifted me to my feet despite my brain shrieking warnings about people who are bleeding from their torso making such exertions. "The curse is not of your making, Bee. Unless you are really Asmodeus in disguise, and since we saw him earlier, I suspect that can't be."

"Of course I'm not Asmodeus. But I did Charm the curse, and clearly, I did something wrong and it blew up on us—"

"And what of this?" He held up my hand.

I gave a little shriek at the sight of the ring. It was black now, as black as coal. "Get it off! Hellballs, it's stuck!"

Constantine examined my hand closely, touching the now-black ring. "Does it hurt?"

Slowly, I stopped panicking at the thought of the ring turning my finger black, and wiggled my fingers. "No."

"Is it uncomfortable?"

"Not really, no. I mean, I'm aware of it." I twisted the ring on my finger. It didn't seem to want to come off, but at least it moved. "My hand feels a bit heavier with the ring on it, but it doesn't bother me."

"Can you remove it?"

"Probably, if I really worked at it, but it doesn't feel like it wants me to do that. Should I be worried about it changing color?"

"No," he said after a moment's thought. "It must still have power; therefore, we must keep you safe from demons. Asmodeus would likely kill you to get the ring."

"Great," I said waspishly, and would have continued, but at that moment, an unearthly moan came from the other side of the room, followed by a hacking cough.

"Gary!" I whirled around to see if the head had been hurt. Evidently my own head, knocked around as it had been, protested such movement, and I weaved to the side and would have fallen if Constantine had not caught me up against his chest.

Constantine *tsk*ed at me. "You see? You are deranged. You have been hurt. You will stop fussing over me and let me see how badly you are harmed."

To my horror/surprise/secret swooning delight, Constantine scooped me up and, stepping carefully over the debris from the curse's percussion blast, set me down onto a clear section of the bar.

"Glorious green goddesses, what happened?" Gary groaned. "Did the demons set off a bomb?"

"I'm fine, Constantine. Stop trying to undress me," I said, slapping off Constantine's hands when he attempted to pull my shirt off. "That's seriously over the line, you know. Besides, it's my head that was hurt, not the rest of me."

"You're bleeding," Constantine pointed out, nodding

toward my shoulder, and with a speed I hadn't seen in a man, he had my nice linen shirt unbuttoned and tossed aside before I could blink. "You've been injured. I must ascertain where and how badly."

"I'm hurt, too. At least I think I am. Oh great, I lost a tooth," came Gary's feeble voice.

"You must *ascertain* nothing. For one, I'm not your responsibility, and for another, I'm a big girl and if I say I'm not hurt, then I'm not—ow." I turned my head to reach my shirt, when my ear brushed against my shoulder. Pain burned for a few seconds, causing me to reach up. My ear-lobe was wet with blood, and pierced by a jagged sliver of glass about the width of a pencil.

"Stay still, I will remove it."

I flinched, and was about to tell him to leave it be, that I'd get a professional to look at it, when there was a brief zing of pain from my ear, and Constantine was tossing the shard of glass onto the floor.

"Ten lords a-leaping!" I shouted, trying to clutch my poor, abused earlobe, but Constantine's head was in the way. "That hurt!"

"Stop being such an infant," he said sternly, peering close at the ear. "I have had much more grievous wounds, and never did you see me shrieking like a woman."

"I *am* a woman," I snarled, and gestured toward my breasts, exposed as they were in my bra. "Which should be pretty obvious to you since you were so fast to get my shirt off. Give me a cloth or something so I can stop my ear bleeding. I've got blood all over my shoulder now."

"It was my favorite tooth, too. Do you think I could get a gold replacement?"

We both continued to ignore Gary. Constantine pursed

his lips for a moment, then leaned in and blew on my ear. At least that's what I thought he did at first, but the momentary sting that followed quickly melted into a warm, tingling sensation that made me jerk back in fear.

"Did you just breathe fire on me?" I gasped, snatching up my shirt and holding it like a shield in front of me.

"I cauterized your wound, yes. It has stopped bleeding, and will now heal." He eyed my chest. "I should probably examine the rest of you to make sure you are not further injured."

"Over my dead body!" Hastily I hurried into my shirt, outrage pouring out of every gesture. "You are the deranged one if you think I'm going to allow that!"

A soft voice drifted over the bar. "He could breathe fire on me any time."

"You ogled my chest," Constantine said, giving me a half smile. "It is only fair that I have the same opportunity. Or do you not believe in equal rights?"

"Don't you even try that bullcrap on me," I snapped and, with my shirt buttoned, tentatively touched my earlobe. It felt numb, but didn't seem to be bleeding. "I'm as equal rights as they come, but that doesn't mean I don't know a manipulation when I see one."

"I'd love to have a gold tooth manipulated into my mouth."

"Gary," I said, turning my head to glare over at where the cage teetered perilously on the now drunken line of crates. "I appreciate that you lost a tooth, and I'm sorry about that, but really, Constantine and I are trying to have a serious discussion and—oh, hairy hellballs!"

It seemed like just the act of my looking at Gary spelled doom, for his cage suddenly lurched to the side, bounced twice on crates, and hit the floor with an audible crash, which was almost immediately followed by a fleshy splat.

Gary groaned pathetically.

I closed my eyes for a moment, asking Constantine, "Is he splashed all over the floor?"

"No." I cracked open an eye to see Constantine watching with interest as the cage rolled a few feet, and ran into a chair that, with exquisite slowness, rocked a moment before toppling over onto the cage. "Well, he wasn't. He might be now."

A faint, ghostly voice emerged from the mess. "Ow. Oh, so much ow. I think my dose id broken."

"It's like one of those insanely complicated Rube Goldberg machines," I commented, opening the other eye. "You okay, Gary?"

"Do," he answered, and the cage shook with a little tremor. "Hurty."

"You stay put," Constantine said, moving off to lift the chair from Gary's crushed cage.

"And you stop giving me orders. I don't like it, and I don't have to take it. Oh, dear, Gary, you are a mess."

"I feel like a bess." The head that looked up forlornly through the cage had a black eye, a nose that was bleeding freely, and a gaping hole where one of his front teeth had been.

"You poor thing. Hold tight, and we'll get you fixed up. I just want to make sure that Constantine isn't going to pass out from loss of blood first."

Constantine put his hands on his hips and glared at me. "I am a wyvern! Wyverns do not bleed to death unless you decapitate them first, and that is difficult to do. The blood you see is nothing."

"It's not nothing." I leaned in and eyed the fast-drying lines of blood on his chest and belly. "On the contrary, it's very something. I must have done something horribly wrong to make the curse revenge itself on you that way. I can't begin to tell you how sorry I am."

"It will heal," Constantine said without any concern for what must have been a very painful injury. He hoisted Gary's cage up and propped it up on the bar. The cage was dented and twisted almost out of recognition, and immediately began to roll off the counter until Constantine pulled it into a rough approximation of its former shape. "Cease fussing over me, woman. I will survive this, although I assume it means the curse is not lifted, as we thought?"

"No," I said sadly, still looking at his chest. It was almost as if the curse had seared itself into his flesh, but almost immediately began to heal over. The blood had dried and began to flake off as he moved, leaving behind an intricate pattern of reddened lines on his silky smooth skin. Even as I watched, the redness began to fade to a faint pink. "No, I'm afraid the curse is still there. Why, I have no idea—I must have done something wrong, taken some false turn in the Charming. But I swear to you I'll figure it out. I don't care how long it takes, or how many dragons we have to beat off...oh! Guillaume!"

"What about him?" Constantine buttoned his shirt and started pushing the crates back in front of the door.

"He didn't come running. He could be hurt or something." I hurried down the little hall to the office area, heading straight for the room with the safe. No one was there.

I checked the room across the hall, and was just about

to check the remaining two rooms when I heard a thump from the room I'd just left, and voices. I peeked in the room only to see a man with his back to me, bending through an open window, obviously helping someone else into the room.

"Demons," I whispered to myself, and was about to call for Constantine when I realized that would give the demons warning we knew they were here. I closed the door gently and dashed to the office, scanning the room wildly for something that would serve as a weapon.

There were no obvious swords or battle axes, or even a handgun, but there was a small wooden chair, and I hefted it and raced back to the hall, parking myself just outside the door with the chair hoisted over my head. My plan was to slam it down on the first demon, and then bolt while screaming like bloody hell for Constantine before the second one could grab me.

I took a deep, but silent, breath, and prayed to any gods I could think of to make the plan a success.

Seven

The door opened and a man emerged from the room just as Constantine, wondering what Bee was up to, wandered into the hallway.

He was just in time to see Bee start a downward swing with a heavy wooden chair. Constantine leaped forward, assuming the man was a demon, but just before reaching him, he realized the intruder was his godson, Kostya.

"No, Bee!" Constantine yelled at the same moment she obviously saw she'd made a mistake. It was too late for Kostya, however, since the bulk of the chair hit Kostya across the side of the head.

"Kostya! Mother of balls, I'm so sorry! Are you okay? Is Aoife here?" Bee danced around the now-staggering Kostya, wringing her hands in despair.

Constantine grabbed his sagging godson, and hoisted him upward, propping him against the wall. He examined the gash on the side of Kostya's face and gave him a brusque pat on the shoulder. "You'll survive."

Kostya started to slide down the wall, leaving a smear of blood behind.

"I've killed him!" Bee wailed. "I didn't mean to! Constantine, you know I didn't mean to, right? It was an accident! I thought he was a demon, and I had a plan, and was going to yell for you after I bashed the demon on the head, but now I've killed Kostya, and oh gods, my sister is going to murder me!"

Constantine shot her a pointed look, wondering if Bee did not see the irony of the situation, and debated pointing out that she was acting much the drama llama, but decided that on the whole, it would be better not to point out her obvious failing.

"No one is going to murder you," he started to say, but just as he did so, a smallish woman emerged from the room, one with long brown curly hair and clear gray eyes. She looked from him to Bee, then her eyes widened when she saw Kostya.

"What have you done to him?" The small woman leaped at Constantine, her fingernails raking down his front. "You'll pay for this!"

"Aoife, wait!" Bee tried to pull the woman off him, jerking her back by both arms. "Constantine's chest is all hurt from the curse striking back. Besides, he's not the one who beaned Kostya, I am."

The woman called Aoife—who Constantine remembered was the name of Bee's sister—released her hold on him and spun around. He thought for a moment she would attack Bee, but she simply snarled something quite rude before hurrying over to where Kostya was leaning drunkenly against the wall. "I might've known you'd feel free to bash Kostya's brains in."

Bee jerked back, rubbing her arms, her sister's words obviously cutting deep. Without considering the action, Constantine put his arm around Bee and pulled her to his side, saying, "She did not attack Kostya intentionally. She thought he was a demon, although I am unsure of why she came to that conclusion." He turned to Bee. "You have a reason for this?"

"Yes, of course I do." Bee, who was still rubbing her arms, leaned into him for a moment before realizing what she was doing, after which she dug her elbow into his side until he released her. Tipping her chin up in a manner he was coming to enjoy, she added, "He crawled in through the window. What was I to think but that he was a demon trying to break in?"

"Ah. That is a good reason." Constantine eyed the woman who was still fussing over Kostya.

"Good reason, my ass. You could have looked before you hit him," Aoife snapped. She gave him a frosty glance. "And just who are you?"

"Constantine," Kostya answered for him, the former reclaiming his wits at last. His voice was rough, but he reached up to stop Aoife from dabbing at his wound and pushed himself away from the wall. "That unfortunate being is Constantine Norka, once a member of the black dragons, and later the traitor who wrought their destruction."

"That is old history, and has no pertinence to the present," Constantine said with a noble lift of his own chin. "You are Aoife, sister to Bee? You do not look like sisters."

"Aoife takes after our father, while I seemed to get

most of my genes from our mom," Bee said, biting her lip. "I am sorry, Kostya, I really am. It's just—the demons are after us, and we have the ring, and then I Charmed the curse, but it backlashed against poor Constantine—well, I just kind of assumed that you were a baddy."

"Why did you think that a demon would be trying to get in?" Kostya asked, frowning.

"Because Constantine got the talisman from Abaddon."

Kostya transferred his frown to Constantine. "I might have known he'd have something to do with the situation. Everything he touches turns bad."

There was a word on the tip of Constantine's tongue, but before he could utter it, Bee hurried on. "It wasn't Constantine's fault. Not that part, anyway. Gary blabbered everything, and Asmodeus put the rest together, and Constantine says he let us escape so that his demons could follow us. Asmodeus's demons, not Constantine's. Ugh, I'm sounding just as confused as you look." Bee put a hand to the back of her head. "I got hit in the head, you know."

"You need not explain further," Constantine told her, wrapping his arm around her again. This time, she sagged into him without rejecting the embrace. "Kostya is clearly in an argumentative frame of mind, and will not benefit from your time. What are you doing here, godson?"

Kostya flinched at the last word. "If it was at all possible to have you removed as my godfather, I would do so, but the last time I broached the subject with my mother, she lectured me about the sins of my father."

"Toldi was quite mad at the end," Constantine agreed. "That does not change the fact that you have not answered my question."

"The front door was blocked. We had a call from the

Venediger's assistant saying that the curse was going to be Charmed without us, and we rushed here to make sure that all was well." Kostya's eyes lingered on Constantine's chest for a few seconds. "I was going to say I assume it ended well, but that looks as if it is a curse."

"The curse wasn't destroyed, I'm afraid," Bee said sadly, and Constantine was pierced with a need to assuage the guilt he knew she was feeling.

"It was not your fault," he said without thinking. "The curse is a powerful one. Asmodeus is a demon lord of much knowledge and skill. Or perhaps it was the talisman—perhaps it was not personal enough to him to act upon the curse as you desired."

"I wish that were so, but it really was my fault," Bee said, turning to face him. The look in her gray-green eyes stabbed deep in his belly. "I'm the Charmer. I'm the one responsible for breaking it. I should have known that the talisman wasn't right—"

"One moment," Kostya interrupted, glancing at Aoife. She was silent, but stood close to him as if she drew strength from the contact, and for a moment, Constantine felt a sense of quiet satisfaction that his godson, his namesake, had found a mate. Then he remembered the many times that Kostya had tried to kill him, and he brushed aside the silly sentiment.

"Did you say *Asmodeus's* curse?" Kostya asked, his eyes narrowing on them.

"Yes. Look, I can try again. Maybe I didn't study the curse long enough before trying to Charm it—"

"But it's not Asmodeus!" This time it was Aoife who interrupted.

Constantine raised his eyebrows. "Who isn't Asmodeus?

I assure you that the demon lord we saw in Abaddon was him. Gary even referred to him by name."

"Who's Gary?" Kostya asked, looking puzzled.

"I am. Ow. A chair fell on be, too."

"A chair fell on Bee?" Aoife asked, giving her sister a curious glance.

"No, on Gary. Or rather his cage. He broke his nose," Bee said, waving away the question. "That's really not important right now."

"I think it is," Gary said softly.

Aoife and Kostya both were staring at Gary with identical expressions of disbelief, but neither made any comment, which was fine with Constantine. He had more important things to do than explain why he had a disembodied head in a battered birdcage.

"It was Asmodeus we saw in Abaddon," Constantine insisted.

"I have no doubt that you did, but that is not what I meant," Kostya said, wincing when he touched the side of his head. "You have it wrong, as I might expect from one who caused so much tragedy amongst your own kin. The curse did not originate with Asmodeus."

"Not Asmodeus..." At that moment, Constantine felt his blood turn icy in his veins. He was frozen, unable to move, unable even to speak.

"Really?" Bee frowned. "But he is the head of Abaddon."

Memories swamped him, as did pain...and fear. The last was an emotion he'd deny until the day he breathed his last, but it didn't make it go away. He was afraid...he was very afraid.

"Yes, but we didn't find out until the day Aoife burned down G&T that Asmodeus didn't cast the curse." Kostya spoke just as if the world were the same as it had been a mere few seconds ago, but Constantine knew the truth.

And Bee, the sometimes annoying, sometimes enticing Bee just stood there with a slight wrinkle between her brows just as if nothing profound had happened. Sick with a sudden prescient awareness, Constantine opened his mouth to speak, but for the first time in his life, no sound emerged.

"Hey, that was a mistake, okay? I didn't intend to burn it down. Plus it's been rebuilt." Aoife glanced around the bar. "Well, almost rebuilt. It looks a bit worse now. What on earth happened in here?"

"The curse backfired. Or lashed out. Or punished Constantine for me trying to break it." Bee shook her head. "I don't know quite what happened, to be honest."

"I do." Kostya's lips thinned. "You used the wrong talisman."

Constantine's gut twisted. It was like he was caught in a nightmare, a horrible dream in which he was helplessly being pushed along to a being that loomed with black malevolence before him.

"How can you say that?" Bee asked, gesturing toward Constantine. "You don't even know what we used—"

"I know that whatever you took from Asmodeus is wrong because *Asmodeus* is wrong," Kostya answered.

"What are you talking about?"

"The demon lord who cast the spell wasn't Asmodeus. Didn't we tell you that?" Aoife asked, not looking at her sister.

"No, you most certainly didn't! You said the premier prince of Abaddon had cast a curse on the demons, and that's Asmodeus."

"Yes, well, we found out later that he wasn't really responsible for the curse. I must have forgotten to tell you that."

Bee looked angry, very angry, but Constantine could do nothing more than absently note that fact. His whole being was consumed with trying not to shriek out loud.

"That makes a huge difference, you know!" Bee said. "What an utter waste of my time and energy, not to mention making Constantine go to Abaddon to get the talisman in the first place. No wonder the Charming didn't work."

"I'm sorry," Aoife said, shooting Bee a quick look. "I thought I had told you about what happened at G&T, but everything was so confused and chaotic, that it just... slipped my mind."

Bee's lips thinned, but she simply said, "Well, now we're back to square one and we still have to get a talisman. So which demon lord *did* lay the curse on you if it wasn't Asmodeus?"

"Bael." The word came out of Constantine's mouth cracked and abrupt, as if it had been chipped from concrete. His gut twisted again at the word. He cleared his throat and tried again. "They speak of Bael."

"Who told you that? Your lady friend who you keep drooling over but who dumped you for someone else?" Bee looked angry all of a sudden. "Wait a minute, are you saying you *knew* Asmodeus didn't cast the curse and you didn't tell me?"

"No, Ysolde did not know any more than I did." Constantine had a sudden mad urge to scoop Bee up and take her somewhere safe, where they could live out their lives in quiet and solitude. It was such a startling emotion, he was momentarily distracted from the sense of horror that threatened to unman him. "She would have told me if she had known it was Bael. And if she didn't, Baltic would have."

Bee was shaking her head even before he finished speaking. "I realize you've been living with this curse for the last couple of years, but I think you're wrong. I know that Bael was banished to the Akasha, which meant Asmodeus took his place as head of Abaddon, a fact which we ourselves saw." A little wrinkle formed between Bee's brows. Constantine had an urge to run his thumb across those glossy red-brown eyebrows.

"Oh, yes, Bael was sent away to the Akasha," Gary said nasally, rolling himself upright so he could look at them through bleary eyes. "Asmo was thrilled aboud it, as you can imagine. He held a party to celebrate. They used me to decorate the top of a congratulatory cake. I wore a little top hat."

"Bael did cast the curse, and just what the hell *is* that?" Kostya asked, staring at Gary.

"I'm a who, not a what," Gary said, sniffing wetly.

"Gary is a knocker. Or he was. Now he's a disembodied head whose nose was broken, but is now healing." Bee's eyes narrowed on Kostya, and Constantine thought she was very close to exploding with rage. "Do you have any idea what trouble you put us to by not bothering to give us the correct information about the curse? Do you know what we've been through?"

"You are a Charmer," Kostya said stiffly.

"We didn't expect you to take off and try to find the talisman," Aoife said at the same time. "Kostya sent word to a thief-taker who was supposed to do that job. We had no idea you were going to try to get it, so really, you only have yourself to blame if you took it upon yourself to find the talisman."

"Silly me trying to do my job my efficiently because you dragons were taking so long." She held up a hand when Kostya started to protest. "Let's just agree that there could have been better communication on both sides, and stop beating that particular dead horse. We have more important things to do than argue. Just how did you find out that Bael laid the curse on you guys?"

Constantine enjoyed watching Bee struggle to rein in her temper. He liked the way that, other than an initial burst of anger, she didn't waste time throwing around blame. She simply reacted, then focused her attention on what needed to be done next. Kostya slid a quick look toward Aoife, who blushed. "That fact came out only after Bael was released."

"Inadvertently released," Aoife said quickly.

"Goddess, you're not going to tell me that Bael is *loose* now?" Bee asked. "Out of Abaddon? In the world with us?"

Constantine closed his eyes for a moment. Life simply could not get any worse.

"He is," Kostya said abruptly.

"I . . . er . . . I tried to break the curse using the ring, and it ended up summoning Bael from the Abaddon," Aoife admitted, meeting her sister's eyes for the first time. "Yes, it's all my fault, and don't think I haven't beaten myself up about it ever since that day, because I have."

"You are not responsible for Bael," Kostya said, pulling Aoife against him. The set of his jaw dared anyone to dispute his declaration.

Bee clearly was not impressed by such a show, and one part of Constantine's mind, the part not busy shrieking and screaming dire warnings, was vastly amused by that fact. She might irritate his sense of what was right, but she was a woman who was not afraid to face difficulty.

"I am, though," Aoife said, looking distressed. "It's because of me that he's out and about, and that G&T was burned down. If only we could get the talisman—"

"Well, you can't," Bee interrupted in her down-to-earth tone that made Constantine want to smile, and if he hadn't been so close to going insane with abhorrence, he might have done so. "Right, so now we have to find Bael, and *then* steal a talisman. Any idea where he is?"

"He *had* been in Asmodeus's palace," Kostya said.

Bee shook her head even before he stopped speaking. "We were just there. All we saw was Asmodeus, right, Constantine?"

Constantine, locked in a world of misery and horror that was rooted in his past, did not answer. He couldn't answer...at least, he couldn't admit the truth. Not to Bee. The thought of what she'd think, of the repulsion that would fill her face when she knew...no. He couldn't bear that.

"He left a few days ago, just before Asmodeus returned from a visit elsewhere, or at least that's what we assume. We had dragons watching, but he escaped our surveillance and went to ground somewhere." Kostya gave a little one-shouldered shrug. "We do not know where."

"Which of course makes it infinitely more difficult to find a talisman. If only I'd known this before—" Bee stopped, and shook her head at her own statement. "Ignore that. I said let's not beat that dead horse, and I won't."

"Speaking of your ghostly ways," Kostya said, giving

Constantine a gimlet eye, "why are you still here? You usually fade away to nothing the second you are wanted."

Constantine dragged his mind from the blackness that consumed it, and glared at his godson. "You forget yourself, Konstantin Nikolai Fekete. More, you forget to whom you speak."

"I speak to the traitor who is responsible for the deaths of hundreds of dragons."

Bee shot him a startled look. He ignored it, focusing his ire on the upstart before him. "I do not have time to teach your place, nor the true facts of what happened all those centuries ago. There are other things more important than you that I must accomplish in order to save all dragonkin."

"That's right," Bee said, nodding her head and surreptitiously taking his hand. He was startled by the contact, not just because she initiated it despite her stated dislike of dragons, but because the touch set the fire smoldering inside him to a blaze. No woman had done that since he had lost Ysolde. "We have more important things to do, like finding Bael, and stealing a talisman from him. I guess we'd better get started on that. Where was Bael last seen?"

"Here in Paris," Kostya answered somewhat sulkily.

"Excellent. Then we can get started right away on the job. We can start at the Paris entrance to Asmodeus's palace, and try to resurrect a trail for him. Sound good, Constantine?"

"No," he answered, and without another word, he released Bee's hand, picked up Gary, and strode out of the G&T.

Eight

"Constantine!"

The voice that chased him was full of disbelief and frustration. He knew both sensations well. He'd lived with them for most of his life. *Both* lives.

"I think Bee wants you, Connie," Gary said helpfully, looking out of the back of the cage. A woman they passed on the street gasped, stumbled, and toppled forward in a faint. "Goodness. Woman down! Maybe you should stop and help her."

"Constantine, where are you going? Why did you just walk out like that?" Bee's voice was breathless as she hurried after them.

"That's definitely Bee," Gary said, squinting against the sun. He turned when they approached a couple of teen-age girls, making a movement that could be interpreted as a bow, and said politely, "*Bonjour, desmoiselles.*"

The girls didn't bat an eyelash at him.

"Constantine! For the love...pardon me, madam, I

didn't mean to step on your hand. Did you fall? Here, let me help you up, and then I really must dash..."

Bee's voice grew fainter as Constantine marched onward, pausing only when he came to a street corner.

"This is fun," Gary chirped, smiling at everyone on the street. "It's been forever since I was out of Abaddon. Paris has changed so much since I was alive. Ooooh, a boulangerie! I would murder for a fresh croissant. I don't suppose you're a bit peckish? *Bonjour, monsieur et madam. Bonjour, bonjour,* everyone!"

Constantine walked on, dark thoughts tormenting him, followed by various gasps, shrieks, and muttered calls for mercy when the patrons of the area caught sight of Gary. Most of them were members of the Otherworld, but Constantine was in such a bleak place mentally and emotionally, he had little empathy to spare the mortals who had no idea that such things as a sentient head existed.

Or rather, he told himself, it was because he had nothing but concern for the mortals that he could spare no time in hiding Gary from them.

"Criminy beans!" Bee burst out as she reached him, panting slightly, and grabbed his sleeve so that he faced her. Her eyes, a bright shade of gray-moss in the Paris sun, were full of questions. "What is wrong with you? Why are you letting everyone see Gary? And more important, why did you leave? Is something the matter? I know you're pissed because Kostya keeps harping at you about some old history—"

"No," he said simply, and lifted her hand from his sleeve. He looked at her fingers for a moment, then bent slightly and pressed his lips to them before dropping her hand and continuing down the street.

"Ooooh," Gary said, blowing a low whistle. "She doesn't

like that, Connie. I think she's swearing. Whoops, here she comes. Act casual."

"Now you just listen here, Mr. Bigshot Dragon!" Bee grabbed Constantine's arm again and dug in her heels. Behind her, a woman stepped out of a small shop, and fell over with a squawk at the sight of Gary. "I don't know what bee got in your butt—and by bee, I don't mean me, because that would be just really unacceptable, not that your butt isn't nice-looking and all—never mind, not going there. I don't know what has upset you to the point where you just say the word 'No!' and then stomp off, but I do know that it's not going to fly. What is wrong?"

Constantine thought about simply walking away from her, but there was something in her eyes that kept him in place. She tried hard to give the impression that she disliked him, but he had seen the softness in her face when she looked at the scars on his chest, and felt the heat of her mouth as it welcomed his. True, she said later she hadn't been welcoming him, but he had a feeling he could change her mind on that point. The idea that he might do such a thing was startling in itself; although he told himself that his heart would ever be true to Ysolde, he had to admit that his body hadn't any such conviction.

The sound of screeching metal, followed by a screams, a car horn, and ultimately, cursing, drove him into looking around for a safe haven. He spied a shop that looked likely and hustled Bee into it.

A middle-aged woman looked up from a long wooden counter. At her feet, an elderly Welsh corgi slept, snoring slightly. "*Bonjour*," the woman said.

"Good day." Constantine set Gary on the counter. The air inside the shop was slightly scented with elements of decades past, tiny little motes dancing in the sun that streamed through the window. "Would you watch Gary for a few minutes? He is causing a disturbance on the street. I can pay you."

The woman blinked, her eyes widening at the sight of the battered cage and its contents.

"*Bonjour!*" Gary chirped, looking around with interest. "Oooh, are you an apothecary? How exciting! I've always loved visiting them, although as a knocker, I never got to cast spells or do anything that needed to use the things you carry. Hello, doggy! What's his name?"

"Her name is Cecile," the woman said, giving Constantine a thoughtful look. "It is not often that I have dragons visit. You are not a member of the green sept, I believe?"

"No. I am Constantine, wyvern of the silver dragons," he answered with a bow.

"Formerly the wyvern. *Now* he's a big pain in the ass," Bee said, giving him a scowl that he supposed was meant to intimidate. "I'm Bee Dakar, by the way. I think we met some time ago at a party the Venediger gave—your name is Emily?"

"Amalie," the woman corrected, and with her mouth half pursed, waved to a corner where a couple of well-worn armchairs sat around a small round table. "You do not need to pay me to watch your...friend. Cecile and I will be happy to keep him company if you wish to sit in the reading corner."

"Awesome!" Gary beamed at her. "My name is Gary, as Constantine said. Well, it's Gareth, really, but no one seems to remember that, and all the demons call me Gary..."

Constantine took Bee's arm and escorted her to the secluded section of the shop. The walls were lined with floor-to-ceiling bookcases that contained few books, but a vast quantity of old-fashioned glass jars of all shapes and sizes. Each bore a label with enticing names like cat's tongues, lilywort, and virgin's blood. Outside, the sounds of the city were muffled and distant, giving Constantine the feeling of seclusion.

"If only it would last," he muttered to himself.

"If what would last?"

"Sanity." He held on to the back of the nearest chair, being prepared to do the gentlemanly thing and seat her first (Georgette Heyer was very strong on male characters following such standards), which is why he was so surprised when, rather than sitting as he expected, Bee leaned into him and lightly pressed her lips to his.

"Was that supposed to be a kiss?" he asked when she pulled back.

The self-satisfied look on her face faded to one of annoyance. "It was very much a kiss, yes. It was supposed to be a comforting gesture since you are obviously distressed about something, but now I take it back. Oafs like you don't need comforting!"

"I am a wyvern, not an oaf. And wyverns enjoy being kissed, but only when it's done properly."

Bee opened and closed her mouth a couple of times, clearly outraged. "My kiss was just fine!"

"It wasn't. It was a mere pressing of lips. There was no passion, no heat, no teasing of the mouth, no whispered promises of pleasure, no hint of the sweet joy that lies within. And then there was the way you leaned forward to do it, ensuring that no other part of your body touched mine. A kiss is more involved—"

"Criminy beans, don't you ever shut up?"

"I assumed you wished to know what elements of your kiss were lacking—"

Bee swore and grabbed Constantine's head with both hands, pulling him forward even as she lunged against him, her belly pressed against his, her hips cradling him in way that would ensure he'd walk funny for at least a half hour. Her mouth took possession of his, a startling change of role that at first shocked him, and then immediately switched to approval when her tongue twined around his. He allowed her to taste him, to tease his tongue and lips, his hands sliding down her back until he held her bottom, pulling her even tighter.

She moaned into his mouth, tugging on his hair in a way that made his eyes cross. His fire, that part of him that seemed as natural as breathing, roared to life beneath the taste and scent and feel of her, and filled every part of his being.

"Fire," she murmured into his mouth, then suddenly shrieked and pushed him back, slapping at her legs.

Constantine, who had been greatly enjoying the kiss, frowned at the little dance she was doing. Yes, his fire was burning up her legs, but since she hadn't complained when he breathed a little fire on her earlier, he assumed she was capable of taking the full brunt of his passion.

Passion, he pointed out to himself, that she had stirred.

"For goodness sake, do something!" Bee demanded, still slapping at her legs.

"Are you hurt?" he asked.

"Not yet, but I'm on fire! Are you blind? Or do you just not care?"

With a flicker of his eyes, he damped his fire, effectively extinguishing the flames circling her. He stood with his hands on his hips, considering her as she muttered to herself while examining the material of her jeans. "You are a woman of many contradictions."

"Yeah, well, you're none too stable yourself. One minute you're looking like someone killed your favorite pet, and the next you're lecturing me about the proper way to kiss."

The heavy burden of reality settled back around his shoulders, threatening to press him into the ground.

"See? You're doing it again," Bee said, straightening up to glare at him. "What is going on, Constantine? Why are you behaving this way? I thought you wanted to help the dragons get rid of the curse."

He thought of many answers to that last question, of the cost of what she asked of him, and his heart sobbed.

"Give me a break," Bee grumbled, and then with a martyred sigh, she wrapped her arms around Constantine, saying into his neck, "Tell mama what's wrong."

He started to laugh at that; he just couldn't help it. The confluence of his raging erection from the kiss joined with her motherly attempt at comforting was too much for him. He gave her a squeeze, pressed a none-too-innocent kiss to the top of her head, and with a brief but enjoyable fondle of her bottom, released her.

"Sit," he said, gesturing to the chair.

She sat. Amalie was busy entertaining Gary at the front desk, and quite obviously not looking in their direction. Constantine took the armchair opposite Bee, and said simply, "I can't help you with Bael."

"Is that what's causing the problem? Then don't worry. I'll get a talisman from him myself—"

"No," he interrupted, trying to pick out what he could tell her, and what he did not wish revealed. "You cannot. He will destroy you."

Bee held up a hand for a moment before dropping it. "Look, we've had this conversation before, and yes, I know that Asmodeus caught me when I tried to get his talisman—really, Aoife has a lot to answer for in not bothering to keep me up to date about the major players in this little drama—but that doesn't mean that Bael will do the same. I've learned my lesson, there, and will be extremely careful."

"He will kill you nonetheless." Constantine was suddenly weary, the sort of weary that built up over centuries of time. He leaned back in the chair, gesturing limply at nothing. "Asmodeus is an amateur compared to Bael. If he even thought you had the idea of trespassing on his private domain, he'd destroy you. There is no leniency in him, no shades of gray, nothing but black and white absolutes."

Bee tipped her head to the side and gave him a long look. "That sounds like you know him."

"I do." His gut twisted painfully.

"How well?"

He hesitated. "Well enough to know that if Bael is the creator of the curse that blights the dragonkin, then it is a curse we will suffer under to the end of days."

"Now who's being overly dramatic?" Bee stopped him in mid-protest. "That wasn't meant to be an insult. But that said, he *was* overthrown and cast into Abaddon, so he's not invincible. And even if he were, we aren't trying to get rid of *him*, we're just trying to break his curse."

For a few minutes, Constantine was tempted by Bee's spirit to be the hero she clearly needed. She was so positive, so convinced that what they faced was a simple matter of taking one little item from Bael, that he considered going against his common sense and casting in his lot with her.

But then he remembered the last time he had crossed Bael, and the cost of such a folly. "No," he said, rising, giving her a long, steady look to let her know he wasn't going to be swayed. "What you ask is impossible."

He started to leave, pausing when Bee spat one word out at him.

"Coward."

He turned slowly, the word crawling across his flesh, burrowing down deep into his psyche, and echoing in his head.

He was a coward. At least, that was the word that Bael had last flung at him. He'd wanted to kill Bael at the time, but Bee was not a demon lord. She didn't even anger him with that accusation, because he knew that were he in her place, he'd do the same.

If only she knew the truth ... he wavered for a moment, wanting to bare his soul to her, wishing with a desire that startled him with its intensity that Bee were his mate. If she were, then she would stand by him, no matter what dark secrets he harbored.

He watched her for a moment, the yearning so strong it stung the backs of his eyes. Bee's eyes glittered angrily. He simply shook his head and said, "If it is cowardly to wish to avoid wholesale death and destruction of both the mortal and immortal worlds, then I accept the name."

"Constantine, wait. I didn't mean that. I'm just frustrated—"

He collected Gary, thanked Amalie, and left the shop before Bee could do more than to splutter a few angry words.

Nine

"I can't believe he just walked out on me." I stood staring at the door of Amalie's shop, half expecting that Constantine would reappear, an apology on his really delicious lips. I stomped my foot before I realized I was doing it. "And he took Gary!"

"He is a dragon and a wyvern," Amalie said, giving me a shuttered look. Her face was placid, as mild as the tone of her voice, giving me no clue to what she really thought. "They do as they please, do they not?"

"Yes, but we're supposed to be working together." I was suddenly struck by the question of just what point in time my job had gone from a solo endeavor to one where I was dependent on Constantine. "Dammit, I don't need him."

Amalie's eyebrows rose in surprise at the two conflicting statements.

"Sorry," I said, gesturing toward the door. "It's…he's… the whole thing is complicated."

"I see." She bent over to pat the fat Welsh corgi who snored in a fleece dog bed. "I rather imagine it would be difficult to be a wyvern's mate. I have known only one other, and she had a very hard time accepting it. I believe it took her some time before she welcomed the role."

"Mate? Oh no, I'm not Constantine's mate. We're not even dating! We were just thrown together in the process of a commission I accepted, and since we had a common goal, I assumed he'd stick around to see it finished." I gave the door a bitter look. "Clearly, I was mistaken in my judgment of his character. The big toad."

"I could not help but notice your activities earlier," Amalie said without meeting my gaze. She scratched behind the dog's ears. "I do not know of anyone, especially a mortal, who can take a dragon's fire without being injured."

"I can't," I said, holding out my wrist so she could see the scar. "I used to date a dragon, and that was the result of a little fire play."

"Your legs were surrounded by dragon fire just a few minutes ago," she pointed out with a gentleness that for some reason irritated me.

"Yes, but that's different. Constantine was being all sexy-man, and it got away from him. My legs were protected by my jeans, and he put it out before it could do more than singe the fabric, whereas the time that Ben Fong—a red dragon I dated for a while before I learned my lesson about dragons—the time that Ben slipped a little with the fire thing, it burned my bare hand."

Amalie stood up. "Indeed? Well, you must know best, but I will say that I have not heard that there is more than one type of dragon fire. However, I am far from an expert on such things." She straightened a stack of small leather-bound journals on the counter. "Can I assist you in anything else?"

"No, thank you. And I apologize for us using your store as a snogging parlor. I don't normally indulge in public displays like that, especially not with dragons, and double especially when the dragon in question is maddeningly obstinate." Sad, I moved toward the door. "I guess I'll just have to do the job on my own."

"Perhaps your friend would help you if you asked him," Amalie suggested.

I shook my head and pushed open the door, allowing sunlight and the noises of the street to stream into the quiet little shop. "He's made it quite clear that he has no further interest in breaking the curse. Well, thank you again. I hope to see you another time soon."

Amalie returned the compliment, and I left the comforting confines of the shop and emerged into the late afternoon sun of Paris. There was no sign of Constantine on the street, which for some reason made my heart sink to the bottoms of my feet.

Three hours later, I was escorted into a pleasant living room of a large house in a high-income section of Paris, and was welcomed by a woman with a genuine smile, and a large black dog.

"You must be Bee. I'm Aisling Grey. Kostya says that you are looking for a demon?"

"Yes, that's right. I have to find Bael, and since he's slipped away from the dragons' watching eyes, I had an idea that perhaps a demon could track him down where you guys couldn't."

"Hmm," Aisling said, considering that. "It's possible, I guess. Although I haven't heard of it being done before."

"Sometimes you have to make your own fate rather than waiting for others to do it for you," I said, trying to look wise. "I figured it's worth a try since you were in Paris, and my only other option is to hire a tracker to find him."

"Drake tried that," she said, speaking about her dragon mate. "He said the trackers lost Bael almost immediately. But a demon...hmm." She glanced at the dog sitting at her feet. "Jim, you may speak now."

"Whew!" the dog said on a whoosh of breath, leaving me momentarily surprised to find that he was obviously not what he appeared. "Hiya. Name's Jim. You have dragon scales on you. Been necking with a dragon?"

"What? No!" I glanced down at the front of my shirt and brushed off a few of the translucent, minute scales that dragons seemed to exude like a fine pollen. "I just kissed him, nothing more. Not that it's here or there."

"Dragon mate," Jim said, nodding, and got up to sniff at my shoes. "Which sept?"

"I have no idea, and I'm not a mate."

"No, of course you're not," Aisling said with a nudge to the dog's backside. "If you were, the curse would make sure we wouldn't be able to talk. Jim, stop being so nosy."

The dog narrowed his eyes in thought. "Man, it's a familiar scent...at least I think it is, but I just can't place it. Gotta be that memory loss I suffered earlier. Okay, I give. Who's the dragon?"

"That's none of our business, Jim," Aisling said primly,

then ruined that impression by adding, "although I am human enough that I have to admit I'd like to know. Not just for the sake of knowing—there're very few mortal women who dare date a dragon, since their fire can be deadly."

"I'm not *dating* Constantine—"

"Constantine Norka?" Aisling interrupted, her eyes big. "Wow. I didn't think—that is, he's a ghost, so I didn't imagine he could...er...perhaps we'd just best let that whole subject go."

"Perhaps we should." I squashed the irritation that rose every time I thought of Constantine walking out on me. "Can you help me summon a demon so I can find Bael?"

"Yes, but I should warn you that this plan is pretty dangerous."

I shrugged. "I have no problem with that."

She watched me thoughtfully for the count of eight before continuing. "You know, Constantine might be a good solution to the problem. He's a ghost, and he can slip in and out of our reality."

"Not anymore he can't." I gave Aisling a brief explanation of the bête noire. "Now he's stuck in the world with the rest of us."

"Hmm." Aisling gave me an unreadable look. "I don't think I've ever tried to break a bête noire. I could try, but it could be that Constantine is happier the way things are. He was always running out of energy at the most inopportune moments..."

"I don't know what he wants." For a moment or two, I was beset with an odd emotion: part frustration, part protectiveness. I knew exactly what Aisling had been subtly hinting, and while the idea of Constantine in a permanently corporeal form was pleasant, less so was the idea that he might use that fact to engage in sexual acts with other women.

Dammit, I did not want to get involved with him. Not romantically. I wanted a nice, normal man, one who wasn't complicated, and who wouldn't drive me crazy.

"Perhaps we could ask him to find Bael anyway," Aisling said, following her own train of thought. "He's still a ghost even if he's in physical form, so he can't be killed if he is caught again. And if we locate Bael, he could steal the talisman you need."

I laughed a short, harsh, and very bitter laugh. "Oh, that's been tried, and failed pretty spectacularly, let me tell you. When I asked Constantine about getting Bael's talisman, he just turned into a block of ice and then stomped out."

"A block of ice? Constantine?" Aisling shook her head. "I don't know him very well, but I find that unlikely."

"Regardless, it's true. I don't mean to rush you, but can we get to the demon summoning? I'd like to get this over before the night is gone."

Aisling thought for a moment, then stood up. "We don't have to summon a demon. I'll have Jim do the job. It's much safer than any other demon I could summon."

"Jim is a demon?" I watched him a bit warily.

"Fifth class," Jim said with pride.

"Yes, it is. It belongs to me, so there won't be any risk of a demon two-timing you, although I'm not sure one could if I summoned it for the express purpose of following your commands."

I was reminded that most people referred to demons by gender-neutral terms, but I couldn't bring myself to do that. I patted the dog on his head while he gave me a once-over: both visually, and with his nose. "Cool," he said after a few seconds' silence. "I can try, although I'm going to need food to do any sort of tracking. Lots and lots of food."

"You've had lunch, and we won't have dinner for another few hours," Aisling said. "Effrijim, I command thee to aid and assist Bee Dakar by any means necessary. There, that ought to do it. May I offer you a beverage, Bee? Some tea? Coffee? Dragon's blood?"

I stared at her in horror for a few seconds before I remembered the dark red, heavily spiced wine that no one but dragons drank, commonly referred to as dragon's blood. I stood up and slung my bag across my chest. "No, thank you. I'd like to get started, since I hope to find Bael by morning. I'll bring Jim back to you as soon as I can."

"Oh, it won't be going with you," Aisling said, smiling benignly. Before I could ask what she meant, she muttered a few words, her hands dancing in the air as she drew two wards, after which Jim disappeared in a puff of oily black smoke that lingered in the air before slowly falling to the floor. "Jim'll check around Abaddon to see what it can find out there about Bael."

"But...but I thought..."

"Trust me, I know demon lords, and if anyone knows Bael's location, it's the princes of hell. Jim'll just do a little covert sniffing around, as it were, and pick up the gossip on what Bael's up to."

"If it's that easy," I couldn't help but ask, wondering just what sort of people these dragons were, "then why didn't you locate him before now?"

Aisling made a face. "I told Drake that we'd find Bael when we needed him. He was all, 'let the dragons handle this, and stay out of Abaddon—we don't need anything to do with them since they are warring with us,' and so on." She gave a little roll of her eyes and laughed. "You coming to me is the perfect excuse to show him that we don't necessarily have to do everything the hard way. Luckily, he's in the country checking on our kids, so I have tonight to help you before he comes home and finds out we fixed things without dragony intervention."

I smiled, not convinced, but grateful for any help I could get. "How long do you think we'll need to wait?"

"Hours." She glanced at a clock. "You're welcome to stay, but if you have other things to do, I'd suggest coming back around midnight. That will give Jim a good six hours of poking around Abaddon, and by then he ought to have an idea of whether the demons and demon lords know where Bael is, and how willing they are to talk."

I left agreeing to return at midnight, and slowly made my way to the arrondissement containing the hotel I stay at when I'm in Paris. The Hôtel de la Femme Sans Tête is known more for its budget nature rather than fabulous accommodations, but it was my Parisian home away from home.

At the reception desk was a familiar face.

"Bonjour, Luc," I greeted the man behind the latest copy of *Charlie Hebdo*. He was round like an egg, with pomaded black hair, a nose ring, and alchemical symbols tattooed on each of his fingers.

"Eh? Oh, it is you," he grunted at me, setting down his magazine only when I asked if there were any messages for me.

"Tch," he said, sucking his teeth as he heaved himself out of the chair and padding over to where an old-fashioned pigeonhole arrangement housed room keys, mail, and phone messages. "There are three."

I waited a minute. It was a game that Luc and I played, although I had a sneaky suspicion that the game aspect was solely on my side. "Might I have them?"

He *tch*ed again, but deigned to pluck the three sheets of pale canary paper from the pigeonhole, and slide them across the desk before resuming his seat and magazine with the air of one who has been well martyred.

The first message was from the coordinator of the local Charmer's chapter, reminding me of the annual conference coming up in three weeks. The second was dated two days ago, and was from Kostya informing me that a dragon had been sent to fetch the talisman.

"Old news," I muttered, stuffing the two messages in my pocket. The third was not dated, but I figured it had to be recent.

Help! The message read. *Connie's stomping around muttering to himself and swearing a lot. In Latin. Also, he refuses to feed me, saying he's too upset to eat, although he did get me a new home. It's very fancy. Hugs and kisses, Gary. P.S. We're staying at the Hôtel du Monde au Balcon—some sort of house of prostitution. Connie has depths to him. Dark depths. Rescue me?*

"Hôtel du Monde au Balcon...Hotel of people on a balcony?" I translated aloud.

Luc shook his magazine, but didn't look at me when he spoke. "It means large breasts. It is the street talk, no?"

"Ah, gotcha." I crumpled up the message and tossed it on top of the other two in the metal trash bin next to the reception desk. "Trust Constantine to park himself at a brothel."

Luc pursed his lips. "Why is it I am taking the messages of much importance if you are throwing them away? It is trouble for me, you know? First, I must answer the phone. Then I must find the paper so that I may record the message. After I have done that, I must find a pencil. And then I must arrange the message in the correct hole of pigeons." His nose ring twitched. "This service, it is not one every hotel offers, you know. You would not get such at the Hôtel du Monde au Balcon."

I bit back the observation that all hotels did, in fact, take messages for their patrons, and instead smiled. "Sorry. Thank you for taking the message, but it's not one I care about."

"I will remember that the next time you get a call," Luc said with a righteous sniff.

"Sorry," I repeated.

Luc retreated behind his magazine and did not answer other than rustling it in a meaningful way. I started for the elevator, made a face at the sign that announced it was "not marching" (and noting to myself that it had never been working in all the years I had stayed there), and made a beeline for the stairs. I had one foot on the bottom one, when I spun around, walked quickly to the desk, snatched the topmost message from the trash, and quickly retreated to my room on the second floor before Luc could do more than snort a triumphant "Ha!"

"Fine, so I do care. But only because he risked his own welfare to get me out of a bad situation. So sue me." I ran up the stairs to my second-floor room, wondering what Constantine was doing at that moment, which just made

126 Katie MacAlister

me angry with myself, because the man clearly didn't give a damn about what I was going through.

"I can't believe that he just walked away after making all that fuss about being the one to get the talisman," I said out loud, pacing the length of my hotel room. I glanced out of the windows as if I expected to see the man himself standing on the street. "He's just a big phony, that's all he is. One who really knows how to kiss. Hoo. Say what you will about dragons, they do that very well."

Guilt pricked me when I thought of his chest, that lovely warm chest with the two adorable nipples, and the soft, golden hair scattered across it. That beautiful chest was now scarred thanks to my ineptitude. Oh, sure, Aoife and her dragon were partly to blame for not keeping me up to date about the source of the curse, but I should have listened to my inner voice when it said something was wrong.

I snatched up the phone next to the bed, pulled out Gary's note, and had dialed the number written before I realized what I was doing.

"Yes?"

"It's me, Bee. How's your chest?" The minute the words left my mouth I felt like an idiot. He was a dragon! Immortal! And he hadn't seemed bothered by the curse searing itself into his drool-worthy chest.

"What chest? I have a rolling suitcase that I liberated from Baltic, but I did not bring my chest of toys with me to Paris."

"No, not that chest—"

"To go to all that trouble and expense would be folly," he said dismissively. "There is a very accommodating shop here that sells many items to denizens of the Otherworld. They have a particularly fine display of nipple devices."

I stared at the wall in blank confusion. "They do?"

"Yes. I particularly enjoy their nipple suction tortoises. They are not real tortoises, you understand—they simply are shaped like them. But they have quite pleasing amount of power to them."

"Just how many women do you use them on?" I couldn't help but ask. "Sorry, that was rude. I just...for a man who says you are in love with another dragon's mate, you sure seem to talk about sex toys a lot. Are you...are they for you? Or someone else?"

"I am pleased that you are interested in them," he said by way of a non-answer. I ground my teeth together a little over the fact that dragons seldom answered questions in a straightforward manner, especially when you really wanted to know the answer. "Would you like a set? I would be happy to accompany you to the shop so that you might pick out a set of your own."

I opened my mouth to correct his false impression, to tell him I wasn't interested in kinky sex toys (even if I couldn't help but wonder at the fact that he had an entire trunk full of them), or point out that he hadn't answered my question, nor even to ask him if he was feeling any after-effects of the curse. What came out of my mouth, of course, was, "Sure."

"I will pick you up in an hour. Where are you staying?"

"At the Hôtel de la Femme sans Tête, but Constantine, I don't really want—"

"Do you have sunglasses? Wear them. How big is your head?"

"I...I...I don't know—"

"Never mind; I'll make a guess. I will meet you on the street outside your hotel in an hour."

"But—"

The phone went silent. I banged my forehead softly on the wall, swearing at my stupid libido for being unable to resist a sexy dragon even though I knew better. "Cripes, Bee, you'd think you'd never met an attractive man before. Get a grip, girl!"

It took a concerted effort, but I managed to avoid thinking about Constantine while I took a shower, checked with Aisling that there was no word yet from her demon, and then tackled some overdue paperwork regarding the last case of Charming I'd done a few weeks before.

It wasn't until I was trotting down the stairs at the appointed time that I paused and asked aloud, "How big is my head? The man is deranged," much to the amusement of the couple slowly proceeding ahead of me.

The street outside the hotel wasn't busy, it being one of the smaller off-the-beaten-path streets in an area given over mostly to folks who may not be strictly mortal, but I heard the low growl long before I saw its source.

I didn't know what I expected other than, perhaps, one of those low-slung Italian sports cars, but when the growl—and Constantine—rounded the corner, I realized why he had inquired after my head.

"I brought this for you," he said, handing me a glossy black helmet. I took it, pursing my lips in a silent whistle as I eyed the motorcycle that rumbled beneath him. It was mostly black, like the helmet, but had an intricate silver dragon painted on the body, starting with a tail that coiled over the rear tire, to iridescent flames that spewed out over the handlebars.

"That is a hell of a bike," I said, pulling on the helmet without bothering to worry about how it would squash my hair.

"I enjoy riding it. I was seldom able to because I was never sure when I would run out of energy, but now..." He made an indefinable gesture. "Now that is not a concern."

"Doesn't it bother you that you've lost some indefinable part of what makes you, you?" I asked, climbing on behind him when he gestured toward the rear. Without even asking permission, my body hugged his, my thighs sliding with apparent familiarity around his, my arms around his torso before I knew what they were doing.

"Being a spirit, you mean?" He gunned the engine, making the machine roar into life before it settled back to a low growl. "No. I am a wyvern. Wyverns do not disappear into nothing because they've run through their available energy. *Allons-y!*"

"Oooh, are you a *Doctor Who* fan, too?" I yelled when the bike leaped forward. Constantine, being all immortal and such, didn't bother with a helmet, which just meant I could surreptitiously bury my face in his hair.

"A what fan?" he yelled back, not turning his head.

I bit back the urge to start an Abbott and Costello "Who's on First" bit, and simply yelled back that it didn't matter, and then settled down to enjoy the sensation of my arms around him, and his hair caressing my cheeks with little silken whips.

The combination of wind and his hair made my eyes stream, so I closed them and concentrated on trying to pinpoint just what his scent was. It reminded me of a walk through the woods, with pine needles crunching underfoot, and sunlight streaming through the branches to touch upon dark, rich earth. Pine, I decided, with a hint of moss, and just the faintest whiff of a rare, exotic spice as a top note.

I sucked in vast quantities of air, enjoying the smell from his hair, and was indulging in a little bit of fantasy wherein neither one of us had to deal with a demon lord, when he pulled up at a red light and turned his head to speak.

"Why are you snuffling in my ear? Are you trying to bite it?"

"Me?" I recoiled for a moment, almost lost my balance, and grabbed his belly again. "No! I would never do such a thing."

"Then you must be excited about visiting the Curiosités Demonia shop. I do not blame you—the proprietor is most comprehensive in his range of merchandise."

"I really don't care about—"

A blast of a taxi horn interrupted my protestation, and given that Constantine had to swerve up onto the sidewalk (scattering the few people contained thereon) in order to avoid hitting the taxi, I decided that it would be better for him to focus on driving.

Ten minutes later we pulled up in front of a small white stone annex to what looked like a miniature version of Sacre Coeur in Montmartre. "Mother of marmots, is that a church next to the sex shop?" I asked, nodding to the glorious white three-story building. It was all small domes and gorgeous stone columns, and detailed stonework that included fleur-de-lis, six-pointed stars, and various symbols of the moon.

"That? No. This way." He opened the door to the annex

building (uninspiring décor-wise compared to its compatriot), and ushered me through a jet-black curtain.

I've been in sex shops before, so I was expecting bright lights, tacky plastic packaging around items of all shapes, sizes, and colors, along with a rack of cheaply made costumes, and possibly even a back room where the whips and restraints were kept. What I found was something altogether different.

"Wow." My voice was small and hushed as I looked around the open floor. Long, low umber benches sat before items displayed in recessed wall cases, the kind with tasteful lighting from above and below. Next to each recess was a discreet label that, upon closer inspection, gave the item name and price. "It's like a museum, or a high-class art gallery."

There were a few people in the shop, a couple of ladies who sat with their heads together in front of a red leather harness that was draped over what looked like a classical Greek marble statue. At the far end, a curved desk sat, with two tiny modernistic chairs, which were occupied by a male and female couple who reminded me of beatniks from the 1950s—they wore hipster sunglasses, were all in black, had long, straight hair, and the man sported a long amber cigarette holder that was (thankfully) empty of a cigarette.

"The tortoise-shaped nipple teasers are over here," Constantine said, pulling me over to one of the lit mini-alcoves.

"Yes, indeed they are," I agreed, trying not to raise my eyebrows at both the price (two hundred euros) and the subject matter (your basic nipple suction devices made out of tortoiseshell). "So, now that we're here, I wonder if we could have a little chat."

"Would you like a set?" Constantine didn't wait for an answer; he turned and lifted his hand in the air. As if by magic, a small, dark man with black hair that was slicked back on his head glided out from behind a section of the wall that must have led to another room. "Ah, Balzac. I wondered if you were about."

"Balzac? You're kidding, right?" I asked softly, but had to school the disbelief off my face when the man stopped in front of Constantine. He made me a bow, then repeated it to Constantine, saying, "Monsieur Wyvern of Norka. The sight of you here, in my humble shop brings joy to my heart, and tears to my eyes. The Curiosités Demonia has missed your presence."

Constantine inclined his head graciously, and waved a hand toward me. "This is Bee Dakar. She is interested in your nipple teasers."

"No, really, I'm not—"

"Ah, Madame has exquisite taste," Balzac said, giving me an oily smile. He clapped his hands, and a tall, thin woman with a pixie cut and two eyebrow piercings sauntered over, her hands held together as if she was in prayer.

"Master?" she inquired.

Balzac waved to us. "Monsieur Dragon and his mate would like to try out the nipple teasers. Would you see to their comfort and pleasure?" He simpered for a moment, touching one long, pale finger to his mouth. "That is, within the reason. Any other services would have to go through Madame Claude, of course."

"Of course," Constantine answered.

"I don't even—" I started to say, but Constantine, with a hand on my back, hustled me forward and into a small room that contained just one display alcove, and a mossy green fainting couch. There was nothing else in the room, not even a light fixture, the ambient light seeming to come from the ceiling tiles themselves.

"Sir." The woman placed the turtle-shaped nipple devices in the softly lit alcove, then inclined her head at Constantine. "I hope you and madame enjoy your exploration."

I counted to seven after the door closed behind her, just to make sure she wasn't going to pop back in and present us with a restraint system, or paddle, or any of the other myriad sexual devices that I'm sure were common in places like this. When no one entered the door, I turned to face Constantine, who was tapping on his phone, evidently entering in a text message. "That was interesting. Not enough for me to even want to touch one of those things—" I nodded to the alcove. "But still, interesting. Educational, even. I had no idea that such things as artistic sex shops existed."

Constantine put away his phone with a distressed expression. "You don't want to try the nipple teasers?"

"No." I crossed my arms protectively across my chest, and was about to go on when he continued.

He picked up one of the devices and plunged the top button up and down quickly. "But they are shaped like tortoises."

"Regardless—"

"The suction is most stimulating."

"I don't like—"

"They are the highest rated of all the nipple accoutrements. Balzac himself endorses them."

"I really couldn't care less who endorses them!"

He started toward me, one of the little turtles in his hand. "You should try it first before you decide."

"Stop!" I ordered, my hand up, and the meanest look I could manage on my face.

He stopped.

"Don't you even dare think of coming closer to me with that thing. No, Constantine, I do not want my nipples suctioned. Not by a tortoise-shaped thingie, thank you very much."

"Is there something else you wish to try, then?" he asked, placing it back on the alcove. "I will call Balzac and ask for whatever fuels your fantasies."

"Okay, first, I don't know who made you king of making sure my toy-related fantasies are fulfilled, and second, I don't have any such fantasies. So just chill, and sit down. I want to talk to you."

Constantine looked horrified. "You don't have toy fantasies? Did you suffer from some sort of sexual abuse?"

"No, thank the gods."

"Then you must have had bad lovers who did not fully understand just how enjoyable it can be to add toys into sexual play," he said with a dismissive gesture at who knows what. "It will be my pleasure to help you overcome such neglect."

I gawked at him, an outright gawk, but I was sadly aware that the reason behind such a reaction was the surge of joy that rippled through me. I got that under control and asked, "Are you saying you want to have sex?"

He was silent a moment, his eyes narrowing in speculation. "If I said yes, would you consider that a sign that I was inappropriately interested in you, or would it be a welcome revelation?"

I couldn't help but laugh. "I would consider it flattering, but not a sign that you were making improper advances, no."

"Ah, good." His expression cleared and he smiled, his eyes glowing with an inner heat that made me feel very warm. "Then the answer to your question is yes. It would be my utmost pleasure to introduce you to those objects which can emphasize the delights to be found in sexual congress."

"You must have been extremely dangerous before you were killed," I said, shaking my head and unable to keep a little smile from my lips.

He took a couple of steps forward, and I was intensely aware that he might be a physical plane–bound spirit, but the man moved like a jaguar stalking prey. Instantly, my breasts decided that they really wanted an introduction to his hands and mouth, while deeper parts of me suddenly woke up and took interest in the goings-on.

"I *am* very dangerous," he said, his voice pitched low, with a roughness that I swore slid along my skin like a caress. "In all ways. Shall we return to your hotel?"

The scent of pine trees touched by the moonlight drifted around us. I breathed it in for a few seconds, so very tempted to just throw all caution to the wind and say yes. He moved even closer until his chest was a hairsbreadth from my breasts, the heat of him making my pulse kick up a few notches. He tipped his head down, his breath brushing my mouth, a strand of his hair moving like silk against my cheek. His eyes were pure molten gold, the little flecks of black and brown swimming in a shimmer that started a fire deep inside, and spread rapidly out to every extremity.

"Bee?" he asked, his fire threatening to burst free and sweep us away.

I tried to remember just why it was I had banned all romantic entanglement with dragons from my life, but failed. Constantine, I told myself, was different. He was a former dragon, a man who had witnessed death and triumphed over it. He was a caring man, one who rescued damsels in distress, and helpless sentient heads. He was sexy as sin, but didn't seem to be aware of it. He was... perfect.

One golden brown eyebrow rose. "Has the cat got your tongue? Or are you simply so overwhelmed by me that you cannot speak?"

And that did the trick—it broke the spell that had just about claimed me. I put both hands on his chest and shoved him backward. "You are *so* not overwhelming, except where your ego is concerned. Oh. Sorry, I didn't mean to hurt your chest when I shoved you. How is it? Is the curse still hurty, or has it disappeared?"

He snorted. "I am a wyvern. I am above mere pain. So you wish to spurn my offer?"

"Yes," I said firmly, ignoring that part of my brain that sent up a cry of dismay at the loss of carnal fun. "I am spurning your offer of sex. I do, however, want to talk to you, as I've said several times now. I think we have some things to discuss."

"Sexual things?" he asked, a hopeful look in his glittering eyes.

"Curse things," I corrected, and sat down on the green couch. "Most specifically, what I can do to get you to change your mind about helping with breaking the curse. I know you don't want to have to hunt down Bael, and that's actually taken care of. But I could use a hand getting an artifact from him, and you are the best choice of person to do so."

He looked around the room for a moment as if seeking insight, cocked his head for the count of six, and then finally gave it a little shake while saying, "No."

"Don't you dare walk out on me again," I warned, prepared to go all sorts of medieval on his (very attractive) butt if he even thought of stomping off for a third time.

"Come," he said simply.

"I beg your pard...oh. Come with you, you mean. I thought you were making a risqué...never mind." I took the hand he offered, and allowed him to escort me out of the sex shop.

Ten

There were a surprising number of people out on the street. I thought at first it was people heading home, but most of them were dressed up, as if they were going to a club. Constantine plowed through them at a pace easy for his long legs, but less so on my shorter ones.

"Are we out for a job, or are you intent on exhausting me so you can ply me with nipple turtles?"

Constantine, paused, his face expressing puzzlement. "I am not jogging."

"You're doing a damned good impression of it, then," I said a bit breathlessly, whapping him on the arm. "Okay, we're out of the sex shop. What is it you have to tell me about the curse that you don't want anyone to hear? And don't get that obstinate look on your face, the one that says you don't want to talk about it. You volunteered to help your people, and you can't do it alone. Spill whatever it is you're thinking. Oh, man, now I have a stitch in my side." I doubled over, one hand on my side, the other on my thigh as I tried to ease the sharp pain digging into my ribs. "Can we go somewhere that we can sit down to talk about what's going on?"

"Always you want to talk," he said with a noticeably martyred look. "I have never met a woman who wishes to discuss my thoughts so much."

"The only reason I'm pestering you about them is because you hardly ever tell me anything. If I didn't ask you questions, I'd sit around wondering what was going on, and why you were being the way you were, and if there's one thing I live by, it's not sitting around wondering something when the answer is right out there."

"Dragons do not like to answer questions," he said simply, just like that was that. "We ask, we do not tell." And with that, the damned man turned on his heel and walked on.

"I never thought I'd see the day when I saw a dragon who was afraid of anything, let alone a little conversation," I said loudly as he walked away.

He stopped, his shoulders twitching a couple of times before he poked his elbow out.

I smiled to myself, and strolled up to him, sliding my arm through his.

"I do this under protest," he said, a thin little stream of smoke drifting out of one nostril. "And only because if I do not, you will continue to yell out on the street every thought you have."

"Not every thought. Just the ones concerning dragons."

"Have you never heard of circumspection?"

I pinched his arm, ignoring the snickers of the passersby as they streamed past us and up the steps of the mini-church. "You drove me to extreme acts. Where are we going?"

"To a place where we can talk without being overheard."

"We *were* in a private room," I pointed out. "Although I admit a sex shop isn't the most comfortable location for an in-depth discussion."

"Just because you could not see anyone there did not mean we were not being monitored. Here." He stopped on the far side of the church, and opened an innocuous door that was partially hidden by a column. "It is not well lit. Be careful on the stairs."

"Is this part of the church?" I blinked a couple of times once I entered the building, squinting to make out the stairs in front of me that led upward. A mass of black to the right indicated stairs going downward into an abyss of nothingness. Cautiously, I climbed the stairs, aware of the faint sounds of music coming from above, and a distant hum of conversation. The air itself had a closed-in feel to it, as if the building didn't have adequate circulation, with faint overtones of a spicy incense, chalk, and, oddly, disinfectant.

"This is not a church," Constantine corrected me, stomping up the stairs right behind me. "It is the Hôtel du Monde au Balcon."

I stopped at the landing and peered down the hallway. It contained a couple of wooden chairs and doors leading to a half dozen rooms, but nothing else. "This is the brothel you're staying at?"

"They have excellent room service," Constantine said, moving past me to the far end of the hall, where he stopped and unlocked a door. "And I know the owner. She does not allow magic within the building. We will be able to speak in confidence."

I hesitated for a couple of seconds while I weighed

the idea of being in close quarters alongside the far-too-tempting Constantine against the need to discuss the situation and engage his help. In the end, I decided that I had a better grip on my own desires than I had confidence in Aisling and her demon dog.

The truth was, I needed Constantine. *We need his help*, one part of my mind corrected, while the other part giggled and thought lascivious things about him.

"Bee!"

I stopped just inside the door, looking around at the available tables for where Gary had been set, glancing down in amazement when a buzzing noise grew louder.

"It feels like it's been forever, and it's only been a few hours, really, but they do say time flies, and I believe that's so true, don't you? Do you like my new digs? I think they're just awesome."

"Hi, Gary," I said, watching as he pulled up before my feet. "Your new…home…is indeed pretty unique. I can honestly say that I would never in a million years have thought of putting you in a gerbil bowl, and mounting it on a remote controlled truck."

"Well, I don't want to say you lack vision, because that's rude, but I do have to say that Connie's strong point is thinking outside of the box." Gary leaned forward, bumping the stick of the remote control that was taped to floor of the big round clear plastic gerbil ball so that the truck drove a circle around my feet. "Now if he'd just feed me, I could die happy. Not that I'm going to die, because hello! I'm a knocker! But you know what I mean." He beamed happily at me.

I looked at Constantine. He had the smug look of a man who was pleased with his creativity. "Well, other than being surprised that they made hamster balls large enough to hold your head, I think we'll just move past all of that and get to the point. Which is Bael."

Constantine's jaw flexed, finger twitching. "Drive yourself downstairs and ask Madame Claude to feed you," he instructed Gary, opening the door for him. "Tell her to bill me for the meal."

"Oooh, I get to see the doxies? I hear they have both women and men. How exciting! You see, this is going to work out very well," Gary said as his little truck buzzed out the door. "I don't suppose my credit would extend as far as—"

"No," Constantine cut him off. "You must make your own arrangements if you wish to patronize other services of the house."

Gary sighed dramatically, but winked as he said, "I'll rely on my skill as a storyteller and my innate charm, then."

Constantine closed the door on him, leaning against it, his face shuttered, his arms across his chest.

"You cannot get more classically *don't want to talk about it* than you are now," I told him, glancing around the room, and picking out a window seat. I sat on it and patted the cushion next to me. "But that's not going to work. What is bothering you that you keep making cryptic comments and walking out on me?"

He held his position for a full minute before he unbent and sat down on the window seat, his leg warm and solid next to mine. "What I tell you, only three living beings know, and one of them was my mortal enemy for most of my life."

"Goodness," I said, feeling a sudden surge of empathy. "If you're worried I'll spill your secret—"

"It matters not," he said with a sharp gesture, looking at the floor with such an expression of bleak misery that I scooted over so I could put a reassuring hand on his shoulder. "After this day, all will know the truth. I will be censured, but I have lived in fear too long. It is true that I hoped to delay it for a few centuries, but that is not to be."

"Constantine..." A sense of guilt overwhelmed me, driving out the overwhelming urge to kiss the breath right out of his lungs. What right did I have to force the man to bare his soul, just because I wanted him to help me? "I don't know what it is that you're afraid of, but I've changed my mind—we don't have to talk about that, or your reasons for not wanting to deal with Bael. I would appreciate any advice you have, however, since I have a job to do, and with all respect to Aisling and her dog, I just don't have a lot of faith that they can help with Bael. They may find him, but it's not fair to expect them to do any more than that."

"I will tell you my reasons. You will understand then why I have avoided this, but you have made me see that refusing to lend my aid will only end in more destruction." He looked up, the emotion in his eyes now flat and cold. "The deaths on my soul were ones obtained honorably, obtained in the course of the wars between the dragon septs, but I do not seek to have others added to that total. Not when they could be avoided."

"Good lord. Who do you expect is going to be killed? More dragons? Or someone else? And by whom? Bael?"

"Yes." Constantine kept his gaze firmly on the wall across from us, his hands fisted where they sat on his thighs. "Bael is...he was not always known as Bael, nor was he born a demon lord."

"I assume not, since demon lords are made, and not

born into the position. Most were mortals that morphed into that via some demonic means or other. Do you know who Bael was before he was a demon lord?"

"He was a dragon." Constantine took a deep breath.

"Mother of martyrs! A dragon? Why would he curse you guys if he used to be one of you?"

"It is for that reason that he wishes to destroy us. He was not just any dragon. He was a firstborn."

"What's that?"

"One of the children of the First Dragon, the progenitor of all dragons who ever were, and who ever will be."

I edged my hand along his side until it rested on his thigh next to his fist, trying to provide what comfort I could. The pain on his face was etched deep; oddly, I could swear I felt his dragon fire condense down until it was almost extinguished. "I've heard of the First Dragon. He was like a demigod, wasn't he?"

"Yes. He was literally the first dragon. His children formed the dragon septs. All of them but one—Kashi, who was not given a sept because his father did not see in him the signs of a wyvern."

"What exactly are the signs of a wyvern other than..." I bit back the word *stubborn*. "...being dominant?"

"Wyverns have many traits that signal their suitability for the position. Kashi wished to control all around him, and a wyvern does not control—he guides, he mentors, he advises—but he does not treat the members of his sept like they are minions, there only to serve him."

I gave his leg a little squeeze. "Was Bael—Kashi—part of your sept, then?"

"No. He belonged to no sept." Constantine took a deep breath and turned to face me. "Kashi is my father."

That was the very last thing I was expecting Constantine to say, and I will admit that my jaw sagged a bit at that statement. "Holy crows, Bael is your *dad*?"

His expression went blank, just as if a curtain had fallen in front of his face. "Yes."

"But—couldn't you—I mean, wouldn't he listen to you?"

Constantine's lips twisted into a wry smile. "I don't know why he would. He never has. Bee, you must understand, he mated with my mother, a mortal woman, but when he realized that he would never be given a sept, he destroyed everything he could—he tried to kill me, but my mother sacrificed her life to save me. She convinced the wyvern of the black dragons to take me in, and make me a member in order to protect me from Kashi's wrath."

"But how did you—"

"No." Constantine interrupted me by standing up, taking a few paces, and turning back to face me. "No more questions about that time. What is past is past. What we must focus on is how to stop him without destroying more innocent lives. I told you the truth so you would understand why I wanted nothing to do with Bael, but that point is no longer valid." His eyes narrowed, and even sitting across the room, I could feel his fire blossom into life. "You said the green dragons were searching for him?"

"Yes." I summarized my meeting with Aisling, musing to myself that Constantine had depths I'd never guessed at. What seemed like a self-centered, frivolous man turned out to be one who cared deeply for others, from someone as vulnerable as Gary to the mortals who might possibly get caught in the crosshairs of Bael's wrath. My heart melted a little at that, and I began to think that perhaps I'd been overly hasty in setting a ban on any romantic relations with dragons.

Constantine was definitely a man worth investigating further.

"When will you speak with the green mate?" he asked.

I glanced at the clock. "Two hours. She said her demon dog would need some time to check around Abaddon for word of Bael."

"I do not know that there is much we can do until we have an idea where he is." Constantine rubbed a hand over his lower face as he thought. "I suppose we will just have to wait until we hear from her. Are you hungry?"

"Not really, no." *Not for food, anyway.* I was a bit startled by that thought, and shifted a bit uncomfortably on the window seat, aware that I was having to restrain myself from moving closer to Constantine. When had I gone from wanting to hit him on the head with a blunt instrument to seriously considering pinning him against the wall and nibbling all along his jaw?

"Would you like to return to Curiosités Demonia?" he asked politely.

"I don't think so. I know you think toys are all that, but I've never really seen the need for them. Plain old normal sex is perfectly fine with me."

"To each his own," he said amiably, then looked thoughtful. "Was that an invitation, or a statement?"

I do not need another dragon in my life, I told myself. *We all know how it's going to end up, and I just don't need that heartache again. You've set your limits—now hold to them.* "Possibly both," my mouth said without me approving the act.

His eyes lit with a golden glow, and instantly his fire

overwhelmed me. I blinked at the sight of it spiraling up my body, bracing myself for the burn, but amazingly, it felt warm, not hot. Pleasantly warm. Tingly warm. It made me very aware that I was female, and he was male, and we were alone in a room with a sizeable bed.

"You want me," he said, moving toward me in a slow saunter that reminded me of a jaguar about to pounce.

"Yes, but you want me, too," I said, lifting my chin, and holding out my hand. His fire swirled up onto my arm, then poured onto my palm, forming an orb. I tossed it into the air, caught it, then flipped it onto him. "In fact, I'd say you're wild for me."

He smiled as he stopped before me, the fire spreading out across his chest before evaporating into nothing. His heat made the hairs on my arm prickle, and my nipples harden in anticipation. "I won't deny it, but I *will* take it as a challenge to make you just as wild for my attentions."

I drew a finger across his collarbone, and down the V of exposed chest. "We only have two hours. Are you sure that's going to be enough time?"

He moved forward, causing me to back up until the wall pressed against me, as cool as he was hot. He leaned forward, his lips brushing mine. "Is it my prowess you doubt, or your ability to gain pleasure?"

I slid my fingers down his shirt, unbuttoning it, and trailing my fingers across his belly. His muscles contracted in a little intake of breath just as I leaned forward and gently bit his lower lip. "I have no doubt of your prowess. I just don't know if there's going to be enough time to do all the things I want to do."

"Then I shall simply have to make sure that you are satisfied with the time we have." His breath was hot on my neck, his lips burning when they kissed a path from my ear down to my shoulder.

I was aware that his hands were moving, but it wasn't until cool air rippled down my back that I realized he'd removed my shirt. A noise from outside the room made me pause and cock an eyebrow.

"Gary?" I asked.

"He will no doubt be availing himself of the amenities of the house," Constantine murmured, reaching out blindly to flip the lock on the door. I shivered when he nibbled on my earlobe for a few seconds before moving on to find the spot behind my ear that sent goose bumps down my back.

"I keep thinking that this is wrong, and I should stop, but then I see your chest and arms and shoulders, and I just want to bite you."

"Really?" Constantine pulled back, his eyes bright with interest and passion. "Bite me where? How hard? Would you want to restrain me first? I do not wish to be restrained, and normally I do not care for my partners to be tied down, but if that's something you want, that would be acceptable."

"You really are the strangest man I've ever been interested in," I told him, sucking in my breath when he cupped my breasts. "Oh, I do like that, though. No restraints, Constantine. I told you that I'm not into toys and things like that."

"Have you tried it?" he asked, breathing fire on my breasts. The heat sank immediately into my chest, and pooled lower, down to my belly, leaving me feeling as if I had a fever.

"No, but I don't have to try leaping off a building to know that I don't want to do it."

His hands were busy around my waist, removing my jeans with the minimum of effort. I took the opportunity to kick off my shoes before rubbing a leg up his.

"Let me try to change your mind?" he asked, stroking one hand up my leg. "So soft, so very soft."

"I'm a girl. I'm supposed to be soft." I leaned forward and bit his shoulder, gently. "What sort of thing did you want to do?"

"I want to show you that there's no reason to fear trying new things," he answered, giving me a slow smile that I felt right down to my toenails. "I won't do anything that you don't like."

I had been leaning in to lick one of his pert little nipples, but stopped to slant a glance upward at him. "Do I need a safe word? Are you going *Fifty Shades of Grey* on me? Because I'll tell you right here and now that I do not find that sort of thing at all sexy."

"Nor do I. I am not talking about controlling you, Bee. I simply want to share some of my pleasures with you." He leaned in and kissed me, his mouth sweet and hot and so enticing that I squelched my inhibitions. "Tell me that you trust me."

"Trust was never an issue," I said, sidestepping the question. Instead, I peeled off his belt and put my hand on his fly. Behind it, he twitched. "All right, you can try one thing. Just one. And if I don't like it, I will tell you and you have to stop."

"I agree to your terms," he said, his mouth moving down to my chest. I shivered again when he removed my bra, leaving me in nothing but a pair of underwear that was fast making me feel like I had too much on. "Tell me what you like, my little honey bee."

I smiled at the term of endearment, arching my back when his mouth took possession of one breast. "Oh, I like that. Do the other one."

"It shall be as you order. You see? I am letting you dominate me without complaint. That is because I am the most obliging of lovers."

"You're something, all right," I said, laughing and unzipping his pants. I didn't even look as I slid them down over his hips. "Luckily, I like quirky men with odd sexual tastes who can turn into dragons at the drop of a hat. Wait—that's not what you're planning on doing, are you? Because I hate to be sexist... no, I guess that would be specist... but I don't get into the whole sex with a dragon thing. Dragon form, that is. Oh, you know what I mean."

He looked hurt for a few seconds, actually looked hurt, which would have been bad on its own, but he stopped molesting my breasts in order to do so. They immediately complained about the lack of attention. "You do not like my dragon form?"

"I haven't seen your dragon form. I'm sure it's quite nice, but I really don't want to have sex with... with... well, balls. If I say animal, that's offensive, because you're not an animal. Let's just say that I'm not comfortable getting it on with you if you're not in human form."

He looked thoughtful for a moment, then shrugged. "I believe we'll leave that discussion for another time, when I can show you just how interesting dragon form can make things. For now, I promise not to shift forms. I will, however, have to prepare you for what I have in mind."

"Prepare how?" I asked, suddenly wary.

He smiled again, and after kicking off his pants and shoes, dropped to his knees, his hands sliding up the backs of my thighs before pulling off my undies. "I'll show you."

"Oh, yes please." I clutched the wall when he pulled one of my legs over his shoulder, and turned his face into my thigh. He had a slight amount of stubble, not enough to give me whisker rash, but enough to create a delicious friction prickling along my flesh. I squirmed in anticipation when he moved upward, his breath hot on my various hidden secrets.

I managed to stand there without melting into the wall while he worked magic on my girl parts, his fingers teasing and dancing against me, his mouth doing wickedly wonderful things, but when he blew fire on me, I lost the tenuous grasp of control, and grabbed his head, urging him on.

He pulled back, asking, "Are you multi-orgasmic?"

I stared down at him, my brain trying to come to grips with the fact that he stopped his wonderful mouth magic. His lips were moving again, making noises that I knew must be words, but at that moment, dangling as I was over the precipice of an orgasm to end all orgasms, I couldn't decipher what he said. Instead, I whimpered, hoping against hope that he'd take pity on me and finish the job.

"Needy, are you?"

Those words filtered through the fog of lust and desire and yes, need that clogged up my brain.

I nodded, digging my fingers into his hair to tug his head back where I wanted it. He pressed a hot kiss complete with dragon fire to my pubic mound, then stood up, scooping me into his arms at the same time.

"Good. Then you should enjoy this even more." He carried me to the bed, but rather than laying me upon it, and following me down, he set me on the edge. "Hold onto that demanding look that I see in your eyes, Bee. This will only take a minute to set up."

The buzz of the near orgasm faded quickly when he moved over to a dresser, and extracted an apparatus of blue silk rope, the middle section of which was long and flat like a cummerbund. I watched him stand on a chair to hang two ends of the rope off a hook in the ceiling, the rest of the device trailing next to me. "Is that a swing, Constantine? A sex swing? I don't think I'm going to like that—"

"Not a sex swing, no, although that is something to consider for another time," he said, eyeing the device. He adjusted two sides of it so that the flat part swayed a little above the bed. "I can think of many games we could play with a swing, but for now, we'll try this."

Before I could ask just what he had in mind, he pulled me upright, his hands on my butt urging me closer to him. His body was as hard as mine was soft, and I gloried in the difference, moving against him restlessly, hoping he'd use his magic mouth on me again.

"Tell me what you want," he demanded, his breath hot on mine.

I tangled my fingers in his golden brown mane, and tugged on it. "I want you."

"And?" His mouth trailed fired as he kissed a path first across my collarbone, and then down to my breasts, his hands nudging my legs apart. I could feel his erection against my belly, and stood on my tiptoes when his fingers found my sensitive parts.

"More," I said on a gasp, my inner muscles trying to grab desperately at him.

"More what?"

I released his hair and reached between us, stroking the hard length of him. "More of you. Inside me. Pretty damned quickly, too, because I feel like I'm going to explode if you don't finish what you started."

He smiled again, a wicked smile full of intent. "I find I like you in this bossy mode. However, I'm going to like this more."

"Like what?" I started to say, but before I could finish the last word, he spun me around, positioning me so that I was directly in front of the rope contraption. With one hand on my back, he pressed me forward until I was bent down, my breasts on the bed, while my backside was right there exposed to anyone who cared to look.

"Constantine!" I shrieked into the sheet, and tried to twist around. He hitched the rope system up a few inches so that my hips and butt were propped upward, while my hands remained on the bed. "I do not like where this is headed! My butt is off limits. Safe word! SAFE WORD!"

He laughed, the bastard, and nudged my knees open wide. "Do not fear, my little honey bee. I will not make you do anything that does not give you the most immense pleasure. Like this, for instance."

"Like whaaaaaaieeeeeeeeee!" Without so much as warning me, he put his hands on my hips, pulled me back slightly, and thrust into me in a manner that not only made me scream with pleasure, but caused every single muscle I possessed in that region to suddenly come to life. "Grace of the goddess, Constantine! You're so—and it feels—I think I'm going to—you're going to move?"

Not being a monster (or, as he'd be the first one to mention, an inconsiderate lover), he hadn't penetrated very far into me, just enough to delight the aforementioned muscles, and to warn me that he meant business.

"Movement is integral to this, yes." He sounded as breathless as I felt, his hands gripping my hips hard. I grabbed at the sheet beneath me, my body moving gently as he worked up a rhythm that allowed him to slide in deeper, opening me up in a way that almost made my eyes cross with pleasure. "What do you think? Do you enjoy this? Unlike restraints, you are free to move, but the support elevates you in a way that is supposed to enhance the experience."

"Oh, it enhances, it enhances," I said, aware that I was babbling, but unable to keep from doing so. I wanted desperately to hold on to him, but at the same time, I didn't want him to stop what he was doing. He was winding me closer, ever closer to the moment when I felt I'd explode into a million pieces, and even though the position was somewhat awkward, and I had thoughts that my butt did not offer a particularly scenic view of me, I let that all go to simply enjoy.

And when my muscles tightened around him as I slipped over the edge of rapture, I reveled in the moan of sheer ecstasy that he gave before collapsing down onto my back.

Unfortunately, the belt or swing or whatever the rope system was called was not built for two. It gave way underneath me, sending both Constantine and me tumbling onto the bed.

Which also gave way, crashing to the floor with a noise that was so loud, it made my ears ring.

Constantine's jaw clipped the back of my head, making us both swear.

"Are you hurt?" he asked, scrambling off of me, and flipping me over to examine me. "Did I crush you? Tell me I didn't crush you. I heard the air whooshing out of your lungs. Can you speak? Can you breathe? Christos, let me call for a healer."

He was up and at the door, standing naked in it as he called down the hallway for a healer when I caught my breath back and managed to speak. "I'm fine. Not hurt, although yes, a little winded." I looked up at the ceiling, shrieked, and rolled to the side just as a chunk of plaster bearing the swing hook came tumbling down onto the bed. I looked from the plaster on the bed over to Constantine, still naked at the door, and burst into laughter.

"What are you laughing at?" he demanded, stomping over to me, his hands on his naked hips. "You find the situation funny? You find *me* funny?"

Outrage gathered in his eyes just as dragon fire burst into a puddle at my feet. I tapped it out with a bare foot, still giggling. Outside the room, voices called, growing louder.

"I find you sexy as hell and an incredible lover," I said, pulling a blanket up from the floor, wrapping it around me. "As a matter of fact, I was just thinking that although I've had boyfriends who've promised to move the heaven and the earth, you're the only one who ever managed to do so."

His smile, as the worried occupants of the brothel burst into our room, was one almost entirely filled with male pride.

Eleven

"Why do you have to leave? The bed is fixed. The debris from the ceiling is cleared. I thought to pleasure you again, and you wish to leave? This is unacceptable. I have many variations of the support system to show you, one of which includes grapes." Constantine waggled his eyebrows meaningfully at Bee. "I'll let you guess who will be the recipient of them."

"Oddly enough, I want to know, but alas, duty calls." Bee rolled off his chest and began collecting her clothing.

Constantine enjoyed the view of her backside and thought of mentioning that fact, but he had found that women of this time did not appreciate knowing that their bodies were viewed with approval. "I am wise in the way of Oprah, and thus won't comment on how charming I find your ass, but I wish for you to know that you need not have negative body issues on my behalf."

"You are wise in the way of..." Bee, in the act of

slipping on her jeans, spun around to stare at him, her mouth twitching in a manner that could either mean intense anger or amusement. He wondered which it was, and decided that it must be the latter.

"Yes. Ysolde insisted that I have feminist training. She said too many dragons thought as they used to centuries before and that she wasn't going to have me running around perpetuating outdated mores and values." He rubbed his chin and wondered what it would take to get Bee naked and in his bed again. "It is for that reason I am so in touch with what women like and need."

"Uh huh." Bee finished dressing before giving him an unreadable look. "I'm surprised you let this Ysolde woman talk you into becoming a feminist. You don't strike me as the sort of man who gives up his dearly held beliefs of masculine superiority."

He donned a noble expression, absently scratching an itch on his groin. "Since Ysolde was once my beloved mate, I am forced by honor to acquiesce to any demands she makes, even if it means reading boring literature and attending with her a few meetings of like-minded women." His mouth twisted for a few seconds, then he gave her a rueful smile. "Although I do admit that I enjoyed the *Our Bodies, Ourselves* seminar. That was quite eye-opening, and not just because some of the ladies had me help them with their ladyplant mirrors."

Bee seemed to have a spasm of some sort. "A what now? Ladyplant?"

"Yes, you know." He gestured toward Bee's ladyplant. "That part of you that is likened to a garden. I do not know what modern terminology is—the ladies at the *Our Bodies, Ourselves* seminar refused to tell me. They claimed ladyplant was their new favorite phrase. One of them said she was going to embroider it on a garment."

Bee blinked at him a couple of times. "And this makes you think you're a feminist?"

"I didn't say that. I said that I am in touch with what women like and need, and you liked me touching you in your ladyplant area. You liked the device despite declaring you wouldn't. We spent an enjoyable hour together, and I thought we might do so again."

"Sadly for my peace of mind, I suspect we will spend many more hours together using that device—" Bee eyed it with an expression that mingled satisfaction with disbelief. "—but that's really neither here nor there. I have to get in touch with Aisling to hear what her demon found out about your daddy."

Pain twisted in Constantine's gut. He made an abbreviated gesture of denial and flung back the sheets to rise. "Do not call him that. The day he tortured and killed my mother in an attempt to bring me to heel he lost the right to be named such."

Bee was in his arms before he had his balance, and the two of them tumbled backward onto the bed. Bee wrapped her arms around him, kissing his shoulder and nuzzling his neck in a way that both inflamed him and brought him a strange sense of comfort. "He killed your mom?"

"Yes. That is one reason why I did not wish to engage him in battle—he strikes quickly and hard, and always at the most dearly held possession."

"What—you don't have to answer this if it's too painful—what happened that he would do that to your mother?"

Her breath was warm and sweet on his neck, and as

he shifted her slightly to the side so that she was no longer crushing his penis, he toyed with the thought of commencing a seduction to keep her in his bed. The memory of that time long in the past drove out all thoughts of pleasure, however. "I was named by the wyvern of the black dragons as his heir—at least I was until Baltic, another of the First Dragon's sons, usurped my position, and claimed the sept for his own. By that time, Kashi was already befriending those beings who would lead him into becoming a demon lord, and he wished for me to follow him. I refused. He struck back in a way that he knew would devastate me: by killing my entire family."

"I'm sorry, Constantine, I'm so sorry." She kissed his jaw, his cheek, and finally his mouth. "I know what it's like to lose a parent. I lost both of mine in a senseless act of violence when they went to help the underprivileged in Africa, but at least I had my sister and brother to share my grief. I can only imagine how terrible it must have been for you to struggle through the loss of your family on your own."

Constantine allowed himself a moment of remembered grief, then set it aside as he had so many times. "I regret that you, too, have had the pain of losing a parent, and I would be happy to comfort you, but you must remove your clothing in order that I do so. Or allow me to remove it. Have you more garments with you?" He lifted a hand and wiggled his fingers. "Dragons tend to show our origins by means of claws when we are sexually excited. I would not purposely shred your clothing while removing it, but you tempt me more than any other woman, and I can't guarantee that your garments might not be damaged."

"Claws, huh?" She pushed herself off him and eyed his hand. "You didn't go claw-boy earlier. I'd have noticed that."

"I retained superior control of myself because I knew you were hesitant over allowing me to demonstrate a toy."

"Is that so?" She got to her feet, rebuttoning the buttons on her shirt that he had just slid open, and made a face at herself in a mirror. "I look like I was dragged through a hedge backward."

"Or you just had an extremely satisfying sexual engagement with a wyvern," he answered, blowing a little ring of fire at her, and throwing as much come-hither into his eyes as was possible.

She resisted it, the little minx. Instead she just laughed and slid the strap of her bag across her torso. "That was pretty slick, and I am truly tempted, but if this curse is ever to be lifted, then I have to put duty before your sexy self. I assume I'll be able to find a taxi outside?"

"No."

"Really? Drat." She frowned. "I'll have to go out a few streets to try to catch one, then."

"No, you will not." He rose and reached for his clothing. "I will take you to the green mate's house. We will deal with Bael together."

"Are you sure?" She watched him dress, her brows still together. "I was wrong to flip you shit for not wanting to help, and I would feel horrible if you let me guilt you into doing something that you'd rather not. You certainly have a solid reason for not wishing to get involved with your fa—with Bael."

"We have already discussed the matter, and I will not change my mind. Bael being loose may not be my responsibility, but I feel obligated to do what I can to end what will only result in a reign of terror for everyone." He pulled on his shoes and, after a moment's thought, picked up a small black box and spoke into it. "Bee and I are going to the green wyvern's house to discuss Bael. Do you wish to stay?"

"Who are you talking to?" Bee asked, reaching for the lock on the door.

"Gary."

She gave him an oddly unreadable look. "You bought him a walkie-talkie?"

"No. That would be ridiculous. It's all he can do to manipulate the remote that controls his truck."

She just looked at him.

He gave a little cough. "I bought a communications earpiece set from a shop catering to surveillance officials. It seems to work quite well for us."

"Uh huh. And this from the man who claims he wants to leave poor Gary on the roadside because he's so much trouble."

Constantine thinned his lips at her at the same time that tinny static came out of the small box, followed by loud music, over which Gary could be heard to say, "Hey, chicky, you ever made it with a disembodied head? Oh, hello, Constantine. Are you and Bee finished? So soon? You must have been very forceful. Did she like the silk lift? Did you?"

Bee whapped Constantine on the arm. "You told him about the silk rope thing?"

"He helped me pick it out. He thought you'd like it. And you did."

"Which is no one's business!" Bee protested.

"I would answer you, but Bee would pinch me again, and I do not wish to distress her," Constantine said into the black box. "However, the answer to the most important questions is yes."

"I knew it!" Gary crowed before adding in a lower tone, "Sorry, monsieur, I must refuse your generous offer. My friends need my help in saving the world."

Bee shook her head and saying, "Somehow, I never thought this day would end up with me hunting a demon lord with an ex-dragon and a head in a hamster ball. Come on, Sir Galahad. If you insist on helping me—and I admit, I'm very grateful for your assistance—then let's get going. It's already midnight, and I told Aisling I'd be in contact by now. Can I use your phone to tell her we're on our way?"

Constantine handed over his phone and busied himself with tidying up the silk rope while she talked to the green mate. He wondered idly if she'd be interested in an electronic device that was said to heighten women's pleasure, but decided that so long as she had him to see to her sexual needs, she wouldn't have need of it.

"All right," Bee said a few minutes later, when he was tucking away a scalp massager for which he found had many other uses, "Aisling says they have a hit on Bael. Well, not hit on him per se, but that he was spotted recently by some green dragons in Italy. Aisling asked my sister and Kostya to talk with us about it, so we need to head over to Aisling's house now."

A thump at the door indicated Gary's arrival. Constantine let him in, saying to Bee as he did so, "Why is she calling a sarkany? The curse will keep her from being able to communicate with everyone but you."

"A what?"

"A sarkany is a concave of wyverns."

"It's like you guys have a different word for everything." Bee gave him an expectant grin.

He just looked at her.

"Not a Steve Martin fan?" She gave a mock sigh. "And to think I'd become involved with a man who doesn't appreciate a good stand-up comedy routine. To answer your question, I have no idea why Aisling's asked us to her place, other than I assume the Venediger won't allow us—well, really, *any* dragons, given that she's pissed at all of you—back in the club after the curse blew up so horribly and damaged the club. So there really is nowhere else safe to go."

"Where in Italy did she say Bael was last seen?"

"She didn't say exactly where, just that he'd been seen." Bee started out the door.

Constantine paused long enough to snatch up the helmet he'd purchased for her, and tucked Gary in his hamster ball under his arm. "I don't understand why we need to waste time talking with my godson and the green mate about Bael. She should provide you with the information on his location so that we can go deal with him."

"Well, we're only after an artifact of his, after all. It's not like you're going to try to take him down personally," Bee said over her shoulder before trotting down the stairs to the street door.

Constantine said nothing, but paused at the door and gave the street outside the brothel a long scrutiny. He pinpointed two women engaged in kissing who he thought had the hint of demon about them. He kept an eye on them as he retrieved his motorcycle and mounted it, watching in the rearview mirror as one of the women languidly parted and moved off into the darkness.

He was recalled by the slight blow on the back of his shoulder. "Hmm?" he asked Bee.

"I said that you'd better keep your eyes on the road or else we'll end up in the hospital. You almost hit two cars at that intersection back there."

"I am a consummate driver. If I almost hit someone, it was because I wanted to do so, and not because I was watching for two women," he yelled.

"The hell?" Bee asked, and pinched his belly. "Why are you watching for women?"

"Your jealousy pleases me, although it is not necessary. I will not betray you to another woman, or even a pair of women, no matter how comely they are."

She pinched him even harder and spent the next eleven minutes lecturing him about how she wasn't a jealous woman, had never been jealous, and didn't have any plans to start at that moment, and if he thought she cared one hoot if he stared at women the length and breadth of Paris, he could just think again, and other such protestations that Constantine knew meant she cared very much about what he thought.

He experienced a twinge of guilt when he remembered the beauteous Ysolde, and how he had pledged her his heart in the best manner of the chivalric stories of his youth, but he told himself he had no time to analyze the differences in his emotions toward Bee (which were growing more and more complicated with each passing hour) and those of Ysolde (chaste, distant adoration). He promised himself a good think about Bee and his attraction to her at a later date, and proceeded to drive to the sixteenth arrondissement where the green wyvern had a home.

His godson and his mate were already there when they arrived.

"I'm supposed to do the honors of translating for everyone," Jim the demon informed Constantine when they entered a long sitting room. It was filled with heavily brocaded antiques and dotted with pools of amber light from various lamps. At one end, a fire burned in a grate, lending ambiance rather than warmth.

"Hi everyone! I'm Gary. Oooh, isn't that a pretty Louis the Sixteenth table. Is that inlaid onyx? Very shiny."

Constantine set Gary's ball down on a small half-moon table.

"Hello again," Bee said, greeting Aisling when she rose.

Aisling's expression was one of shock, her gaze glued to Gary. "That's . . . I'm . . . is that a *head*?"

"Cool!" Jim the demon dog said, strolling over to snuffle the giant hamster ball. "Hiya. Do you get motion sickness rolling around in there?"

"Not at all. I've always been a good sailor," Gary told the demon, then beamed at the room in general. "Well, now! Isn't this nice. A room full of dragons and a demon, and of course Bee, who is the most charming of all Charmers."

Aisling shook her head, closed her eyes for a few seconds, then opened them, saying, "You know, I'm just going to go with the flow here, and not even ask."

"I'm sorry we're so late, Aisling," Bee said. "We—I— we got a bit caught up in things, and I didn't see it was so late. Do you know Constantine? I know you can't talk to him, but I figured you must have met him since he's Kostya's godfather. Oh, hello, Aoife. I didn't realize you and Kostya were here yet."

Constantine watched with interest as Bee's sister, who

had been sitting and petting Jim, leaped up and flung herself in front of Kostya, her hands on his arms as if she were restraining him.

"What on earth are you doing?" Bee asked.

"Protecting Kostya from Constantine. We aren't at G&T, so the curse will make them want to kill each other."

Bee turned to consider Constantine. "Do you feel like killing your godson?"

"Not at the moment, no." He made a bow to Aisling. "I will defend myself if he feels obligated to attack, but I bear him no particular hostility. Greetings. I am Constantine of Norka. I do not believe we have been formally introduced."

Aisling's eyes grew round as she took the hand that Constantine politely held out. "Criminy Dutch! I can hear you! That is, I can understand you."

"I can understand him, too," Aoife said, looking confused.

"As can I." Kostya set aside his mate and came toward them, frowning. "Why can I understand you? You are a member of another sept. Two septs, if you count that which you formed in order to destroy the black dragons."

"Again you bring up old history. Very well, this once I will correct you. Baltic was the one who destroyed the black dragons." Constantine snorted. "I tried to save them, but he—"

"Time out," Aisling said, rising from the brocade loveseat. "Constantine, I don't know if you're prone to lengthy speeches about the glory of the black dragons and how they will rise again, but long familiarity with Kostya leads me to believe that he's about to go on one of his rampages, and quite frankly, I don't want to hear it. Well, I can't hear it, not while the curse is on us, but you know what I mean."

"What is she saying?" Aoife asked him, obviously unable to understand what Aisling said due to the curse.

He was tempted to tell her that she should be asking her sister that question, but decided, in a rare moment of insight, to forestall such a suggestion. Instead, he gave a summary of Aisling's comments, ignoring Aoife when she bristled at the slur against her wyvern.

"I don't know why the curse isn't affecting me," he told them all, one hand absently rubbing a spot on his chest. Bee made a distressed noise and moved closer. "It could be that in trying to break it, Bee had some effect on it. Regardless of the reason, I wish to locate Bael. What did your demon find?"

"I think we should discuss the issue of why the curse isn't affecting you," Aisling said with a little pull between her eyebrows. "It might be important."

"It isn't," Constantine stated, and made an impatient gesture. "Answer my question."

"Please," Bee said softly.

"I do not have time for social niceties. If I am abrupt, it is because I'm trying to save as many lives as possible."

"From the red dragons, you mean?" Kostya took a seat in an armchair, while Aoife perched herself on the arm of it. "They have not been seen in Paris, and all dragonkin are watching for them. We would have had word if they were going to strike."

"Golly!" Gary said, turning his eyes to Constantine. "Red dragons are after us, too?"

Constantine felt as if the weight of the world had settled on his shoulders and was slowly but inevitably crushing him into the ground. "It is not the red dragons I fear, but their master. What did the demon find out?"

"I have a name, you know. It's Jim. Well, Effrijim really, but that's awfully girly, so I've always gone with Jim. At least I think I have," the demon dog said, pursing its lips thoughtfully. "I lost my memory for a bit, so I don't remember anything before Eefers here ran me down."

"Eefers?" Bee asked before shaking her head. "Aoife is pronounced *EE-fuh*, Jim, not *eefers*."

"Ignore Jim, please," Aisling said, giving her demon a stern look. "It's in one of those moods because the trip to Abaddon was pretty hairy."

"Hairy with big fat warts on it," Jim said, nodding.

"I hear you on the full name versus nickname thing," Gary told Jim. "I'm actually a Gareth, but no one seems to be able to remember it."

"Unfortunately, I cannot ignore the demon. Not so long as it has information to give, which I request for a third time," Constantine said, fast losing his patience. Now that he was committed to stopping Bael, it seemed to him that everyone was unconcerned. Did no one else realize just how much time they were losing with the inane conversations? Were they all unaware of the danger that Bael posed? Was no one but Bee interested in stopping the massacre that was sure to happen should Bael continue unchecked?

Bee must have sensed his rising fire, for she moved closer and brushed his hand with hers until he gave in and took it, the touch giving him an odd sense of contentment. For the first time in longer than his memory spanned, he felt as if he was not alone.

"I don't understand why you are involved with the

Charmer," Kostya said, his gaze on Constantine. "You can no longer go into spirit form, so you have no special abilities used in finding the talisman. I don't see why you should be here—"

"Cease this mindless babbling!" Constantine roared, releasing Bee's hand to stomp into the center of the room.

The silence that followed was pronounced.

"Do none of you care that the most dangerous being who ever lived is now free again?" he demanded to know.

"Of course we care," Aisling said, glancing toward Kostya. "But really, our focus is on breaking the curse."

"We want the curse broken, too," Bee said. "It's just that Constantine has issues with Bael being out and about, and we'd like to locate him in order to make sure no one is hurt."

"Issues?" Kostya eyed Constantine suspiciously. "What issues would you have with a demon lord?"

The urge to run was strong, but he knew that he could never again turn away from the responsibility that had plagued him for so long. He was silent for a few minutes, picking out what he wanted to say, grateful that Bee was giving him the opportunity to speak or not speak, as he chose.

"Bael is no ordinary demon lord," he finally said.

"You can say that again," Gary said with a little giggle. "Asmodeus was terrified of him, although he'd never let on to anyone. But oh, how he used to check that Bael was still in the Akasha, and not out where he could mess with him. Asmo, that is."

"Who *are* you?" Aisling asked before shaking her head and answering herself. "No, never mind, I said I wasn't going to go there, and I'm not. But I will say that we all know Bael isn't a normal demon lord. For one, he's a tricky bastard, and for another, he managed to place a curse on all of the dragons while he was still confined to the Akasha. You have to have some pretty big chops to pull off that sort of thing."

"He does have big chops, as you call it," Constantine answered her. The room was silent as he spoke the words that weighed so heavily on him. "As a son of the First Dragon, he was born with abilities beyond the understanding of most beings."

Twelve

"Bael's *what*?" Aisling exclaimed at the same time Kostya burst out with, "He's another son? You are wrong. He can't be."

"Glorioski! That's a plot twist I didn't see coming," Gary told Jim.

"Are you *sure* he's one of the First Dragon's sons?" Aisling asked, and although it took time they did not have, Constantine briefly recapped his history.

"For the fourth and final time, what did your demon find out about Bael's location?" he asked when he finished.

Aisling looked like she wanted to say something else, but in the end, she waved a hand at Jim. "Go ahead. Tell Constantine what you overheard in Abaddon."

Jim stood up and made a gesture with one paw that would have been a salute on any other being. "Aye aye, *mon* dragon *capitain*. At first, I didn't think I was going to find out much about Bael. For one, no one seemed to know he'd been released by Eefies."

"Unintentionally!" Aoife protested.

"Ha!" Bee said with a snort. "I'd say that was worse than being caught sneaking around Abaddon."

"But then I caught wind that all of Asmodeus's wrath demons were out of Abaddon, and in the mortal world hunting."

"Hunting for what?" Kostya asked.

"Well, that's the interesting part. Once I heard that all the wrathies were out in a hunting party, I figured they'd be looking for Bael, and they were, but it also turns out they were searching for some chick named Thala."

"Who?" Bee asked.

Constantine's gaze settled on Kostya. "Baltic's Thala?"

Kostya looked thoughtful. "I assume so. You know why he'd seek her, yes?"

Cold, hard fear filled his stomach. "I do."

"Well, we don't, so enlighten us, please," Bee said, glancing between Aisling and Aoife. "Who is Thala?"

"And why would Asmodeus want to find her?" Aisling asked.

"She holds a valuable weapon," Constantine said, his mind assembling and then discarding any number of scenarios that would explain Bael's actions. "A light sword. Baltic used to possess it, but it was stolen by Thala."

"So you think that Asmodeus wants this sword? Why?"

"Not Asmodeus—Bael. With it, he'll be able to remove Asmodeus from the throne of Abaddon."

"That makes sense," Bee admitted. "But that's not going to help us find out where Bael is and where he is living. We still need to get some kind of talisman from him to break the curse."

Constantine looked pointedly at the demon dog. "Did you find out where Asmodeus's demons were searching?"

"Yup, that and a whole lot more. One of the gate-keepers in Asmo's palace says that he heard that three of the demons went to England, to a small town called Piddlington-on-the-Weld where Bael has set up camp, while the others were sent off to scour Paris for Thala."

"She's here?" Aisling asked.

Jim's lips curled. "According to my gatekeeper buddy, they tracked her from Asia to Italy and then to Paris, but they lost her a few weeks ago. That's what some of the lesser demons are saying, but I wouldn't like to vouch for how accurate it is. You know how it is with those junior demons."

"No, how is it?" Gary asked, donning a fascinated expression.

Jim cocked a knowing eyebrow. "They love to gossip, and if they don't have anything to gossip about, they'll make stuff up."

"Really? No one but Asmodeus's wrath demons were allowed into his private chamber where I lived, but they were always very factual. Sometimes too factual, if you get my drift."

"Nothing a wrathie likes more than to talk tor-ture methods," Jim agreed, nodding. "What were your demons' faves?"

"Oh, it was ghastly, simply ghastly!" Gary said with great relish. "They loved to take a traffic cone, you know, one of those orange and white plastic things, and then grease it up really well—"

"And that's about enough," Bee interrupted with a fierce look at Gary.

"You can tell me later," Jim told the head *sotto voce*. "And I'll tell you what Ash does when she gets PMSy. Bet you my tales beat the pants off of yours."

"I don't know," Gary said hesitantly. "It's pretty bad if someone inserts a greasy traffic cone into—"

"Right, that's the end of my patience," Bee said, picking up the hamster ball and sending it rolling out of the room and into the hallway. Gary's screams followed.

"Where were we?" Bee asked. Everyone stared at the doorway with a shared shock expression.

"I am not a bowling ball!" came an objection from the hall. "Great, now I have a nosebleed."

Bee closed the door. "Constantine?" she asked, appealing to him for help.

He pursed his lips. "I hope you didn't break his nose again. He'll be hell to live with if you did. It's bad enough I had to have it fixed once today."

"I'm sure I didn't." Bee bit her lower lip, and with a muttered curse, opened the door and fetched Gary back. "I said I was sorry! No, your nose isn't broken, that's not even blood. The juice box that Constantine tucked into your little home is leaking, that's all."

Everyone stared at her. She coughed and set Gary down on the half-moon table again. Gary gave an injured sniff and looked noble for a few minutes.

"I've totally lost the thread of what we were talking about," Aisling said, choking a little when Constantine took a few tissues, popped open the lid of the hamster ball, and wiped off the juice before getting Gary settled again.

Bee's shoulders slumped.

"Thala," Aoife said, obviously trying not to laugh. "We were talking about Thala being in Paris. And where Bael might be."

"England," Aisling said, nodding.

"Paris," Constantine corrected.

"Because of Thala?" Bee asked.

"Yes. Thala's sword must be at the top of his list."

"That makes sense to me. If I were Bael, seeking instruments of power would be my priority," Kostya agreed.

Bee looked like she wanted to argue the point. "But that takes us back to the question of why he wants a sword that offers power only to a mage. Why would he want that?"

Constantine didn't answer until Bee poked her elbow into his side. He turned to face her then, hesitating to tell her the truth. He had a sudden, overwhelming urge to protect her, to keep her from continuing with the task of Charming the curse. He wanted her safe, tucked away somewhere peaceful where she would wait for him, greeting him with open arms and laughing eyes. He bowed his head for a moment as blackness blinded him to their surroundings. Arms, warm and solid, slid around his waist. He blinked when he realized it was Bee embracing him, the scent of her driving away the dark thoughts, instantly making him hard with desire.

"If you don't want to tell everyone," she whispered, her breath as soft as a feather against his ear, "you don't have to. You've done enough soul baring for one day."

"Oh, so it's like that, is it?" he heard Aoife say.

Bee stiffened in his arms.

"It's all right," he told her.

"What is, them knowing about your father or my sister being a jerk?"

"Both," he answered, and kissed the top of her head before turning to face the others, one arm comfortably around Bee. "Bael seeks the light sword not because of the power it offers him, but because it *has* power."

"What are you thinking?" Kostya asked, his expression as black as Constantine's thoughts.

"Bael was overthrown before he was banished. His leagues of minions were broken up and divided amongst the other demon lords, and the power he used to maintain control of Abaddon was lost to him. Now that he has been freed—" He paused to give Aoife a look. Kostya growled at him in response. "Now that he is free to move about the mortal world, he must gather power unto him again. He is basically repeating what he did when he first became a demon lord."

"Which is what?" Bee asked.

"He made the Tools of Bael, and imbued into them a good portion of his power. They then focused that power, and allowed him to overthrow the current prince of Abaddon, taking his place and subjugating all the other demon lords."

"I think I heard that the Tools were destroyed," Bee said, frowning in concentration. "There was a rumor going around that they were used to banish Bael."

"I assume something like them must have been used," Constantine said, nodding. "It must have taken extraordinary circumstances to banish him. Logically, then, if the Tools are no longer available to him, he must seek new ones."

"The sword," Bee said, enlightenment dawning in her eyes. "He plans on using it to . . . what, make a new Tool?"

"I can't think of any other reason why he'd want a

mage weapon." Constantine's gaze held hers. "He must not get it."

Her cheeks paled a little. "I can see him getting a hold of it would be very bad. You mean to stop him, don't you?"

"I have to."

"You don't. It's not your responsibility, but I see why you feel like you must do something."

"I don't see why," Aoife said. "I mean, I get that you want to save the dragons, although it sounds like you've done a lot to wipe out the black sept—"

"Ancient history!" Bee said before Constantine could.

He grinned at her. She blushed in response, a fact that simultaneously delighted him and made him want to take her to bed and introduce her to a few of his favorite toys.

"I agree with my mate," Kostya said. "That he would help us break the curse is understandable. But what reason does he have for wanting Bael stripped of his power? Is there something you're not telling us?"

"What are they saying?" Aisling asked.

"Oh, it's all very exciting," Gary said, his hamster ball vibrating with his enthusiasm. "Down, please! Thank you, Bee. Evidently Connie knows something about Bael, and Aoife and Kostya are being a bit terse with him about it. Would you mind?"

Aisling lifted the hamster ball and set it on the cushion next to her, listening while Gary filled her in on the part of the conversation she couldn't understand.

"Are you going to tell them? Don't feel like you have to," Bee whispered to Constantine while Aisling was being caught up. She put a hand on his wrist and gave him a supportive squeeze. "It's really not any of their business."

"Perhaps not, but I can't see that hiding from the truth will do any good." He smiled at her, warmed by her concern. When was the last time a woman took his side? "There is a ball that I think you would like."

Bee blinked at him a few times before wrinkling her forehead. "One of yours?"

"Yes. It is metal, and filled with mercury. It can warm to the touch or be very cold, and has unexpected movements. I would very much like for you to experience it."

She leaned into him, her eyes on Aoife and Kostya as they held a whispered conference. "You mean like a ben wah ball? I'm not going to be into that. It's one thing to have action in your hoohaw while you're engaged in lovemaking, but I don't want to just stuff things in there to be carried around while I go about my daily business. I mean, it's not a purse."

Constantine's lips twitched. "You can insert the metal ball into your ladyplant if you so desire, but there are many other things you can do with it, too. Equally enticing things. For both of us."

"Oh, now that does sound promising."

"Later," Constantine promised, and squared his shoulders before facing his godson. "You asked why I feel responsible to make sure Bael does not harm others. It's not just because he was once dragonkin, or is one of the children of the First Dragon. It is because he is my father."

He had the satisfaction of seeing identical looks of surprise on all their faces.

"You're the First Dragon's grandson?" Aisling asked, her eyes big again. "But that would mean—Baltic is a son of the First Dragon, so you'd be—"

Constantine sighed. "He is my uncle, yes."

"Holy cow," she said, pulling out a mobile phone. "I have to tell Drake this. Or does he know already? I mean, you were close to his dad and all. Judging by the look on his face, I'd guess that Kostya didn't know."

"The only one alive who knows the truth about my relationship with Bael is Baltic, and he cares nothing about it. He is focused solely on Ysolde and his own doings."

"I can't imagine what it's like to have a demon lord for a father. How did he become one?" Aoife asked.

Constantine waved away the question. "It is a long story, and not one I wish to tell now. I must act—Bee and I must act. We must stop Bael from claiming the mage sword, and get the talisman needed to break the curse. He can't be allowed to destroy others as he will surely wish to do."

"You're not going to try to destroy him, are you?" Aoife asked nervously. "Obviously you don't want to kill your father—"

"I have tried in the past, and failed. I would attempt it again if I thought I'd succeed," Constantine said with studied nonchalance.

Aoife took a deep breath. "Okay. Moving past that, he's dangerous. Very dangerous, and I should know because I was in the circle that summoned him for a few seconds before Aisling pulled me out. He was one seriously badass dude then, and if you think he's gathering power now..." She shivered and rubbed her arms. "I don't see how you or even you and Bee together are going to get rid of him. It's got to take an army or something like that."

"Perhaps," was all that Constantine said in response, but privately, he wasn't so confident. He had failed in the attempt to destroy his father centuries ago, when Bael was decimating dragons and mortals alike in response to Constantine refusing to follow his father into Abaddon, but when the assassination attempt failed...mentally, he shuddered at the memory of his mother's death in retaliation. "Bael must be stopped. There is no way mortals or immortals can live in peace with him in power."

"One thing at a time, I think," Aisling said.

"That's sound advice." Bee nodded. "Let's find a talisman and break the curse, and *then* we can gather support to tackle the problem of Bael head-on."

Aisling's phone burbled. She looked at it while Bee was speaking, suddenly leaping to her feet. "Oh man, I don't— Kostya, Aoife, you have to leave." She made shooing motions at them that caused them both to stare at her. "Jim, tell them they have to leave. Right now!"

Jim, who had been chatting with Gary about the latter's experiences in Abaddon, turned a surprised face on her. "Huh? How come?"

"Just tell them!" Aisling ran out of the room, yelling for Jim to do as she ordered.

"K, but I'm telling them that you're the one going crazy, not me. Slick, Aisling wants you and Eefums to get the hell out of dodge. Like, right now."

"What? Why?" Aoife asked, looking a bit insulted.

"Dunno. Ash just went a bit nuts and started yelling for you to go."

"Drake's on his way home," Aisling bellowed from the hall. "Tell them he just landed here in Paris, and Kostya has to get out of the house before he comes home."

"What about Connie?" Jim asked, following Kostya and Aoife out into the main hall. It was a well-appointed room, with walls of hunter green, and a beautiful white marble floor that pleased Constantine. He wondered what Bee thought of it, and decided then and there that he'd have to raise enough money to buy a house with a marble hall floor. Bee would appreciate the floor when he laid her down upon it, and licked her naked body with flames...

"Should we go, too?" Bee asked, pulling him from the delightful fantasy that was building in his mind.

"How do you feel about blindfolds?" he asked her.

She pursed her lips, the corners of her mouth twitching a little. "I don't think I'd like it."

"But you haven't tried it?"

"No."

"Ah." He smiled at her, and added a new pair of blindfolds to his mental shopping list. "Good."

"There's no good about it, buster," she said, whapping him on the arm before striding forward. "I prefer to see what's happening around me. Aisling, did you want us to leave as well?"

"No, I don't think that's necessary, since Constantine appears to be some special exception to the curse rules. Tell them good-bye for me, would you? And that Jim will be in contact when we have some news."

Bee duly repeated the request to Aoife and Kostya, who paused at the door and said, "Do not do anything foolish, old man. I understand your desire to seek revenge, but the good of the dragonkin must come first. The curse must be broken. You have twenty-four hours to locate the talisman. If you do not do so by that time, then the black dragons will do the job for you."

Constantine held onto his temper, despite the overwhelming urge to show Kostya a thing or two about how *old* he was. "Do not threaten me, whelp. I was battling demons before your father even met your mother, and I do not need to be told how to do my job. We will do what we must, but rest assured that Charming the curse is a top priority."

"Twenty-four hours," Kostya repeated, and with a little bow to Aisling, who waved in response, Aoife and Kostya departed.

"The nerve of him giving you an ultimatum like that," Bee said softly in his ear, her hand sliding into the crook of his arm. "He acts like he's all Mr. In Charge, but I don't remember anyone nominating him king of the dragons. I mean, I know there's two sides to every story, but I have to admit that there are times when I really want to punch him right on the snoot." She flashed a quick smile at him, and squeezed his arm. "Don't look so glum, Constantine. We'll get the talisman and take care of Bael, just you see."

Constantine said nothing, but he thought a great many things. And none of them were good.

Thirteen

Constantine appeared to be in deep thought when I asked him if we should take off before Aisling's husband came home. I had to nudge him before he turned to face me. "Hmm?"

"I said, should we hightail it out of here, too? Or are you okay with the green wyvern?"

"Yes, we should leave," he said absently, his gaze directed inward. I wanted to ask him what had him so thoughtful all of a sudden, but at that moment Aisling came bustling back into the sitting room with a tall man with slick black hair and the greenest eyes I'd ever seen on a human.

But of course he wasn't human. This was obviously the green sept wyvern, a man who was known far and wide through the Otherworld as a master thief.

"There were two female demons outside," Drake announced as he kissed his wife. "They ran off before we could capture them. Pal and Istvan are in pursuit, although the way the demons went to ground, I don't hold out much hope they will be located. The house has not been breached?"

"Of course not," Aisling said, giving him a smile that was clearly welcoming in many ways. "You know I have three different layers of wards over every entrance. Nothing can get in that we don't want in."

"See that you reinforce them."

Constantine continued to stand quiet, his mind obviously ticking away along some path that I wasn't privy to. I had a brief review of the conversation of the last few minutes to see if I could pinpoint what had made him so introspective, but came up with a blank.

"Bee, this is my husband, Drake. Bee is the Charmer who Kostya engaged to break the curse," Aisling said, presenting the wyvern. He bowed formally over my hand, as is the wont with dragons, although I thought Constantine did it better. Perhaps it was the green eyes, so very calculating and emotionally distant, or the high cheekbones and the glossy black hair, but everything about Drake left me cold.

My gaze drifted over to Constantine, who was now greeting Drake. What a study in contrasts the two of them made; where Drake reminded me of dark, still water, Constantine was fire and light, the warm glow of his eyes making me think of molten gold. He was sunshine to Drake's shadows, and it made me shiver a little with anticipation when I remembered just how hot Constantine's fire could be.

I was distracted from my smutty thoughts by Aisling giving Drake an update on all the happenings.

Drake looked startled by the information dump. "Bael is one of the firstborn? Why have I not heard of this before?"

"Only the children of the First Dragon know of Bael's true origins, and of them, only Baltic is alive." Constantine shrugged. "It had little relevance until now. Bael must be stopped, no matter who his sire was. I failed to stop him in the past, but I will not fail again."

Drake noticed Gary at that point, giving him a look of pure disbelief. "What is that?"

"He's a who, not a what," Constantine said.

"And his name is Gary," I said, lifting up the hamster ball so Gary could say hello and couldn't keep from adding, "His real name is Gareth, but no one ever calls him that."

"Pleased to meet you," Gary said politely, giving Drake a little nod. "You have a lovely home. My apologies about the tiny dent in the paneling in the hall. I bashed into it earlier when Bee decided to play Bowling with Gary."

Drake's lips tightened.

"And I've apologized twice for that. It was wrong of me, but really, Gary—you know better than to go on about traffic cones after I've made it clear such topics aren't welcome."

"I thought it had interest," he said with an injured sniff.

I set him back down on the couch, saying as I did so, "Oh, balls, Gary, you're all red again. I think your juice box is leaking. I'll take it out, shall I?"

"Please. And might I have another tissue? This juice is a bit sticky."

I removed the offending box while Constantine mopped up Gary again. While we were doing so, I caught Drake giving Aisling an unreadable look.

She batted her eyelashes. "What?" she said finally. "You've never seen a disembodied head who likes pomegranate juice?"

Drake chose to ignore that question and addressed Constantine. "I understand that Baltic and Ysolde asked you to help in the acquisition of the talisman."

"They did." Constantine closed the lid on Gary's ball, and crossed his arms over his chest, at his most formal, something that tickled my funny bone. "Unfortunately, we were given misinformation, and thus the talisman we liberated did not break the curse."

"You do not know where Bael is now?" Drake asked, his arm around Aisling, but a distant look in his cold eyes.

"No," admitted Constantine. "But I'm fairly certain he is in Paris, and if he's in the vicinity, we will find him."

"Hmm."

"What are you thinking?" Aisling asked Drake. "Are you planning on flexing your green dragon skills? Because if you are, you know I want to help. And don't tell me that it's not safe—I feel fine, the twins are in the country with my stepparents and uncle, and you need me."

"I would be a poor green dragon if I couldn't extricate a simple object without aid, even from you." Drake's gaze turned inward as he clearly sorted through some thoughts. "It seems to me that we need two distinctly different things: to keep Bael from finding Thala and the light blade, and to locate his hiding spot. I propose to deal with the latter. You would be hard put to do both, and we green dragons are well suited to the task at hand."

Constantine rubbed his chin, his eyes on me. "I was asked to find the talisman. I hate to go back on a promise to do so. What do you think, Bee?"

I was touched that he even thought to ask me, given that my experience with dragons—and, initially, Constantine— had led me to believe they just did what they wanted without consideration for others. But I was wrong. Constantine was different. Where other dragons were overbearing and insufferable, Constantine was thoughtful, and kind, and considerate. I couldn't think of any other man, let alone a dragon, who would care for a disembodied head, and yet there was Constantine, not only fixing up a new home for Gary (and making sure he stayed hydrated), but giving him a mode of transportation.

"I think you're pretty awesome," I said before I realized I'd spoken that thought aloud.

Constantine's eyebrows rose. I felt my cheeks warming when Aisling stifled a giggle, and Drake looked embarrassed.

"Man, we going to have another mate? Can I watch when he claims her?" Jim asked, snuffling my leg. I swatted at him.

"I am not anyone's mate, and stop wiping your nose all over me. It's cold." I turned to give Constantine a nononsense look, just in case he was listening to Jim's babble. "I am responsible for lifting the curse. That's what I was hired to do, and that's what I will do, come hell or high water."

"Abaddon," Gary and Jim corrected at the same time.

"So my inclination is to say that we will get the talisman, since I'm the best person to know what will work and what won't work. However—" I lifted a hand to stop Aisling at the beginning of her protest. "I am willing to change my mind if you can answer one question, Constantine."

"Forty-two," he deadpanned.

I stared at him for the count of three, then burst into laughter. "If I didn't like you already, the fact that you're a Douglas Adams fan would raise you high in my estimation. Unfortunately, the answer I need isn't going to be as amusing."

"Very well. What is your question?"

"If Bael gets hold of the light sword, will it make it harder for me to Charm the curse?"

"Oooh, good question," Gary said, hopping up and down a little. "And scary, too, because what if Asmodeus gets the light sword? Then we'll have two powerful demon lords going at it, and where will it end?"

"The head has a point," Drake said.

"I have a name!" Gary said indignantly.

"He does have a point," Constantine said slowly, his eyes now dark with thought, with only a few little amber flecks showing bright. "And Bee's question drives home the question of what we must deal with after the curse is broken."

"Assuming it is," Drake said drily.

"Of course it will be broken," Aisling said.

"The Charmer has already tried and failed. There is nothing to say that can't happen again," he pointed out.

"Hey now," I protested. "We weren't told that the curse originated with Bael. The fact that the Charming failed isn't our fault."

"The answer to your question is yes, I think," Constantine said, having ignored us all to focus on what was important. "Bael cast the curse on us. We still don't know how he did that from the Akasha, but the fact that he could warns us that even there he had powers beyond our estimation. But if he were to gather together three new Tools..." He hesitated, then glanced at Drake, who immediately wrapped an arm around Aisling and pulled her close.

"If he gets new Tools, then he'll become unstoppable?" I finished.

"No. Or rather, not in the sense you mean. He will, however, be able to layer curse upon curse on dragonkin, to the point where we couldn't break them. That is just one reason why he must be kept from gaining the light sword."

"That answers the question of what we should do, then, doesn't it?" I asked him.

"Yes." He gave me a long look. "I just wanted to be sure you were happy with the decision, since you must break the curse."

I sensed the pain within him, dampening his fire until it was almost cold, and leaving him pale and drained of energy. I hated to see him like that, since he was so warm and vital, like a personification of his dragon fire. I wanted the feisty, sexy Constantine back, not the man who bore the guilt of a father's sins.

I leaned into him and bit his lower lip before sucking it into my mouth. There was a flash of surprise and pleasure in his eyes before I closed in for a kiss, my tongue demanding entrance, delighting in the spicy, sweet taste of him. He was like an intoxicating honey wine, going instantly to my head, and making the rest of me warm with anticipation.

"Hoo boy, that's what I'm talking about," I heard Jim say. "Where's my camera? He's going to claim her right here in front of us."

"Golly," Gary said, his voice filled with wonder. "I thought you were wrong before, Jim, but gracious me alive! That is quite the kiss, isn't it?"

"Jim! Get out of my purse. No, you may not use my cell phone. Drop it! Bad demon!"

"Aw, Ash, you never let me have any phone. Just a couple of pictures. One or two for my Facebook page. Bet I'd get a ton of likes for it."

"No."

"I hope Constantine does claim Bee. That would mean I could stay with them both, rather than having to be just Connie's sidekick. Not that there's anything wrong with that," Gary said. "But you know, it's better to have a mom and dad rather than just one, although Connie does tend to hang out at some cool places that I don't think Bee would like. But you have to take the good with the bad, right?"

I managed to pull myself off Constantine, who had his hands on my hips, and was kissing me back for all he was worth. It took me a good minute or two to collect my scattered wits. Dear gods, the man had a mouth that could tempt a nun. But pull back I did, and as soon as I could speak, I turned a gimlet eye on Gary.

"If you refer to me as your mom again, I'll see to it that your RC car privileges are revoked for a week."

"Ouch," Jim said.

Gary's eyes widened. "I was just trying to explain that I felt like we were a family."

"Uh huh. Don't call me mom again." I avoided looking at Constantine, and kept my gaze on Drake. "If you would be so kind as to find a talisman, we would be grateful. Just remember that it has to be something of personal importance to Bael."

"I will start immediately," Drake said with a nod and got up from the table. "I'll call for help from local green dragons."

"I think I'll contact my mentor," Aisling said, "and just warn her that her talents will be needed shortly."

"We are leaving," Constantine said, his hand on my back. He tucked Gary under his arm, and gave me a little push toward the door. "We have much to do, and little time to do it in. Drake, do not dally raising sept members to help you. We must have the talisman before dawn."

"Why then?" I asked, allowing him to herd me toward the door.

The look he gave me was enigmatic, which just irritated me. "It won't take Bael long to find the sword, if he hasn't already."

I waved at Aisling, who lifted a hand in response before Constantine hustled us out of the house. I waited until I was on the motorcycle, tucking my hair into the helmet to say, "You sound like you know where the sword is."

"I do."

He started the engine of the bike, making it difficult to hold a conversation, but that didn't stop me from yelling in his ear, "You do not!"

"I do," he bellowed, and the bike lurched forward just as he added, "As do you."

I waited until we were stopped at a traffic light to speak again. "Are you crazy? I don't know where the light sword is. I don't have any idea where it could be, or Thala, or for that matter, Bael. I'm just a Charmer, Constantine, just a simple Charmer."

"You're anything but simple," came the muffled comment from the region around my stomach, where Gary was wedged between Constantine and me. "Don't be afraid to blow your own horn, Bee. If you don't do it, who will?"

Constantine said something, but it was lost when the motorcycle bucked and we zoomed off into the night again. At first I thought he was returning us to his accommodations, but when he passed the street the brothel was on, and turned down a familiar block, I realized what he was doing.

"How do you expect to get inside?" I asked some three minutes later when Constantine left his motorcycle in a small area containing trash bins, and walked us around the perimeter of the building that was Goety and Theurgy. "You know full well that the Venediger is likely to be angry with us, and probably all dragons. She won't let us in. And speaking of that, why are we *here*?"

We were about to round the corner of the building to the front when Constantine held out his hand and stopped me from proceeding forward. I peered around him and gasped silently at the sight of a handful of people guarding the front entrance.

"Who are they?" I asked in a whisper.

Constantine tipped his head back and sniffed a couple of times. "Demons."

"Hellbeans," I swore.

"Abaddonbeans, I think, would be more apropos," Gary said softly, whistling as he did so. "Those are Asmodeus's wrath demons. I recognize three of them."

"What are Asmodeus's demons doing here?" I asked, obediently turning and following Constantine when he retraced our steps to the rear of the building. "They can't get in, can they? I thought the Venediger had the building protected from demons unless they are summoned there."

Constantine slid me a look, stopping next to a window. Due to the light from the building next to us, half his face was in shadow, giving him a dangerous appearance that sent a little jolt of adrenaline through my body. *What did I really know about him?* my brain demanded to know. He was a dangerous being, a wyvern, a man who was used to fighting and killing for what he wanted. His eyes glowed with an inner light that, for a moment, had me fighting the urge to flee into the night, but then the smart part of my mind, the part that remembered how gentle he was with Gary kicked in, and I stood where I was.

"You have answered your own question" was all he said before pulling off his jacket and shirt, and wrapping the latter around his hand.

"He's not going to do what I think he's going to do, is he?" Gary asked, his voice high with excitement.

I moved back a few feet. "I think he is. Close your eyes in case any shards go flying and crack the hamster ball."

"All right, but I don't want to miss anything good. This is the most exciting thing I've seen since the behemoth ate my body!"

The tinkle of glass that followed Constantine punching a hole in the window seemed inordinately loud to my ears, but there was no reaction to it from within. Judging by the placement of the window, I guessed that Constantine had chosen a small storeroom, a guess that was validated when he brushed off the glass, raised the broken window, and climbed inside before offering me his hand.

"Keep quiet," I told Gary when I gave Constantine the ball, then hoisted myself up and over the window into the room. The door to the room was closed, although large, bulky, black shapes could be made out from the light coming in through the alley. I caught my breath, standing still next to Constantine as we both listened intently. A distant rumble of voices warned that we were not alone in the building.

Constantine waved at me in what I assumed was a silent warning to stay put. I made a face at his back when he opened the door and peered out into the lit hallway, moving up immediately behind him.

"Hey!" Gary whispered loudly. I shushed him. "What about me? Don't leave me behind."

"Keep quiet, then," I said, and tucked him under my arm before hurrying out of the door that Constantine had left barely open.

Blood splattered the walls, dribbled on the floor, and even arced onto the ceiling. It was empty of people, however. I covered my mouth to keep an audible gag from being heard, as I tiptoed to where Constantine stood peering around a corner to a second hallway that crossed the first. It must have run parallel to the main body of the club, with a small garden space in the center.

A long, gruesome smear of blood led to a closed door at the end of the hallway, the room that had held the Venediger's safe.

"I don't think I want to know what's in there," I whispered to the back of Constantine's head.

"Stay back," he growled softly.

"No, sir. We're safer with you."

"You are nothing of the sort, not so long as you bear the ring."

I curled my fingers into a fist and said nothing, but stuck close to the back of Constantine as he walked quietly down the hallway, avoiding the blood smears. He paused at the door, listened for a moment, then made an almost noiseless exclamation, and opened the door.

There were four people in the room, two men, two women, and...I slapped a hand over my mouth to keep from screaming at the sight of the fifth person. It was Guillaume, clearly dead.

"Don't look," Constantine said gruffly, standing in such a way as to block me from the rest of the room. "There is nothing we can do for him now."

"Poor Guillaume," I whispered, and hoped fervently that he hadn't suffered. He had been an officious little man, but certainly didn't deserve to be killed.

Of the other four people in the room, I only recognized one: the Venediger. She stood facing us, her expression as black as night, her fingers twitching as if she wanted to strangle someone. A woman with long blond hair and a man with shoulder-length dark hair stood facing the fourth person, the man clearly in a defensive pose.

"Do you know these people?" I asked Constantine in a whisper.

"Yes. They are Baltic and Ysolde."

So that was the Ysolde he kept talking about. I made a mental note to have a chat with her another time. Right now, it was the man they were facing who worried me most.

As soon as I looked at him I felt as if I'd been punched in the gut. He wasn't even looking our way; he had clearly been speaking to the Venediger, and didn't bother to see who'd entered the room. He was a demon lord, that was clear enough from the blackish-blue aura that seemed to shimmer in and out of view, and there could only be one person who made Constantine's fire suddenly roar to life with a vengeance.

I touched the back of his shoulder, saying almost soundlessly, "Is that—"

"Yes. Keep yourself to yourself," he whispered back.

The words sounded like rock grinding on rock, and for an instant, irritation flared to life within me. Keep myself to myself? What sort of chauvinistic, micro-managing sort of comment was that? And as soon as I found myself bristling with ire, I realized what he meant.

We were in the presence of Bael, a demigod so ruthless, he thought nothing of destroying countless people, including Constantine's own mother.

I set Gary down on a chair and folded my right hand over the left, concealing the black ring from view.

"I wondered when we would see you," the dark-haired man said casually, giving Constantine a little nod. His gaze brushed over me without interest, paused at Gary for a few long seconds, then returned to Bael, who sat on the corner of the Venediger's desk, casually fingering a dagger that had most likely been used as a letter opener.

"What are you doing here?" Constantine asked, addressing Baltic. "He should never have let you come here, Ysolde. It is not safe in Paris."

Baltic gave a short, humorless bark of laughter at the same time Ysolde made a little face. "You know nothing of women if you think you can control their actions. My mate does as she wishes."

"That said, I sort of wish I wasn't here right now," Ysolde said, casting a pained glance at the body of Guillaume. She scooted closer to Baltic before turning her worried gaze back on Bael.

The Venediger made an inarticulate noise, her face now red with fury. She snarled something very rude at

Constantine, adding, "I should have known it would be folly to get involved with dragons. The blame for Guillaume's death goes squarely on your shoulders, and for that, I will see to it that you never have another day's peace so long as you live!"

"That's hardly fair," Ysolde said, glancing at the Venediger. "Considering that Constantine and his friend weren't even here when Bael forced his way in and slaughtered your secretary." She shuddered, which caused Baltic to shift slightly so that he was more than half blocking her.

"One moment," Bael said, pulling out his cell phone when it burbled at him. "I have a text I must answer. Instructions regarding the princes of Abaddon, you understand. Feel free to talk amongst yourselves until I can once again give you my full attention."

"Talk amongst..." I shook my head and stopped speaking. It wouldn't do to point out to a demon lord just how annoying he was.

"None of this would have happened if that one had not attempted to Charm the curse." The Venediger made an awkward, abrupt gesture toward us. I was filled with sympathy for her, and didn't even dispute the unjust claim. She was no doubt grieving heavily for poor Guillaume.

Slowly, with studied indifference that I didn't for a moment buy, Bael looked up from his phone and turned his head to consider us. I took a long look at him, and immediately wished I hadn't.

He was of medium height, with pale blond hair and washed-out blue eyes. If you discounted the black aura of power surrounding him, he looked perfectly normal, even attractive, although I had heard that he could change his appearance at will.

"Constantine," he drawled, his face a mask devoid of emotion. Even his eyes were flat and uninterested. His gaze crawled over me for a few seconds, causing little bits of my soul to tear off with cries of anguish, and then suddenly I was free, and he had turned his attention back to Constantine. "So you have come crawling out of oblivion. You will not be surprised if I say that your presence is not needed or welcome."

I had my hand on Constantine's back, and thus felt when he reeled backward into me, just as if he'd been dealt a physical blow. It took every ounce of restraint that I had to keep from yelling at Bael to leave his son alone, but the pressure of my fingers around the ring reminded me that in this situation, the lowest profile possible was going to be the best for all of us.

"You know Constantine?" Ysolde asked, looking confused and suspicious at the same time. "What's going on, Baltic? Why is Bael here?"

"He is here for the light sword of Antonia von Endres," the Venediger said, her voice choked and rough. Behind her, I could see the safe, its door blasted off the hinges. On the shelves I could make out a fertility statue, a cerise crystal, and the glint of silver metal.

The sword! Of course, that's why Constantine brought us here—he remembered seeing the sword in the safe and must have realized what it was.

"How did *you* come by the sword?" Constantine asked, getting a nod of approval from me. I very much wanted to know the answer to that question, too. "It was stolen by Baltic's guard, Thala."

"I would be a very poor mage if I left something so valuable as the light blade in the possession of a half-dragon," she replied with a little scornful curl of her lip. "Naturally, I did what was necessary to find her and took the sword into my possession."

"Well, that solves one problem," I murmured to Constantine. He gave a barely perceptible nod. "The big elephant in the room is how to keep Bael from taking the sword."

The Venediger must have had very good hearing, because she gave a disgusted snort, her gaze holding Bael's (something that gave me the willies just thinking about it). "He is mistaken if he thinks there is any way I would give the sword up to him. All mages swear an oath to protect it with their lives, and I will use every ounce of my powers to ensure its safety."

Bael's head snapped around to pierce her with his horrifying gaze. "If you desire it, then so shall it be."

The Venediger didn't even have time to scream—one minute she was standing there, bristling with anger, and the next, there was nothing but a pile of ash and a few bits of tattered yellow material.

"You monster!" I yelled, anger bursting to life within me. I had been sickened and saddened by the sight of Guillaume's body, but to see a living, breathing human being suddenly and very literally turned to ash right before our eyes—my brain couldn't cope with it. I started forward, no idea in my brain other than that I had to tell Bael what I thought of him, but I was stopped almost immediately.

Constantine grabbed my arm in a grip that I feared would leave a bruise, and shoved me toward Baltic and Ysolde. "Stay with them," he ordered, not taking his eyes off of Bael.

"Oh?" Ysolde asked, her expression shifting momentarily from horror to speculation, but the hideousness of the moment quickly regained her attention.

Baltic raised one eyebrow, gave me a long look, and then flickered a glance at Constantine.

I desperately wanted to tell Constantine that we had to do something; we couldn't allow the Venediger to be wiped out without so much as a second thought, but the weight of the ring on my finger reminded me that I had to think beyond my own desires.

With my gaze on the ashy remains of the Venediger, I scooped up Gary and moved over to stand next to Ysolde.

"You had no right to take her life," Constantine said, his voice colder than the Arctic wind.

Bael looked mildly bored. "She threatened me. You all witnessed that."

"She was defending herself," Constantine snapped, his fire hot within us both. I swear his eyes were just about glowing. "You came here and slaughtered her minion, then stated your intention to take a relic important to mages, which you cannot even use. Of course she threatened you—anyone would, given that circumstance."

"I do not need to explain myself to anyone, least of all you," Bael said in his bored voice that said we were all tedious beyond belief.

"The entire Otherworld will seek justice for the death of the Venediger," Baltic said.

"Given the threat you pose, I would not be surprised if Abaddon joined forces in order to contain you," Constantine added.

I wondered for a moment why the two men were baiting Bael, but realized they were simply trying to get him to retreat. I'd rather we tackled him right then and there, with the remains of two people who had been alive a half hour before, than wait until a later time. It struck me that I wasn't feeling just my own desire to make Bael pay for his actions, but also Constantine's. And that was a bit shocking in itself—at what point had I become so in tune with him?

Bael's lip curled. "I will soon rectify the situation with Abaddon, of that you can be sure. Asmodeus possesses a ring that I desire, and I make it a policy to obtain that which I seek."

I hid my ring-bearing hand behind my back, almost sick with fear that Bael would somehow sense it was here.

"You will not get the light sword," Constantine said, moving to stand beside Baltic. "The demons at the front of the building will already have caused alarms to be set off around Paris—reinforcements will already be en route."

"Demons?" Bael's face showed an emotion at last, one of speculation, but it was gone almost immediately. "Those of Asmodeus, I assume. They are of little concern and will soon no longer exist."

I bit my lip to keep from blurting out something rude.

"Regardless of your idle threats, your presence here is doomed." It was Constantine's turn to sound bored, although I could feel by the tension running through him that he was barely restraining himself. "Stay, if you wish, but you will bring upon your head your own destruction."

"Don't be tedious—" Bael started to say, his voice dripping unconcern, but at that moment, Constantine lunged at his father, a massive ball of fire preceding him that slammed Bael through the wall and into the next room.

Baltic leaped to the side, snatched up the shiny sword from the safe, and with a yell of warning tossed it to Constantine. He reached back into the safe to grab something else, but by then, Bael threw himself into the room, his face a vision of wrath that I swear took a few years off my life just to witness.

"Constantine! Run! Don't let him get the sword!" I yelled, trying to get around Baltic, who now took up a stance in front of Ysolde and me. The latter was muttering to herself, clearly drawing on some inner power to cast a spell.

"Yes," Bael said, in a voice so horrible it caused little cracks to appear in the walls. His head lowered, but his eyes were firmly fixed on Constantine. "Run away, Constantine. You of all dragons know what will happen if you try my wrath. Or do you care so little that you are willing to risk the lives of everyone here?"

In a move that showed more bravery than I thought possible, Constantine took up a fighting stance and gave his sword a twirl that was pure bravado. "You cannot fight us all and win, Bael. Not in your weakened state. Leave us, if not in peace, then at least with your pride intact."

Ysolde sucked in her breath at the brash words.

"Golly!" Gary whispered, his eyes round, his expression one of utter admiration. "He's really wonderful, isn't he?"

I shook my head. "Wonderful, but foolish. He needs to get the sword out of here, not stand up to his father."

"Father?" Ysolde goggled at me, then gazed at Constantine. "He's Bael's son? Did you know this, Baltic?"

"Yes," he answered, his body tense with anticipation. In his right hand he held the small cerise-colored jewel.

I wondered why he wasn't doing something to help Constantine, since obviously it would be better for everyone to keep Bael from gaining the power the sword held. "I am aware of most of the offspring of my brothers."

Ysolde goggled again. I felt a twinge of sympathy for her. "I—he's your—you mean the First Dragon is his— Why didn't you tell me?"

Baltic managed to shrug even while looking like he was about to pounce. "It never occurred to me that you didn't know."

"Well, I didn't!" Ysolde turned to me, and asked softly, "Who exactly are you?"

"My name is Bee Dakar. I'm a Charmer."

"I do not believe my situation is as dire as you would like to believe," Bael said, brushing off dust from drywall before slowly sauntering forward. I wanted to scream at Constantine to get the sword away, but he just stood there until his father stood a couple of yards in front of him. "In fact, I believe the odds are with me."

Constantine raised the sword so that it stood between them. "You will not find us so easy to overcome."

Bael pursed his lips for a moment, glancing from Constantine to Baltic, and then to Ysolde. His gaze touched me for a moment, but since I was now behind both Ysolde and Baltic, I managed to stand the experience without flinching. "Perhaps not. Very well, have it your way."

And with a gesture like that of someone sweeping back the door to a tent, he simply waved open the fabric of space, and a handful of demons leaped through, each brandishing a sword. They skidded to a stop, looking at Bael for instructions.

"Run, Constantine! Save the sword!" I yelled again,

trying to get around Ysolde and Baltic in order to grab Constantine and forcibly drag him from the room.

"That is not the light sword," Baltic said calmly, moving forward to block my path. In his hand, the crystal thrummed for a few seconds, then elongated into a beautiful sword that appeared to be made of blue-and-white light. "Only a black dragon can handle arcane magic."

Ysolde finished casting her spell, flinging her hands wide just as Bael gave the command to attack.

Constantine and Baltic, side by side now, lifted their swords and prepared to defend us from the demons. My heart seemed to contract with fear, and I realized something profound: I was falling in love with Constantine.

I didn't have time to do more than to admire him as he flexed his hands, ready for the attack, before a flash of insight struck me: we didn't have to look anywhere else for Bael's talisman.

The ring suddenly grew hot and heavy on my finger, dragging my attention to our immediate surroundings. I pulled hard on the ring's magic, planning to focus it on Bael, but a fraction of a second before Bael brought his hands together in a dramatic gesture, I knew with every ounce of my being that we were about to be destroyed.

The resulting shock wave not only threw us all backward, it flattened the building, sending walls, bricks, roof, and timber down on top of us.

Fourteen

"I'm seriously tired of having this building coming down on top of me."

Bee's voice was strained and thin, but Constantine could have greeted the sound of it with cries of joy. Instead, he carefully levered off a part of the wall that had collapsed down onto a long desk and flung rubble out of the way until she was revealed to him.

"You're a mess," he said, not wondering at the way his heart lightened just by the sight of her dust-streaked face. Her hair was sticking out all over, partially turned white by plaster dust, bits of paper and wood, and bits of upholstery from an armchair. Her shirt was torn off of one shoulder, with little speckles of blood, but his quick gaze reassured him that it was minor scratches, and nothing more. She was filthy, dirty, and blood-streaked, and coughed and spat up bits of dust, wheezing like an asthmatic at a cigar bar.

And the world was a better place because she was in it, swearing like a stevedore in between coughing attacks.

He kicked aside a broken bit of chair and gently helped her up, rubbing her back in an attempt to ease the distress.

"Is everyone—" Bee broke off to cough again. Her voice was as rough as sandpaper. Even that seemed charming to Constantine. "Is everyone okay? Ysolde? Baltic? Where's Gary?"

"I'm here. I think. Golly, what happened?"

Constantine waited until Bee had her balance before releasing her to toss aside a painting, part of a settee, and a chunk of Sheetrock, pulling Gary out of the remains of his hamster ball. He, too was covered in dust and dirt, his hair resembling a porcupine's back with slivers of wood and glass poking out at all angles. Constantine picked the worst of it off and propped him up on the remains of a chair before turning to look to the other side of the room. He'd seen Baltic and Ysolde as soon as he hauled himself out from under the part of the roof that had fallen on them, so he knew they were alive, at least.

"Are you hurt?" he called to them, wondering that he wasn't panicked with worry about Ysolde's state of health. He felt vaguely guilty over that, but decided that since Bee wasn't immortal or mated to a dragon who would give his life to protect her, it was only right and proper that he be more concerned about her.

"Ysolde was struck on the head, but she appears to be unharmed," Baltic answered.

"Thankfully, I have a thick skull," Ysolde said with an attempt at a smile.

Rather than rushing to her side to make sure that she wasn't overestimating her state of health, Constantine simply nodded, then proceeded to clear a path before up-righting the remains of a chair so Bee could sit down.

"I'm fine, really," she protested when he insisted that she allow him to tend her wounds. "I think the ring did something to protect us, because I had this flash of insight right as Bael did whatever it was that brought the place down around our ears. I mean, we shouldn't have survived that, should we?"

"You shouldn't have," he agreed, pulling out the tail of his shirt and tearing off a piece of it. He dabbed gently at the bloody specks on her shoulder and upper arm, pleased to see that none of the wounds were deep or serious. "The ring definitely protected you and quite possibly cushioned the rest of us as well."

"Except the Venediger and Guillaume," she said sadly, and reached out to pull Gary onto her lap. Constantine was horrified to see her eyes well up with tears. "I can't help but feel partially responsible for their deaths. I know that it was Bael's decision to kill them, and ultimately the blame must lie squarely on his shoulders, but he wouldn't have been here if we hadn't tried to break the curse. And speaking of that, I've had an idea."

"Why on earth would you say that?" Ysolde asked, carefully picking her way over to Bee, Baltic at her side. Around them, sirens began to wail, while the noises of the city, normally a constant background, slowly began to filter through the residual ringing in Constantine's ears. "The part about the curse, I mean. Didn't the Venediger already have the sword? Aisling's demon, Jim, said you tried to break the curse and failed, but I don't see how that would lure Bael out of hiding. He certainly didn't seem concerned about the curse at all."

Constantine noticed Baltic hunting among the rubble. A chill clutched his guts. "What are you looking for?" he asked quietly.

Baltic turned a stricken face to him. "The light sword. It was in my hand when I was knocked backward, but it is not here."

The two men stared at each other in horrified comprehension.

"That's one," Constantine said finally.

"One what?" Bee asked, moving over to where they stood.

Both men were silent for long enough that Bee poked Constantine in the side and repeated her question.

"Bael has the light sword," he admitted.

"Oh, no!"

"I suspected he'd gotten it after blasting us nearly to kingdom come," Ysolde said tiredly. Immediately, Baltic moved to her side.

Bee stroked his arm in an obvious attempt to comfort him. "I'm sorry, Constantine. Yes, I know it wasn't my fault, but I'm sorry that he got the sword after all. It just means we have to keep him from getting anything else he can use to build power. If only we'd gotten here earlier, perhaps we could have saved the Venediger and the sword . . ."

A shout from behind them had Constantine lifting his hand in acknowledgment. People had begun to gather outside the remains of G&T, as well as the buildings on either side, both of which were missing walls. "The deaths are not anyone's fault but Bael's," he said, giving her a quick reassuring squeeze. "They are regrettable and will not be forgotten by anyone in the Otherworld, but they do not stain our souls. We must leave. The mortal police will be here shortly, and we have much work to do."

"Yes, we do, but the most important thing we can do is right here and now." Bee unbuttoned his shirt, making Constantine both instantly aroused, and mildly shocked.

"You wish to make love now?" he asked, glancing around. "I must tell you that I do not find such acts in public places exciting. Outside, yes, but I really must demand a little privacy. Others watching is unsavory."

Bee gave a little laugh, shook her head, and looked startled when a small bit of wood flew out of her curls. "I'm not into voyeurism, either, so as good as it is to know I won't have to fight you over that, I wasn't actually trying to seduce you. I need to see the curse to Charm it."

A little frown pulled his brows together. "We do not have a talisman."

"Oh yes we do." She leaned forward, brushing her hair back in order to stare at his chest and belly, finally putting a finger on a spot on his side. "Right, let's see if I can do this without any other catastrophe."

"Did you steal something from Bael?" Ysolde asked, looking around them. People on the street started to work their way through the debris and rubble, calling out questions. In the distance, sirens grew louder. "Or did he leave something behind?"

"You could say that," Bee said, her focus on Constantine's chest as she traced the pattern seared into his flesh. It was like being touched by a hummingbird's wings, soft and light and fleeting, but with each passing second, he felt as if a heavy weight was being lifted off of him. "The talisman is Constantine."

"You're kidding," Ysolde said at the same time that

Constantine shook his head. "Bee must have struck her head as well."

"I did no such thing." Bee slid a glance upward at him, and inexplicably grinned, warming him down to his toenails. "Think about it—what is a talisman but something that has a strong relationship to the person in question? Often it's a possession, but it can just as well be something that is a part of that person. Well, you're Bael's son. You can't be more a part of something than related by blood."

"That's really smart thinking," Gary said, somewhat muffled since Bee still held him clutched to her front. "And to think that Connie was the answer to the problem all along!"

"But why didn't it work the first time, if that's the case?" Ysolde asked.

"Most likely because we didn't just use Constantine alone—we had Asmodeus's talisman as well, corrupting things." Bee was frowning now, her attention focused on his chest, her hand shaking a little as it traced the pattern of the curse.

He watched her for a moment, concerned by the strain that was showing in her tightened lips. He was about to ask her if she was all right when he noticed that her finger had turned black, an inky color that moved slowly up her flesh as if it was a flush. Her hand shook harder as she struggled to unmake the curse. He wanted to stop her, but he knew it had to be done. After a moment's thought, he placed his hand on her arm to give it support, and breathed fire onto her hand.

She gasped and looked up at him, a flash of gratitude in her eyes. The dragon fire sank into her flesh, driving back the black stain until it was confined to just the tip of her finger.

He stroked her arm, aware that it was cold, ice cold. She continued unmaking the curse, the blackness leeching up her hand until he drenched it with more fire. And so it went on for several minutes until she straightened up, her gaze intent on his chest as she followed the swirls leading up to his collarbone. "Almost done."

He bathed her entire arm in fire, not liking how the chill was creeping up her flesh. "If it is too much for you—"

"It's not," she said quickly, taking in a shuddering breath. "I blame myself for not thinking of you earlier, to be honest. I got there in the end, but I just wish I could have done so before the Venediger and Guillaume were killed. Is everyone ready? I'm coming to the heart of the curse. I don't know what it will do when it's broken, but I want everyone ready for some reaction."

Constantine braced himself as Bee's finger finished tracing out what appeared to be an overly complicated Celtic knot on his right shoulder. Just as she traced out the last curve, her eyes met his.

He decided then and there that he would spend his life trying to thank her for everything she'd done for him, for bringing warmth back into his life, for reminding him that even he had a future, and most of all, for standing by him despite all the trials they'd endured. And with that thought, the world seemed to contract before suddenly releasing its breath and sending him staggering backward a few steps.

Ysolde and Baltic did the same.

Gary cheered.

Bee slumped for a moment before straightening her

shoulders and lifting her chin. She shook her hand, and Constantine was pleased to see the black color slowly fade away. "And that, lady and gentlemen, is how we Charm a curse. Even one made by a bastard murdering demon lord. If you will forgive me for referring to him like that, Constantine."

"He *is* a murdering bastard, at least in the sense of his character," Constantine said, taking his first free breath in what seemed like a lifetime of bondage. He looked down at his chest. The curse itself was no more, the dark discoloration having evaporated away with the movement of Bee's finger, but his flesh still bore faint scarred traces of it. He touched his skin, not feeling anything but a profound sense of relief. And joy. So much joy he couldn't contain it.

"Ow!" Gary protested when Constantine hoisted up Bee and spun her around jubilantly, Gary caught between them.

He kissed her hard, his lips softening almost immediately. "Thank you," he whispered before reluctantly setting her down. "Is your hand damaged?"

She flexed her fingers, making a rueful face. "No, just a bit stiff. Curses are always cold on the hand. Your fire helped a lot, though. Thank you for that."

The passersby had reached them, mostly denizens of the Otherworld, but enough mortals that Constantine did not wish to have to explain what happened. He pulled off the tattered remains of his shirt and wrapped Gary in it before escorting Bee out of the debris.

"It's done? It's over?" he heard Ysolde ask before she whooped with joy. She flung herself on Baltic, the sight of which would have normally sent him spiraling into depression, but now he simply gave Baltic a nod and lifted Bee over a large chunk of splintered wall.

"I have to say I'm glad that's done," Bee said, lightly touching his chest. Her pleased expression melted into one of regret. "The curse has scarred you, though. I'm sorry, Constantine."

"Sorry about what?" He stopped beside the remains of his motorcycle, mentally sighed, and took Bee's hand to lead her to the street in search of a cab. "You lifted the curse that has plagued all of dragonkin for more than two years. You have done that which we doubted could ever be done. You have given back to us a future, one where we can restore the weyr and live in peace."

"I did my job, and that was only after screwing it up big-time first. And now we've lost the light sword." She rubbed a hand across her head, looking so tired that it wrung Constantine's heart. He stepped out into the street, stopped a passing cab, and demanded service.

"I am just going back to the depot—" the driver started to say in French, but Constantine cut him off with a particularly potent look.

"You may do so after taking us to my rooms," he said firmly, urging Bee into the cab. She was clearly too exhausted to protest and slumped against the seat in a limp way that made him swear to himself that he would allow her food and rest before he seduced her.

That noble intention lasted until he got her into his room at the brothel.

"Go to bed," he said, pointing at the bed that had, thankfully, been made up since they had last used it. "I will fetch some food."

"I have a hotel room—" she started to protest weakly.

"Bed," he said firmly, and with Gary in one hand, and the RC truck in another, he went downstairs.

"I take it I'm *de trop* again," Gary said conversationally, wagging his eyebrows. "I know you said you don't like onlookers, but how do you feel about a threesome?"

"I don't share my women," Constantine responded, amused despite himself.

Gary's eyebrows went into overtime. "I wouldn't actually be interested much in Bee, charming though she is. I mean, I like women, I truly do. I'm totally in touch with my feminine side. I even like some of them more than others, if you know what I mean. But not Bee. She's like a big sister to me."

"Bee doesn't strike me like the sort of woman who is willing to share, either." Constantine made a mental note to tell Bee just how Gary viewed her. He had a feeling she would find it as entertaining as he did.

"That's a shame," Gary said sadly.

Constantine thought for the time it took to trot down the flight of stairs to the ground floor. "Although I can recommend a light dragon who might be willing to entertain your offer. Baltic's friend Pavel is back at Dauva keeping it safe from any attacking red dragons, but he is like you—he enjoys both sexes."

"Hmm. I'll remember that if I'm ever in the area." Gary heaved a dramatic sigh. "It's just a shame that you couldn't expand your circle of experience to include me, but if you insist..."

Constantine ignored the hopefully coy look the head was giving him, and instead stopped by the brothel office and requested a pair of scarves, which he proceeded to use to strap Gary onto the RC truck, tucking the remote joystick under one of the ties, but within reach of Gary's mouth.

"Whee!" Gary said, zooming down the hallway in a ragged line. "Whoops, drifting to the right...my apologies sir. Er, madam. Oh, you're both? Apologies, nonetheless. Woohoo, freedom again! This is even better than in the ball! You go ahead and love up Bee, Connie, and I'll catch you in the morning. Beep beep! Coming through! I wonder if I could do a wheelie? Hey, guys, I'm back! And what an evening I've had. I'll tell you all about it, but first, check me out! I'm burning rubber!"

By the time Constantine collected food, made arrangements for Gary, and told reception not to disturb him unless the zombie apocalypse hit (and then only if the zombies were within biting distance), and made it back to his room, he expected Bee to be fast asleep.

He wasn't disappointed.

She lay facedown on the bed, fully clothed, covered in soot, dirt, and plaster dust, one shoe on the floor while the other dangled from her toes. Her mouth was open, and she snored slightly.

Constantine couldn't recall when he had last seen such an attractive woman.

"Not attractive," he said aloud, shaking his head while he pulled Bee's shoe off and placed a duvet on top of her. "Beautiful. Gorgeous. Downright breathtaking."

He thought about that while peeling off his own filthy clothing in the bathroom, mentally pulling up a picture of Ysolde and comparing it to Bee. Where Ysolde was tall and blond and willowy, Bee was of medium height, a build that he would have thought of as stocky on anyone else (but modified it to pleasingly round), and with freckled skin that demanded to be stroked and kissed and licked.

Although Ysolde's ethereal beauty might attract most men, he had to admit that there was something else about Bee that appealed to him. She was an earth goddess, a woman who was straightforward and honest, and who was clearly devoted to helping others.

"I could fall in love with her," he told his reflection, rubbing his whiskery chin. "But then she'd fall in love with me in return, and I'd end up breaking her heart because she would want a proper wyvern, and I don't have a sept. That wouldn't be fair to her at all."

He sighed, momentarily feeling sorry for himself. All those centuries ago, when he had lost his heart to Ysolde, he swore he'd never love another, and he hadn't. But sometimes, the thought crossed his mind that unrequited love wasn't as satisfying as the chivalric texts promised, and once or twice he'd wished that he had a woman in his life whom he could love, and who would love him in return.

Wouldn't it be nice if that woman were Bee?

He shook his head at that rogue thought. "She enjoys my body, but nothing more. She deserves a mate who will be able to provide her with everything she desires. No, I'll just have to keep her at an arm's length, emotionally speaking. We can enjoy each other physically, but nothing more. We'll both be happier that way."

His reflection looked doubtful and more than a little disbelieving of that statement, but Constantine didn't give himself time to dwell on the subject. He finished removing the last of his garments, turned the water on as hot as he could stand it, and stepped into the shower.

Cold air hitting his back was his first warning. Bee's

scream echoing in the small bathroom was the second, but by that time, he had her up against the wall, holding her by her neck a good foot off the ground, his claws pricking into her flesh.

"Ack!" she said, grabbing at his arm.

Instantly, he released her, worriedly watching her take a couple of deep breaths of air. She was now naked, but he tried not to notice that fact while preserving an expression that was both contrite and concerned. "I'm sorry, I did not know you would surprise me like that."

"It's okay," she said, her voice a croak that she cleared with a little cough. "It's my fault. I should know better than to startle a dragon."

"Especially one who left you sound asleep," he agreed, dabbing at a little spot of blood where one of his claws had scratched her. "Did you want something?"

She made an odd gesture, an embarrassed expression fighting with a smile. "Yes. You. I heard the shower, and thought I'd join you. I'm a mess, and I thought we could—er—I thought—"

"Ah," he said, delighted. "You wish to engage in sexual activity in the shower. I applaud such a spirit, but I am a silver dragon."

He waited for her to say she understood.

Instead she looked puzzled. "And?"

"The green dragon's element is water. It is not mine."

Her forehead wrinkled. "And that means what?"

"Silver dragons don't like water. We like the earth and the forests and plant lore. We are master gardeners and healers. If you'd like to make love outside, I would be happy to introduce you to the dragon chase."

Bee blinked her brown lashes a couple of times, then

waved him aside, and stepped into the shower, cocking her hip as she struck a pose. "No? All right, then. I'll just take a shower by my lonesome."

"Water is a necessary evil, and not at all enjoyable," he said, but as if he was pulled, found himself following her into the shower. There was something about the sight of her standing there, all slick, silken skin, and hips and breasts and legs, and all those other bits of her that he loved.

"Perhaps, but soapy skin can be so very, very slippery." She soaped up a cloth, and ran it across her chest, and instantly his head was filled with thoughts of his fingers doing a soapy dance across slick, satiny skin.

He sucked in his breath, inhaled a little water, and spent a moment coughing it out of his lungs before he gave up his desire to talk her into lovemaking in another room, and took possession of the soap and cloth.

"Sorry. Are you okay now?" Bee asked, her expression full of remorse.

"Yes. But you see the danger of doing this in the presence of water. Why do we not get dressed, and find a nice private park—"

"There's no such thing in Paris." Bee moved around him so that the water was to his back, and stroked a hand across his shoulder to his chest, and down to his belly. "But don't let me stop you if you need to get a breath of fresh air. Personally, I much prefer the privacy of a cozy room. And I have to say, making love in the shower has always been one of my fantasies, but that's not really your problem, is it?"

"I shall make it my problem," he said nobly, well aware of the fact that she was fast driving him to distraction, no matter if they were in the shower. He took both of her breasts in his hands, enjoying the weight of them, as well as the wet flesh that slid so enticingly across his palms. He also enjoyed the way her breath hitched when he bent down to flick his tongue across the nipples. "I have always been in support of fulfilling sexual fantasies, so it would be only right for me to fulfill yours. If you touch me there again, however, I will not be responsible for what happens."

Bee, who had been gently tugging at his testicles while stroking his penis, paused. "Touch you where? Which hand?"

"Both." He took a long, shuddering breath that had nothing to do with being in the shower, and everything to do with the enticing woman who was even now trying to rub herself all over him in an attempt to drive him insane with lust. "If you won't let me chase you outside in a park, then let me at least take you to my bed."

"Tempting, but here we are undressed," Bee said, releasing his genitals, but now doing a little shimmying move against his body that was almost as bad. "Don't you want me, Constantine?"

"More than anything else I can think of," he said in absolute honesty.

"Good, because I want you to take me here. Right now. In the shower, where we're warm and steamy and wet, and I can slide against you."

He opened his mouth to tell her how much he liked her making demands of him, but nothing came out other than a little whimper of sheer sexual desire.

Bee smiled, damn her arousing self, and slid her hands around behind him until her fingers dug into the heavy muscles of his ass. "I suppose I should ask you about this. Some men like—"

"No," he interrupted and, wrapping his hands around the backs of her thighs, he hoisted her up. "But I know you like this."

"Glorious goddess, yes!" Bee gasped and writhed against him when, pressing her against the wall, he released her legs and allowed his fingers to find her sensitive flesh. "Oh, yes, yes, that, do that again. No, not the pinching thing, the swirly bit with your thumb."

He smiled a wicked smile, one full of manly intent, when she closed her eyes in bliss, her wet hair streaming down those delicious breasts that bobbed so enticingly in front of him. He wanted to touch them and taste them, to taste all of her, but he couldn't release her to do that. Her fingers dug deep into his shoulders as he dipped two fingers inside her, enjoying the feel of her intimate muscles clenching around them.

"I want a turn," she panted, her eyes open again. He was lost in the green-gray depths of them, warmed by the emotion he saw in there, feeling almost invincible. "I want a turn to make you insane with pleasure. No, I take it back, I want you to do that again. Hrm!"

She almost purred when he rubbed his erection along her woman parts, her legs wrapping around his waist as she tugged on his hair and demanded, "Fire! Or wait, can you do that in the water?"

"I can do anything," he swore, and proceeded to set her alight. His dragon fire licked up between them as he tilted her hips and slid into her, groaning with the sensation of her heat even as she moaned his name.

Her hands moved down his back, dragging her nails in

a manner that was not painful, but stirred him on to more vigorous motions. He pressed her against the shower wall, mindless of the water now, needing only to give her the pleasure that he knew would spill over onto him. She kneaded the muscles of his ass even as he set up a rhythm that had them both struggling for breath, his fire burning around them despite the water.

"I hope...you aren't...going to be long," he panted, trying to keep from just plunging wildly into her, as he wanted to do. "I'm not going to last much— Bee!"

"Sorry. My hand slipped. I didn't mean to encroach on unfriendly territory. And if you keep doing that little lunge to the left, I won't last either."

He lunged. She squealed in happiness. Her hand slipped again, but this time he didn't care. She bit his shoulder as she shuddered into a climax around him, making a thousand little muscles inside her tighten on him in a manner guaranteed to push him past all control. He lunged forward three times, then gave himself up to the joy that was Bee.

And when his legs gave out from the strain of holding her up, combined with an orgasm the likes of which left him feeling as weak as a newborn kitten, he managed to get them out of the shower and onto a soft, welcoming bathmat before he collapsed entirely.

It could have been a few minutes later, or it might have been an hour. For all Constantine knew, eons might have passed before he managed to recover.

"The bathroom is on fire," Bee said, not sounding in the least bit concerned.

He cracked open one eye and turned his head to look at her. She lay rosy, wet, and flushed with the satisfaction of a woman well loved, lying on her back on the thick oatmeal-colored bathmat. He, being a naturally chivalrous man, had let her have the rug while he made do with his discarded clothing.

"The room is not on fire. My dragon fire does not get away from me like that. I am fully in control of it at all times. It is a fact I have long prided myself—"

He stopped when she pointed at something behind him.

He looked. He pursed his lips. He considered her. "I blame you. You distracted me with your ladyplant and your breasts and your mouth that I want to kiss over and over and over again. Even now, I want to kiss you, and I am so exhausted by your demands for loving in the odious shower that I cannot even stand, let alone think, or work my mouth enough to do all the kissing."

She giggled when he waved a hand and tamped down on the fire that had, in fact, escaped him. "You have the best pillow talk. I want to kiss you, too." She rolled over and slid herself on top of him, cradling his head in her hands as she leaned down and bit his lower lip. "I like your mouth a lot, you know. I like all of you a lot. You have nice legs. And thighs. And your chest is gorgeous, although I feel bad about the curse scarring it. And your butt! I could write odes to your butt."

He raised an eyebrow, and tolerated her kissing him, letting her twine her tongue around his, tasting him even as he tasted her. That lasted for about three seconds before he couldn't stand it any longer, and taking her hips in his hands, he slid her up so that she could torment him more effectively.

"You are a sublime kisser," she said after some minutes, snuggling her face into the crook of his neck. "Even without the fire, although I like it when you do that, too.

Why is it your fire doesn't hurt me, and the other dragon I dated had fire that did?"

"He was clearly inferior. What sept was he from?"

"He had a red dragon parent and a blue dragon parent. Does that make him purple?"

He drew little circles of fire along her back. "No. It means he belonged to one of the two septs. Neither of which is as superior as my silver dragons."

Bee was silent for a moment, then lifted her head and, resting her elbow on his shoulder, leaned her chin onto her palm. "But they aren't your silver dragons any more, are they? Do you miss being a wyvern?"

"Yes," he said without thinking, then paused, frowning. "No. Sometimes I do. Sometimes I enjoy the freedom from responsibility. Other times I miss the camaraderie, the sense of belonging. I miss having someone to protect."

"Maybe it's someone else's turn to protect you," she said, combing his wet hair with her fingers.

"I was born and raised a warrior. It's in my nature to protect." He looked down at the top of her head and said something he never expected. "I would take you under my protection if you would allow it."

"Is that a proposal?" she asked, touching the tip of his nose, a little half smile curling her lips. Those delicious, tempting lips. "And if so, is it a proposal for illicit activities, or are you desiring my hand in marriage?"

"Marriage is a mortal convention." He tried for a light tone, but regretted the words when she slid off him and got to her feet, taking a towel with her when she returned to the bedroom. He watched her walk away—admiring her legs and ass as she did so—frowning to himself over the unpleasant emotion that was filling him.

Regret. It burned with a dull ache. He disliked it intensely. He also didn't care for this sense of insecurity that gripped him when he watched Bee climb into his bed. Had she been serious about him binding himself to her via mortal conventions? Was she simply testing him? Or was she teasing? Dammit, he didn't know the answer to any of those questions, and that annoyed him most of all.

"What are you doing?" he asked after he toweled off and went to stand next to the bed.

She was on her side, the sheets tucked around her, watching him. "I'm going to sleep. Unless you're going to kick me out of your room, but I assume you won't do that because you enjoyed yourself a lot a few minutes ago, and also because you're a gentleman. And you don't strike me as someone who gets into a wham, bam, thank you ma'am mindset. Do you want me to stay, Constantine?"

He hesitated, unsure of whether she meant permanently or just for the night. Wyverns, he decided as he strode to the other side of the bed, did not do unsure any better than they did insecure and regret. "Forever, or for tonight?" he asked.

She gave him a long, unreadable look before answering, "Either I'm more tired than I thought I was, or you're being deliberately enigmatic. No, that's not the word I mean. Inscrutable? My brain is too frazzled right now— let's leave the talk for the future of our relationship aside for the rest of the night. Or morning, rather, since it's almost dawn now."

He thought about that for a few minutes, decided that she had a point, and slid into bed beside her. "Very well. You'd tell me if you hurt." It was a statement, not a question, and Bee took it as such without animosity.

"Yes, I'd tell you. And yes, I'm human and vulnerable to things like buildings being blown apart around us, but not many of us have magic rings that protect us, so you don't have to worry that I'm about to collapse. To be honest, the scene in the shower did more to wear me out than any of the other activities of the night, including Charming the curse." She smiled, rolling over so that she was tucked against his side, one arm draped across his belly. "Be honest, now—you enjoyed the water, didn't you?"

"I enjoyed you," he qualified. "The water was a necessary evil."

"Hrmph. Obstinate dragon." She snuggled in even closer, and he gave a heartfelt sigh of contentment as he wrapped an arm over her and breathed in her clean, sunshine scent.

Fifteen

"I don't know why you think we need to meet with every-one. I mean, we know Bael is in Paris, or at least he was last night, and I can't think why he'd leave unless some-thing called him away. So why aren't we tracking him down instead of talking with your dragon friends?"

"A sarkany has been called by Drake. I am a wyvern, thus I must attend."

I got out of the cab that stopped at Aisling and Drake's house, and gave Constantine a side-eye as he paid off the driver before he hefted the box that had sat next to us on the seat. "If I pointed out the obvious, would you find it obnoxious?"

"What obviousness do you mean?" he asked, throwing grammar to the wind.

I followed him to the front door. "That you're not a wyvern anymore, and therefore, you don't have to be a part of this dragon meeting thing. Why don't you just admit you want to be a part of the meeting? I can go make a few contacts and see if anyone knows exactly where Bael went after he blew up G&T."

"You will not face Bael alone."

The look he turned on me was stark and filled with pain so deep, I instinctively took a step forward and wrapped both arms around him, kissing along his jaw.

The door opened, the demon dog eyeing us critically. "Heya, Connie. Heya, Bee. 'Sup, Gare."

"So many exciting things!" came the answer from the cardboard box, now sitting at Constantine's feet while I kissed him. "I spent the night with a poltergeist, and Connie bought me a new remote-control truck, and Bee insisted I get a helmet because I kept falling out of the truck, and oh, so much more."

"Dude," Jim said in a general acknowledgment. He eyed us, then turned and yelled over his shoulder. "Connie and Bee and Gary are here. They're snogging in the doorway. Not Gary—for some reason he's been put in a box."

"It's so the mortals don't see me." Gary's voice was muffled, but the box bulged in a way that indicated he was getting restless.

"Uh huh. That's how it starts, man, and then the next thing you know, they have you locked into a closet with the vacuum cleaner."

"Bee—" Constantine said, his eyes shiny and hard.

"I won't go without you, okay?" I don't know why I felt so compelled to reassure him other than perhaps witnessing the depths of Bael's depravity frightened me. "If you want to talk to the dragons before we tackle Bael, then we can do that."

The look of fear faded from his eyes, replaced with an emotion that left me feeling hot and extremely pleased. "Do not believe that I have lost my interest in dealing with Bael now that you have broken the curse."

"Ash is coming," Jim announced, and nudged Gary's box inside. "Istvan, the box has Gary in it. Don't know why they couldn't use a head carrier like a normal person. Gary's a head. No, just a head. Don't ask me, he never said. I mean, there's all sorts of reasons why someone could lose their body, but I'm not the sort to pry. "

Jim, pushing Gary's box in front of him, entered the house at the same time a red-haired man appeared to block the door, giving us each an exaggerated examination. "Constantine Norka," the redhead finally said. He had a Slavic accent, pronounced but not unintelligible.

"Istvan..." Constantine said, then stopped and made an irritated face. "I do not know your surname. I cannot call you by your full name."

Istvan smiled. It was a smug sort of smile, the kind that makes your palm itch. "That is so."

"You will tell me your surname so that I might use it, and then we will be even."

Istvan glanced upward in thought for a few seconds. "No, I don't think I will."

"I will remember this," Constantine warned, his eyes narrowing. I could feel by how high his fire was that he was irritated, but had to admit I found the posturing more than a little amusing.

"As will I."

"I find it rather ironic," I interjected, unable to keep quiet any longer, "that for two and a half years, you guys have been unable to talk to each other, and when you finally can, you start a verbal pissing contest. Honestly, what happened to saying hi, how are you, nice to be able to chat again?"

Both men stared at me in disbelief.

I sighed and made a conciliatory gesture. "Right. Silly me, expecting dragons to act reasonable. Proceed with your posturing."

Constantine's lips thinned, while Istvan, with a pinched look about the nostrils, said, "You wish to enter the domicile of the green wyvern?"

"A sarkany has been called, has it not?" Constantine took my arm and hustled me inside, pushing Istvan aside as we passed through the door. I thought for a moment the latter wasn't going to give way, but evidently he thought better of antagonizing Constantine any further.

We entered the same sitting room that we'd been in the day before, only to discover the room had been rearranged. Where before there were couches and loveseats and chairs, now a large circular table dominated the room, around which sat three chairs. Against the walls sat more dining chairs, arranged in a row clearly intended for an audience to the meeting.

Kostya was there with my sister. Aoife shot a quick glance at us, her gaze skittering away as soon as I tried to catch her eye. My heart grew heavy at that, and I wondered if there would come a day when Aoife would forgive me for the extreme lengths I'd gone to in order to keep her safe two years ago.

I set aside that worry, and went to help Jim unpack Gary from the box, setting the head up on his shiny yellow motorized dump truck, and making sure that the new pink-and-purple bicycle helmet—the only one we could find at a moment's notice—was strapped on securely.

"The truck is fully charged and has backup batteries installed," I told Gary, who was trying out the new remote with its tiny joystick. "Don't run into anyone, and don't damage any of the furniture here. It looks like it's all antique."

"Thanks, Bee, I'll be extra careful. Jim, do you want to see me do a wheelie? I was practicing this morning, but kept rolling off the back of the truck bed and smashing myself into the wall, which is why Bee insists I wear a helmet, but really, I think I have the hang of the joystick now. The truck is quite quick, too."

"Cool story, bro," Jim said, a slight look of envy crossing his furry face. "I wonder if I could get Aisling to get me a car?"

"She might if you asked her."

"Yeah, but Drake wouldn't like it. He thinks I'm a bad influence on the spawn. Which, of course, I am, because hello! Demon sixth class here. But still, a car would be cool."

"Connie got me this truck without me even having to ask," Gary boasted.

"You have better parents than me," Jim said, nodding.

"We're a good team, that's for sure. Hey, if you got a car, we could have races!" Gary's voice was filled with enthusiasm.

I left them discussing the various routes such a race would take if Jim was able to possess himself of a vehicle.

"Bee! How nice to see you again." Aisling, with the other dragons at the far end of the room, bustled toward us, Drake on her heels. "You must excuse me for being so slow to welcome you, but it's been forever since we've been able to speak to anyone outside of the sept, and there's a lot to catch up on. Have we thanked you for breaking the curse? If not, consider us profoundly grateful. We're thrilled that the curse is finally gone, all of us. Ysolde and Baltic were telling us what horrible events happened last night. Everyone is talking about what Bael did, and how he tried to kill you four, and the fact that he has claimed the role of the Venediger."

"You're kidding." I glanced at Constantine, who was making a stiff bow to his godson. "Why would he do that?"

"Power." Aisling's expression turned dark. "The bastard tried to take the job of Venediger once before, but I ended up with it. I didn't want it, naturally, and gave the job to Jovana—poor woman—but clearly he hasn't forgotten."

"Nor will he," Constantine said, glaring for a moment at the table with its three chairs. He turned on his heel, marched over to the line of chairs against the wall, and hauled one over to the table, giving the other three wyverns a hard look as if he was daring them to make a comment.

"What's all that about?" I asked Aisling. Ysolde joined us just as she answered. I couldn't help but notice that Aoife stayed next to Kostya.

"Only wyverns are supposed to sit at the sarkany table."

I thought about that for a few seconds. "But Constantine was a wyvern."

"You know it, and I know it, but the other men don't consider him one anymore. I mean, he did give up his life for Ysolde, but still, I gather once you're dead, you're no longer considered a wyvern."

I may have gawked at Ysolde for a few seconds before I realized that I was doing far too much gawking of late for my peace of mind. "He died to save you? When was this? He never said anything about that to me—" I stopped before I gave away too many of the emotions that even now I didn't want to examine.

"He didn't really. Well, he might have. I'm still a bit unclear about that, because all the First Dragon said was that someone had given up his life for mine, but he never said it was Constantine. And now that we know Constantine was his grandson, well, that makes it seem so much more unlikely, doesn't it?"

I opened my mouth to say something, decided it was incoherent, and contented myself with saying simply, "I'm confused."

"Don't worry, you'll get used to it," Aisling said, putting an arm around me. "It happens to all of us, dragons being what they are. Present company excluded, Ysolde."

"I'm still more human than dragon," Ysolde said with a little shrug, although she managed to give me a fairly shrewd look at the same time. "Would you mind if I asked you something, Bee?"

"That depends on the question. You can ask anything you like, but I won't answer unless I want to."

"Smart girl," Aisling said.

Ysolde nodded. "Rightly so. I wanted to know what you think of Constantine."

"That's not what you want to know," Aisling told her, whapping her gently on the arm.

"It is, too."

"You said they were an item, so it's pretty clear what she thinks of Constantine. What you want to know—what we both want to know—is whether she's Constantine's mate."

"You don't just blurt something like that out!" Ysolde said with a frown at Aisling. "You work up to it, gently, cautiously."

"Pfft," Aisling said, waving away that idea. She turned back to me. "We don't have time for that. What we want to know is if you're just shacking up with Constantine or if you're his mate. Have you taken his fire?"

"Taken it where?" I asked.

Both women wore identical expressions.

I sighed. "Look, I'm a Charmer. I like Constantine. A lot, as it happens, and yes, we're an item, or at least I think we are, but beyond that, I don't know, and I don't particularly care."

"She's taken his fire," Aisling told Ysolde, who was studying me with intensity.

"Fire does not a mate make," the latter said, and possibly would have grilled me more but at that moment Istvan and another redheaded man entered the room, along with a dark-haired fellow who moved over to Baltic.

"That's Pavel," Aisling told me, pointing to the last man to enter the room. "He's Baltic's friend who just got into town. The other man is Pal, who with Istvan is Drake's elite guard. Kostya doesn't really have any guards. They were mostly killed by the red dragons, but I assume he'll appoint some out of the handful of black dragons who are left."

The dragons did something odd then. All three of the wyverns fetched chairs and set them next to each of the chairs at the table. Aisling and Ysolde, with knowing looks at me, took the additional seats next to their wyverns. Aoife evidently knew what was going on as well, because she sat next to Kostya without a word.

Constantine watched them all, then cocked an eyebrow at me.

I raised mine back at him.

He gave me a little nod, went to the wall, and grabbed a chair which he set down next to his, and proceeded to stand beside it, obviously waiting for me.

I didn't know what the others would think about me taking a place at their dragons-only discussion, but after a moment's thought, I decided I didn't care. If Constantine wanted me there, then I'd sit there and be supportive. It was the least I could do for a man who was as thoughtful as he was.

The other men present took up spots behind their respective wyverns, and Baltic aside, all the male dragons reacted with surprise when I took the seat Constantine held for me.

"Is there something you wish to announce?" Drake asked Constantine, nodding toward me.

"Yes."

You could have heard a pin drop in the silence that followed.

Constantine looked at each person there before speaking again. "Bael is my father. He is also the son of the First Dragon. I have sworn to destroy him, and will do so with or without the help of the weyr. Also, I wish to know the surnames of all your guards. I dislike not knowing them. That is all." He sat back with the air of a job well done.

All hell broke out around us, verbally speaking. I ignored the outbursts of surprise from the dragons who hadn't known the truth about Bael, giving Constantine a little smile.

"You're a troublemaker at heart, aren't you?" I said softly, taking his hand.

His fingers were warm and strong, and they sent little shivers of delight skittering down my back. "I do what I can to keep things interesting. I have a system awarding points for how much I can irritate Baltic on any given day."

"I like that you don't say what I expect you to say. Will me being here create a problem for you?"

Two lines appeared between his brows. "I don't understand why you would think that. I've told you that I welcome your help with Bael—"

"I meant with the dragons." I nodded toward the other end of the table, where Kostya was arguing with Baltic. "I can see that they're letting you join in the fun because you used to be a wyvern, and you have a tie to Bael, but I'm just a simple mortal Charmer. I'm not your mate."

"Do you wish to be? I could name you so in front of the weyr, although Kostya did that with a naiad—before he met your sister—and it did not end well." He looked thoughtful, ignoring the chaotic conversation around us. "Still, if it would make you happy, I would tell the others you were my mate."

A little pain zinged through me at his words, and I realized that what bothered me most about that statement was not the offer to be considered a dragon's mate...it was that it would be pretense and not real.

Since when had I wanted to become part of the dragonkin? I shook my head at my foolish thoughts, but Constantine interpreted it as a negative answer. His eyes lost a bit of their brightness when he turned away with a murmured, "I would never force you to do anything you did not wish."

"That's good, because I wouldn't do something I didn't want to do," I managed to tell him before Kostya, with a loud exclamation, leaped to his feet.

"I don't care if he helped the Charmer lift the curse; he is no longer a wyvern, so he should not have a place at the table. Especially with the mortal at his side." Kostya shot an angry glare our way. "The curse is lifted, yes, but we have much work to do. We must discover if there are any red dragons left who have been untainted by Asmodeus. We must rid the world of the demon-dragon hybrids, or at least confine them so they can do no more harm. We must form the weyr again, and for that, we need the First Dragon."

"I'm getting a little fed up with your negativity," Ysolde told him, much to my surprise. I hadn't expected anyone to stand up for Constantine. "And your bossiness. We're trying to get something accomplished, and you're just making a fuss about nothing."

"Baltic, control your mate," Kostya said, looking daggers at him.

"No," Baltic said, leaning back in his chair. There was something about him, perhaps the line of his jaw or the way his chin was shaped, that reminded me of Constantine.

Kostya goggled at that answer. "You must!" he finally said.

"Have you learned nothing from Aoife?" Aisling asked, shaking her head. Drake put a warning hand over hers, causing her to say in a whisper that was heard by everyone there, "I know I shouldn't say it, sweetie, but honestly, sometimes your brother is the biggest boob who ever lived."

"Hey," Aoife said, sitting up straight. "We can hear you, you know."

"Good," Aisling said with a bright smile.

I stifled a giggle.

"My mate can say whatever she likes," Baltic interjected, still looking mostly bored by the proceedings.

"It is against the rules of the—"

"Perhaps it *was* against the rules of the sarkany," Baltic interrupted, leaning forward to pin Kostya back with a warning look. "But the old weyr is gone. Destroyed. This new weyr will have new rules, and one of those should be that mates have a voice."

"Here, here," Aisling said, applauding.

"Well done," Ysolde said, kissing Baltic's cheek.

Kostya looked like he wanted to argue, but evidently caught a glimpse of Aoife's face, because he shot her a puzzled look.

"Sorry," she told him with an apologetic gesture at the rest of the table. "About this, I agree with them. If you want me to be a part of your life and a member of the black dragons, then I think I should be able to say something."

"It is not the way we have done things," Kostya argued, but the fight had gone out of his body language, and he sat back down when Aoife patted his arm, and said, "I know it is, but now is an excellent time to change things, don't you think?"

Kostya might have realized he had to give in on that point, but he stuck like a burr to another one. "Even if we do change the rules to allow mates to have input, that still does not address the fact that Constantine is here with an outsider."

"Look," I said, standing up and putting my hands flat

on the table. "I know I'm an outsider, okay? I'm human, and I'm a Charmer, and I don't particularly like dragons." I slid a fast glance at Constantine. "Well, I like one dragon. The rest of you are a bit much to take in close quarters. That said, Constantine and I have just as much a right to be at this planning session as you do. More, since we're the ones who broke the curse."

"Which you bungled the first time you tried," Kostya snapped.

"Because you two didn't bother to give us the proper information!" I slapped the table hard enough to make Aoife jump. "Dammit, do you think I'm here because I don't have anything better to do with my time than listen to a bunch of scaly human-shaped beasts bicker with each other? Bael killed the Venediger and her assistant, Guillaume. They saw it." I pointed at Ysolde and Baltic.

Ysolde went a little pale. Baltic put his arm around her and hauled her onto his lap.

"Now, I may not be a big, tough dragon like Constantine, or even mated to him, but I did know Jovana for almost three years. She passed along many jobs to me over that time and was never anything but thoughtful. She cared about the Otherworld. She wanted to protect not just them but the mortals from any bad influences on the immortal side. And she provided us all with a safe haven where everyone could meet without fear or danger." Tears came to my eyes, making me blink rapidly. "So yes, I'm only a mortal Charmer, but I'll be damned if I let Jovana be snuffed out of existence like she's nothing more than a cigarette. I will do everything within my power to see that Bael pays for his crime, and if that means he has to be destroyed, then by the gods, I'll help cut him down!"

Silence fell on the room. It was a stunned silence, one that was eventually broken by the slow clapping of one pair of hands.

I turned my head to look at Constantine. He smiled at me, then rose and stood at my side, his hand on my back. "And so too do I swear. I will rid this world of Bael, or I will die trying. I have died once, and did not enjoy it. I don't wish to do it again. Especially now as I am responsible for Gary's well-being and Bee's sexual needs."

I smacked him on the arm. He turned a startled expression to me.

"We have a new rule: you don't announce to people I've just met that we're doing the sheet tango. It's hard enough getting respect without them wondering which of your many toys we've been trying out that day."

"Ooh, Constantine has some excellent toys," Ysolde said, nodding. "I helped him pick out a couple of them from a fabulous shop where I got a really wonderful toy shaped like the letter U."

"Is that for a he or a she?" Aisling asked, leaning forward to see around Drake.

"It's sold for women, but a little creativity can do wonders with it," Ysolde answered.

"Battery operated or electric?" Aoife asked.

Kostya shot her an indignant, "Aoife!"

"It doesn't hurt to ask," she told him soothingly.

"Batteries," Ysolde said with a private smile. "Take my recommendation and get a few extra packs. You definitely don't want to run short, and using both ends of the U shape takes a lot of battery power."

Aisling clearly agreed with that sentiment, because she leaned forward again to ask, "And where did you get—"

Her question was cut short when Drake, who had evidently been holding his temper in with a not very patient hand, suddenly roared for silence, and slammed his hand so hard on the table that it sent a long crack out from the center. "Enough!" he cried, sharing a truly magnificent glare among us all. "This is a sarkany, not a sexual aid discussion! We have important things to discuss and decide upon—"

Constantine tapped the table until Ysolde looked over to him. He held a tablet of paper in one hand and a pen in the other. "What shop was the U device sold at, and do they take bulk orders?"

Sixteen

I had to take a little break after that, strolling out to a small park across the street from Drake's house, along with Ysolde, Aisling, and Aoife.

"I can't believe they kicked us out like that," Aisling said, sniffing in a faux-injured manner. "It's my house, too! I'm definitely going to have words with Drake later about them giving us the boot. Jim! Don't you dare do that right next to that flowerbed! Honest to Pete, I can't take you anywhere!"

"What do you think they're going to talk about?" I asked Ysolde. I kept glancing over at Aoife, expecting her to be giving me the usual cold shoulder that she'd adopted ever since she found out the part I had played to keep her safe from the demon lords, but she walked at my side with an abstracted expression on her face.

"Kostya will argue about unimportant things for a bit. Drake will try to calm him down. Baltic will enrage everyone with his opinion that none of it matters, and Constantine—" She stopped, frowning down at the ground. "I was going to say Constantine would instigate bad behavior in the others, but he seems to have changed since I last saw him." She looked up and beamed at me. "I believe we have you to thank for that."

"I'm not a dragon's mate," I told her.

"Perhaps not," she said with a little one-shouldered shrug. "Perhaps so. Time will tell."

"We don't *have* time, that's the whole problem," I pointed out. I stopped, looking around the park. It was full summer now, which meant the flowers were bobbing their colorful heads in the gentle breeze, while children screeched and shrieked with joy as they ran around chasing each other. Dogs barked excitedly, the ever-present hum of traffic provided a low droning background noise, and above it all, the faint, thin twitter of birds floated above. It wasn't idyllic by any meaning of the word, but it was pleasant, and I hated the idea that it could be wiped out by a wave of Bael's hand. "We have to stop him. We have to *do* something."

"And we will," Aisling soothed. "You know, it's a shame you aren't Constantine's mate, because if you were, you could join the Mates' Union."

"You've unionized?" I asked, somewhat scandalized at the thought, although I couldn't put my finger on exactly why that was.

"It's just a name, really," Ysolde said quickly. "It provides us mates—and we're missing one, a delightful woman named May who was in Australia with her wyvern, but now is coming to Paris to discuss the ramifications of the breaking of the curse—where was I? Oh, yes, it's just a way for all the mates to get together and have lunches and bond. Aoife will join us now, of course, and we'd be delighted to have you, only..." She stopped speaking, and I felt highly uncomfortable.

"I thought the meeting today was supposed to discuss the curse being broken," I said after a few moments' awkward silence. Ysolde and Aisling had been sending each other telling glances, but I couldn't see them well enough to read them.

"It is. But there are two other wvyerns who weren't in Europe when you Charmed the curse, and they will want to have their say. May and Gabriel, that's the silver wyvern, were holding down the fort in the South Pacific as best they could. The blue wyvern was in the U.S. for a while, then I think he went to Canada."

"Interesting," I said politely, even though I didn't particularly care about where the other dragon septs were. I had enough trouble with the ones present.

"I need to talk to you for a few minutes," Aoife suddenly said, tugging on my sleeve with a look toward Aisling and Ysolde.

I was surprised; Aoife hadn't said more than a half dozen words to me of her own will since our last argument, so I paused, giving her my full attention.

She glanced around us, biting her lower lip for a minute before finally meeting my gaze, and saying, "What you said back at the sarkany—about the Venediger—I thought that was nice."

"Thanks," I said, my heart filled with pain for the way our relationship had been destroyed. Was this a sign that it could be mended? "I meant every word."

She nodded. "You always were the altruistic one of the three of us."

"Pfft. I'm the oldest child."

"Rowan is older than me," she pointed out.

"Yes, but he's a man," I said lightly. "He gets the double whammy of being a brother and a male, which pretty much guarantees he is always thinking of himself."

"Not all men are self-centered." Her expression turned guarded again. "Kostya isn't like that. Well, he is sometimes, but most of the time, he's very devoted to his sept and his brother."

"Well, if we're going to be pedantic, then neither is Constantine. He may seem like a big goofball, but he really is the sweetest, most thoughtful man I've ever met—" I stopped at the look of surprise on her face.

"You've fallen for him, haven't you?"

I glanced around us. Ysolde and Aisling had gone on ahead of us, and evidently realized we'd been left behind, because they had turned and were strolling back toward us, Jim snuffling the grass beyond them.

"I don't know what I feel for Constantine other than I like him, and I like being with him. And honestly, I don't think the question of my emotions is very important given the situation we're facing."

She tipped her head to the side, her long brown curls swinging to the side. It was such an Aoife move, one that brought back memories of our childhood, that tears pricked behind my eyes. "It's kind of ironic," she said, "isn't it, that we both ended up with dragons? I mean, five years ago we didn't even know they existed."

I looked away, not wanting to hurt her feelings any more now that she was finally making an effort to talk to me.

"Wait..." Her eyes narrowed on me, and she clutched

my arm with a hard grip. "You knew about them five years ago?"

"I dated a red dragon when I was twentyish," I admitted, wishing like hell I could lie to her, but I'd never been good at it. "It didn't last long, but yes, I knew about dragons then."

"And you never told me?" The outrage was stark in her face. Her fingers tightened on my arm. "What the hell, Bee?"

"I couldn't tell you. Not at first—the Charmer's League doesn't allow that in their apprentices, and by the time I was made a full-fledged Charmer, you'd gone off to university."

"That was years ago," she argued, then made an effort to control her temper, and said in a tight, level voice, "What about Rowan? Did you tell him?"

I hesitated again, which was the wrong thing to do.

"He knew, too? Did *everyone* but me know?"

"Of course not, don't be silly. And for what it's worth, I didn't tell Rowan. He ... er ... he found out by chance one night."

Her lips were so tight, they were just about nonexistent. "I see. And it didn't occur to you to tell me once our brother found out?"

"It's not like that, Aoife. It's not something we discussed—"

"Never mind." She was spitting out the words with sharp little barbs aimed right at me. "There's no sense in hashing over old injuries."

"I didn't mean to injure you. I was trying to protect you from the dangers of the Otherworld. I had to keep you out of it, all of the family away from it. If the Otherworld knew about you, all of you could have been used by unscrupulous people to put pressure on me. Don't you see? I had to protect you and the rest of the family—"

She held up a hand as Aisling and Ysolde approached. "Yeah, heard it, did the time in the nut house because of it. What I really wanted to say was that since you finally broke the curse, you won't need my ring any longer."

Instinctively, I clutched my hand, twisting the ring around my finger. "Your ring? You do know it used to belong to a demon lord, right?"

"*Used to* being the key phrase," she said acidly, holding out her hand. "It was evidently remade and then given to me. So I'd like it back."

"What's this?" Aisling asked, coming to a halt in front of us. She was momentarily distracted when Jim, who had loped off to chase after a couple of Dalmations, suddenly turned and raced back toward us, his black ears flopping in the wind. "What on earth has gotten into him, I wonder? Jim!" She raised her voice and gestured toward the demon. "Slow down or you'll plow into those people— Oh lord. Excuse me, ladies. I have to go apologize…"

Aisling started off at the same time Aoife tugged at my arm.

"My ring?" she said, her face set in a stubborn expression I knew well.

Reluctantly, and with a heartfelt sigh, I started to pull the ring off my finger. I hated to admit it, but I had become attached to it and really regretted giving it up.

Just as I dropped the ring onto Aoife's palm, Aisling, who had gotten within range of the people Jim had knocked down, suddenly turned and screamed at us, her hands waving as she dashed toward us.

"What the—" I squinted into the sun to see what was going on.

Ysolde must have had better eyesight than me, because she stiffened and said one word. "Demons!"

"Run," I said, shoving Aoife toward the entrance to the park. "Go back to your dragon. Don't just stand there, you idiot, *run*!"

Ysolde, in the meantime, had run forward a few steps, and was standing with her head down, her hands dancing in the air as she wove magic. Aisling had spun around as well, and was evidently casting grounding wards that stopped three of the five women whom the demon Jim had knocked down in his impression of a hundred-pound furry black bowling ball.

"I am not going to run away and leave everyone else here," Aoife said stubbornly. I was looking around for something I could use as a weapon, but the park was sadly lacking in swords, two-by-fours, or convenient tree branches.

"You have the ring!" I snarled at her, not wanting to do more damage to our already fragile relationship, but knowing I couldn't let that ring fall into Bael's hands.

"Here, you take it. I was being rude in demanding you give it to me—clearly, the ring is happy being with you," she said, hastily shoving it back at me before bolting past, dipping down to grab a couple of stones from a flowerbed as she ran to where Aisling stood casting ward afterward. Jim was wrestling with one of the demons, while Ysolde was sending out balls of arcane magic that mostly missed everyone.

"I don't want it!" I yelled after Aoife, and had just slipped it on my finger when a man's voice spoke behind me.

"I am pleased to hear that, since my master very much *does* want it."

I spun around, making an ugly sound when the wrath demon behind me simply slammed his arm across my midsection, driving all the air from my lungs as he scooped me along with him. Four more men behind him strode forward with us, none of them speaking when he gave the order to grab the others.

"They don't have anything to do with this," I gasped when I had enough air in my lungs to get my voice back. "Bael would have no use for them."

"Bael," the demon holding me snorted. "What care we of him? My master does not fear that has-been."

My new dragon friends might have been able to hold off four demons, but nine of them was a different matter. It took less than a minute for them to overwhelm everyone, tear open the fabric of being, and drag us all back to Abaddon.

"This is really getting to be old hat," I said a few minutes later, when the demons dumped us unceremoniously into what appeared to be my old cell. "Although it's made slightly nicer having company— Ow!"

"Sorry," Jim said, scrambling off where one of the demons had tossed him on top of me. "Thanks for breaking my fall, though."

"You are not welcome," I said, rubbing my belly where the bulk of the dog's weight had landed.

"Where are we?" Ysolde got to her feet and brushed herself off, looking around the small cell. "Is this Abaddon?"

"Yes." Aoife glanced around us. "I recognize it from the time I was here. I think this was our cell, wasn't it, Jim?"

"Could be."

"I've never been here," Ysolde said, making a face at the dirt that rubbed off the stone wall when she touched it.

"I have," Aisling said with a sigh. She slumped against the wall and waved a hand in a vague gesture. "Jim, I don't suppose there's any chance of us opening up a tear and getting all of us out of here?"

"You could, but not the others, not without making a deal you probably don't want to make."

"Ugh," Aisling said, wrapping her arms protectively around herself. "I think we'll avoid anything that involves making deals."

"What are we going to do?" Aoife asked, pacing the width of the cell. Ysolde sat down next to Aisling and started speaking softly to her.

"Wait?" I suggested.

"For what? For you to figure out how to use the ring to rescue us?" Aoife made a disgusted noise and turned back to try the door.

I got to my feet, my anger getting the best of me. "You annoying little shit!"

Aoife turned back to me, her mouth an O of surprise.

"Word," Jim said, nodding his head.

Aoife shot him a wicked look before narrowing her eyes on me. "What did you call me?"

"You heard me." I stalked forward, past Ysolde and Aisling, and stopped when I was toe-to-toe with my little sister. "You just got done telling me that you didn't really want the ring, and gave it back to me. Well, I'm sick and tired of this attitude of yours, and frankly, I've decided I'm not going to take it anymore."

Her jaw dropped for a second before it snapped close, and she jabbed a finger into my upper arm. "I am not the one who had my sister condemned to a loony bin for two years. You don't have the *right* to be tired of my attitude!"

"I have explained to you why I had to do that and also apologized that they did not treat you as Rowan and I were told you would be treated. I'm sorry, Aoife, I'm really sorry about what happened. I wish I could have explained to you what was going on, but you were in so much danger... and it had only been a few years since Mom and Dad died, and the thought of losing you was just more than I could stand. I know you won't forgive me, but I truly did what I had to do in order to save you."

She looked taken aback now, blinking rapidly before saying, "I don't think I was in that much danger."

"That's because the Otherworld hadn't really touched you yet." I was suddenly tired, exhaustion pulling at me and making me want to curl into a little ball and ignore the world. "And frankly, I'm grateful for that. But let me reassure you that while you were tucked away safely—if uncomfortably—the rest of us in the Otherworld were trying to stay alive. It wasn't just dragons who suffered from the curse, you know—lots of others got in the way of the demons and were cut down just like Jovana and Guillaume."

Tears sprang to Aoife's eyes, and she turned away from me. My heart hurt as I added, "The Otherworld isn't a magical place of sexy men who just happen to also be dragons—there is blood and death and suffering here because of some very dangerous individuals. Can you blame me for wanting to keep my baby sister away from it all?"

She choked, and shook her head, her eyes closed. Tears

burned behind my own as I hugged her, wishing with all that I had that I could keep her away from the pain that I knew must follow. After a moment, she hugged me back, causing Jim to say, "Awww. Sisterly love. The only way that could be better is if they mud-wrestled out their issues first."

I laughed shakily, sniffing and wiping my eyes, releasing Aoife to face the two other women. "I'm sorry you had to witness our family squabbling."

"Not at all," Ysolde said, giving us both curious looks. "I suspect it's been a long time coming."

She and Aisling returned to their discussion.

Aoife wiped her eyes with the edge of her sleeves, giving me a rueful smile. "I didn't realize...I mean, I know that you did what you thought was best, but I was just so angry about being stuffed into the loony bin that I didn't consider what everyone else was going through."

"It's understandable you feel that way," I said, my shoulders drooping. I wondered if my relationship with my sister would ever be mended. I hoped fervently that it would. "It can't have been easy for you."

"No." Her lips twisted wryly. "But I don't suppose you were out having oodles of fun."

"Far from it." I rubbed my face, wondering how long we'd be held before Constantine and the others managed to free us. "I just hope that someday you can forgive me."

She was silent for longer than I was comfortable with, but eventually she nodded. "I think I have. It doesn't mean I would have done what you did if I had been in your shoes, but I am willing to accept that you acted in what you thought was for my best."

"You had the ring," I said, brushing a strand of her

hair back from where it clung to her tear-stained cheek. "I didn't want you to die for that quirk of fate."

"Are you going to be able to use it to get us out of here?" she asked.

Ysolde and Aisling paused their conversation to look expectantly at me.

I shook my head. "I'm a Charmer. I'm a whiz at working maze puzzles and I can unmake curses, but I can't break out of anywhere, let alone hell."

"Abaddon," Jim and Aoife said at the same time.

"We're just going to have to wait for the men to realize we've been taken by Asmodeus. I have no idea how long that will be, but I'm—"

The door was wrenched open at that moment, the passageway beyond it filled with demons.

"Come," the one nearest the door said, gesturing abruptly. "The master wishes to treat with you."

"Asmodeus is willing to bargain for the ring?" Aisling said, getting to her feet with a hand from Ysolde. It struck me at that moment that she was pregnant, not far gone, but enough that she was no doubt very concerned about the welfare of her unborn child. It made me resolve to do whatever it took to get the others out of Abaddon before I dealt with Asmodeus.

"She's got it on her finger," Aoife said, leaving the cell with a nod at me. "He can't take it off her with force."

"Huh. You learn something new every day," Aisling said, filing out behind us.

We were escorted to the room where Constantine and I had faced Asmodeus before, and sure enough, as soon as we were herded into the center of it, a door at the far end of the room opened and the dark figure of Asmodeus strolled in. He looked more preoccupied than before, although I did notice he was looking pointedly at my hand when he stopped in front of me.

Even darkened as it was, it clearly still held some power that attracted him. He gave the others a quick look before addressing me. "What do you ask of me for the ring?"

I lifted my chin a little, not enough to express arrogance (which would not be tolerated by a demon lord) but just a smidgen to give him the idea that I wasn't a pushover.

"An interesting question," I said, stalling for time. "One that I haven't thought much about. I will put my mind to it momentarily, but first you must set the others free."

"Why?" he asked. "Do they mean much to you?"

"They're my friends, yes," I said, showing a bit of exasperation in my eyes. "Of course they mean something to me. And no, torturing them won't get me to cooperate. Far from it, it will force me to use the ring to protect them and me."

He was silent for a moment, which meant my shot in the dark had found its mark. He snapped his fingers, and two wrath demons marched past us and took up spots in front of Asmodeus. I risked a glance behind us, and was interested to see that all nine wrath demons were present, along with a handful of lesser demons.

"Very well," Asmodeus said after a few minutes of speaking with the two demons. They took up a position on his right side. "I will exchange your friends' lives for the ring."

"Hold on now," I said, shaking my head. "That's not what I said, and you know it. The conditions for me to open up negotiations for the ring are that you release everyone first. Let them go, and *then* we'll talk."

He gave me a look of pure loathing that probably took a good seven years off my life. I was braced and ready for him to consign me to the most miserable of all his cells when a commotion became audible from outside the room.

Ysolde cocked her head for a moment, then smiled. "The cavalry is here," she said with a little smile.

Seventeen

The hellish nightmare began as one of the green dragons who'd just arrived in Paris stumbled through the door of Drake's home and informed the group that Aisling and some other women had been abducted by demons.

"Oh noes!" Gary said from where he was practicing wheelies. He zoomed through the open door before Constantine could stop him, yelling, "Come on, Connie! Let's go rescue Bee!"

"I told you sending them out of the room like they were truculent children was a bad idea!" Constantine snarled at Drake before running off to catch Gary.

"Let's go!" Gary demanded when Constantine picked up his truck. "What are you doing? You're going the wrong way."

"If they were taken by demons, running after them will do no good," Constantine said grimly. "We must have a plan."

"But the demons—"

"They will pay, as will their master." Constantine's voice was as hard as his heart at that moment. He didn't even have to make a mental promise to exact revenge for whoever was responsible for the abduction of the mates— it was as natural to him as breathing.

And judging by the faces of the other wyverns, they felt the same. In short time, Drake organized his green dragons into monitoring the known entrances to Abaddon, picking the likeliest one to storm.

"We will need weapons," Constantine told him, feeling calm despite the desperate need to know that Bee was safe.

"My armory is at our disposal," Drake answered, and opened the door to a walk-in closet that would have filled the heart of a medievalist with ecstasy. In it were swords of all makes and sizes, various morningstars and maces, daggers, and an array of firearms that all the dragons ignored. Guns tended to attract attention from the mortal world and weren't nearly as effective on an immortal as a blade was.

"Oooh," Gary said, following them into the closet. "Can I have a gun?"

"No. You might shoot yourself in the eye."

"I wouldn't! Promise!"

Constantine hesitated, then pulled from the wall three small daggers that in his youth would have been used to eat with, and strapped them in a fan display to the front of Gary's car. He claimed for himself a longsword, the style of which had been his favorite in centuries past.

"You will leave to me whichever demon lord is responsible for this attack," Constantine declared a half hour later as they exited from the cars that dropped them off at the entrance to Abaddon they'd chosen. In addition to the wyverns and their respective guards, there were five green dragons, all equally armed. "I do not tolerate anyone stealing Bee from me."

"On the contrary, it is *my* mate who was stolen, and she is in a delicate state of health. It is for me to avenge this act," Drake said in a low, ugly voice.

"Are you implying that Ysolde is not the most important thing in the world to me?" Baltic asked, bristling. "I died rather than live without her! The honor is mine to destroy whoever dared touch my mate."

"Aoife is the newest wyvern's mate," Kostya argued, swinging his morningstar in a manner that almost took off Baltic's head. "Therefore, she is dearer to me than your mates are to you. It is I who should take the life of the demon lord, be it Asmodeus, Bael, or some other prince of Abaddon."

The bickering that followed lasted long enough for Constantine to pick up Gary in his truck and charge into the building that housed the opening to Abaddon.

"Hey!" Kostya called out. "He's going without us!"

The dragons gathered behind him, and by the time he kicked open the door, smote the demon standing guard, and strode into the part of Abaddon that coincided with that section of Paris, he had Kostya on one side, Baltic on the other, and Drake beyond him. The other dragons streamed behind them, presenting a solid wedge that simply overwhelmed any resistance. They marched forward, swords singing as they went into action, Kostya's morningstar taking down even the most stubborn of demons.

"Whoohoo! Here we go!" Gary cheered, and immediately burst into "Pour Some Sugar on Me."

Constantine made a mental note to get Gary a music player of his own at the same time he separated an oncoming demon from his head and, on the backswing, parted another from his sword arm.

"Who has taken the wyverns' mates?" he bellowed when they reached a central square. He leaped up on a small cart and waved his sword in the air, sending black demon blood flying. "Who dares touch that which belongs to dragonkin? You!"

The demon who had come running in response to an alarm call skidded to a stop at the sight of all the dragons filling the square, and would have turned and run had Kostya not grabbed him by the back of his collar, dragging him forward.

"Who dares declare war on us?" Constantine demanded to know.

The demon, in the form of a smallish man with gold-rimmed glasses, squeaked incomprehensibly until Drake picked him up by one arm and shook him. "Where is my mate?" Drake growled, fire pouring down his body, stretching out into all points of the compass.

"I don't know! I swear to you, I don't know—"

The buildings were now all alight. Drake tossed the demon to Baltic, saying, "You are the best at torturing. Slice off bits of him until he sees fit to tell us what we want to know."

"Asmodeus!" the demon began to babble, his eyes wild as he watched the flames lick up the buildings surrounding the square. "Asmodeus sent his demons out to search for the ring because he heard Lord Bael was back. That's all I know, I swear to you upon his unholy soul—"

There was another squeak, a crash of glass, and then another cheer from Gary. "Right through the window! A fiery bull's-eye, Baltic. That's got to be worth twenty points, don't you think?"

Constantine leaped down from the cart and with the other dragons proceeded to cut their way through the attackers until they were at the gate of Asmodeus's palace. The guards at his door were easily dealt with. By the time Constantine led the way to the ballroom where he had been taken before, all the dragons were singing along with Gary.

Constantine had a moment of feeling kinship, a warm fuzzy emotion that he hadn't ever expected to feel again since he had been demoted to the role of simply a sept member, rather than its wyvern.

"This reminds me of that time when we were young in Ankara. Do you remember?" he said to Baltic. "We went up against that Mongol warlord who'd made a deal with one of the demon lords."

Baltic stopped singing long enough to smile in reminiscence. "We destroyed many demons that day. It was one of the finest battles we ever fought."

"You almost lost your right leg," Constantine pointed out. "And as I recall, you *did* lose a good part of your scalp."

Constantine touched his hair with a hand black with the blood of the demons who had tried to stop them. "My part has never been the same since. Ah. There he is."

His voice turned cold with fury when they entered the room that now held Bee and the other women, as well as Asmodeus and a number of wrath demons. Constantine strode forward, the other wyverns falling into formation alongside him.

"There, you see? I told you they were here." Ysolde smiled at Baltic, a fact that Constantine didn't particularly mind. His eyes were on Bee, checking first her face, then the rest of her to make sure she hadn't been harmed. His heart had leaped at the sight of her, giving him an odd feeling of both contentment and arousal.

The wrath demons instantly surrounded the women, but at a command from Asmodeus, they left them to form a protective circle around the demon lord.

"Are you injured?" Constantine asked, approaching Bee. Just the sight of her made his spirits lighten. "Have you been harmed in any way?"

"Hi, Bee! Look at the cool battle armor Connie made for my truck! I've run into ever so many demon ankles." Gary zipped past them to make a sweeping circle.

"Not harmed," Bee said, her eyes glowing with an inner light. "But we do have to talk."

He thought to himself just how expressive her face was—it was as if he was seeing into her soul. Her light and joy shone like a beacon that drew him with silken bonds. He wanted nothing more at that moment than to scoop her up in his arms and find the nearest bed where he could pleasure her to the tips of her adorable pink toes, but first, he had to attend to the man who had tried to steal her from him.

He turned to face Asmodeus, aware of Bee as she pressed up to his side. "Asmodeus."

The demon lord, barely visible in the circle of wrath demons, all of whom were armed with swords, watched the dragons with a blank expression. "Why do you invade my palace, dragons? What right do you have to slay my legions?"

As he was about to answer, he felt Bee take his hand, but rather than twining her fingers through his, she slid the ring onto his smallest finger.

He turned to glance down at her.

"We have to get the others out of here," she said softly, her fingers holding tight on to his hand. "Aisling is pregnant, and there's no reason they should suffer because of our actions."

It was on the tip of his tongue to ask her to what action she was referring, but Asmodeus continued in a voice that belied his annoyance. "I have no argument with dragonkin. You have attacked my minions without justification."

"You stole our mates," Drake said, his arm around Aisling. "I call that justification of the highest degree."

"A simple mistake," Asmodeus said, spreading his hands. "A miscommunication, if you will."

"A miscommunication that will cost you your life," Baltic answered, stepping forward with his sword held at the ready. "No one steals my mate and lives to tell about it."

Asmodeus rolled his eyes. "Who would I tell? I have just explained that this was a mistake. It was the mortal bearing my ring I sought, not any dragonkin."

"Regardless, you took them, and we will have our revenge," Kostya declared in a dramatic manner that reminded Constantine of Kostya's father.

"Did I ever tell you about Toldi, Kostya and Drake's father?" he asked Bee.

She gave him a look that plainly said she thought he was crazy. "No. Is it important right at this moment?"

"He was dramatic, too," he said, nodding at Kostya. "Everything was fodder for excessive declarations. He couldn't be merely hungry, no, he was starving, nigh unto death. If he was happy, the world was a paradise laid out for his pleasure. If he was sad, then all life had ceased to be important."

"Sounds like he was manic depressive." Bee frowned a little and leaned into him. "Why are you mentioning this?"

"It is keeping me distracted."

She gave him an odd look. "Why do you have to be distracted?"

"To keep from killing Asmodeus. He dared to take my mate. No being, mortal or immortal, will survive that."

Bee went very still. "I'm not your mate, Constantine."

"You are."

"Since when?" she asked, clearly a little irked. He loved that about her—just when he thought he knew how she'd react to a situation, she would surprise him.

"Since you were taken from me."

"I think I'd know if I was your mate—"

He pulled her against his chest, claiming her mouth in a way that should leave no doubt in her mind that they belonged together, that each of them complemented the other, and that joined, they would be unstoppable.

"Golly!" he heard Gary say. "They're on fire."

"Ah, so she is a mate," Baltic said dryly. "There truly is a person for everyone in this world if a dead wyvern can find a woman such as the Charmer."

Constantine allowed his fire to wrap them in its warm embrace, the act of sharing it so intimate, it again roused the need to claim her as only a wvyern could claim his mate.

"Is he going to bonk her right here in front of Asmodeus?" Jim asked.

"Hush, you," Aisling said.

Constantine knew he needed to stop. He had to deal with Asmodeus, and then he could take his time proving to Bee that she was put on the earth to spend her life with him.

He retrieved his tongue from where it was leisurely exploring her mouth, tamped down his fire, and bodily set her from him. Her eyes were soft with passion, her breath as ragged as his own, giving him immense pleasure that she felt the same way he did about their physical contact.

"If your bawdy show is over," Asmodeus said, cutting through his thoughts, "I have business with the mortal. The rest of you, as I have already said, may leave."

"This is not over," Bee told Constantine and squeezed his hand to remind him that he was now bearing the ring. Why, he had no idea, but he assumed she had a good reason for giving it to him. Perhaps she had been impressed by the manly figure he made with the demon-blood–drenched sword?

"We're not going to leave without Bee," Ysolde said firmly.

"Of course not. If we go, we all go," Aisling said.

Drake looked unhappy, but tapped his sword on the ground. "You may not have the Charmer. And we will leave, but not before we teach you for taking our mates."

Asmodeus laughed. The wrath demons laughed. Constantine growled.

"Do you think to frighten us, wyvern?" Asmodeus parted the demons and stepped forward, pausing to address the line of dragons before him. "You forget who I am. I am not some inexperienced, weak demon lord like the Guardian."

Aisling raised her chin but said nothing.

"Nor are my minions as easily overcome as those you slaughtered to get to my palace." Asmodeus's dark gaze pierced them all, but Constantine did not have Bael as a father without learning how to withstand such acts. "You come here, to my house, and threaten me with just a handful of men." He waved dismissively at the other dragons. "Begone. My time is valuable, and I do not wish to waste it on your empty threats."

"Our threats are anything but empty," Kostya said, swinging his morningstar.

Constantine lifted his sword, just as the other wyverns did. He fully anticipated that it would come down to a battle, but he hadn't realized how torn he would be between keeping Bee safe and destroying the man who had taken her from him.

"You do not have the power to do more than irritate me," Asmodeus said in a bored tone. "But if you wish to destroy yourselves, so be it."

He turned, obviously about to order the wrath demons to attack them, but instead, a voice spoke out, causing him to stumble.

"They may not have the power, but I do."

Constantine did not need to move to the side to see who spoke.

"Oh, no," Bee said in a whisper, taking his hand. "I have a bad feeling about this."

"Great. Bael's here," Aisling said, looking weary. "That's just what we need."

"Bee, if I asked you to leave, would you do it without arguing?" Constantine asked her.

She thought for a moment, then shook her head, her fingers warm against his. "No. We're in this together."

He sighed. He had a feeling she'd say that, but at the same time, he was pleased she valued him so highly that she would risk her own safety. He couldn't allow her to be harmed, of course, but until he made that point clear to her, he'd cherish the knowledge that she was, indeed, his mate, the woman who was born to complete his life. He turned to Drake. "Take the others and leave."

Drake hesitated.

"There is no sense in all of us remaining here to deal with Bael," Constantine told him.

"You seem to have forgotten my presence," Asmodeus said, his irritation clearly getting the better of him, enough that he lost his usually cool demeanor. Constantine knew well it was Bael's presence that caused this reaction; no doubt Asmodeus, while the titular head of Abaddon, knew he was no match for Bael. "I am the premier prince of Abaddon, and thus, I am the one you should remained focused on, not the former demon lord Bael. As for the other dragons, I have already dismissed them."

"Why would you dismiss them when you could destroy them?" Bael asked, shaking his head and *tsk*ing in faux dismay as he sauntered forward. "You have ever been weak against dragonkin. I will not make such a mistake when I have retaken my throne."

Constantine ignored the outburst, telling Drake in a quiet tone, "Leave, and if we are not successful, then you may handle the situation as you think best."

"Really? You have nothing better to do than challenge me for what used to be yours?" Asmodeus said, addressing Bael in what was intended to be a dismissive tone, but Constantine was well aware of the undertone of strain in the demon lord's voice.

Bael stopped in front of Asmodeus, little black tendrils of power snapping with every step. Asmodeus's aura ratcheted up a notch as well, until the air was fairly tingling with static electricity. "Your posturing will not save you. I have more power in my little finger than you will ever possess."

Drake clearly didn't want to leave, but after a look at his mate, he turned and gave his men a sharp order.

"Another time it might be amusing to encourage your delusions," Asmodeus told Bael, brushing off a bit of lint from his arm, and donning an expression of boredom, "but I have better things to do than state and restate the obvious facts. Begone before I have you thrown out of Abaddon."

With one eye on the arguing demon lords, Kostya sidled over to Constantine. "I will stay if you need me."

"That says much about your character," Constantine acknowledged. "But it is not necessary. Get your mate to safety."

He did so without arguing.

"Do you think I did not know you were behind the overthrow that sent me to the Akasha?" Bael asked Asmodeus. His eyes, in this incarnation a dark blue, now turned solid black. A sense of dread, smothering and sticky, seemed to seep out of him and cover them all. "I knew what you had planned, of course. You played into my plan perfectly."

"It was all my plan; I meant for it to happen this way," Asmodeus said in a high-pitched, mimicking voice before switching back to his normal tone. "You always say that whenever something doesn't go your way. You may try to save face with others, but it will not work here."

Bael snarled an oath in Latin that Constantine knew

well. He'd had experience of Bael losing his temper, and needed to clear the room before that happened. "Baltic, you must leave, as well."

"Yes, brother," Bael said, interrupting his bickering to shoot a look of loathing at Baltic. "Take my son with you when you run away. We wouldn't want you to have to face the shame of having to bow down to your own brother, would we?"

"Shame?" Baltic uttered a sharp laugh wholly without mirth. "The First Dragon disowned you the moment you embraced the dark power. You were removed from dragonkin and made human. What you do here has no meaning to any of us."

Bael's lip curled. Asmodeus gave a little golf clap and made a shooing gesture toward his rival. "Begone. I have business to conduct."

"Baltic," Constantine said quietly, his eyes on the demon lords. "Leave. This is not your fight."

"Nor is it yours."

"Unfortunately, it is. He is still my sire, no matter how offensive that fact is."

"And I tire of your pretentions," Bael told Asmodeus, the two demon lords now facing each other. Constantine sensed the two men were about to lock horns, so to speak, and he had no desire to witness it, let alone have others there who could be harmed.

"Go," he told Baltic.

"I see that I shall have to have you cast out of Abaddon a second time," Asmodeus said, yawning a little. He gestured toward Bael, which caused his wrath demons to move forward in a semicircle.

Bael's demons responded likewise.

Baltic hesitated, but after a searching look at Constantine, he took Ysolde's arm and escorted her out past them. He paused to say simply, "Remember the lessons we learned at the knee of our wyvern," before following the others out of the room.

"Are you sure we should leave?" Ysolde said as Baltic urged her through the door. "I could set up some spells that would help—"

"Bee . . ." Constantine spoke without turning his head.

"No. I'm staying." Her hand gripped his with a force that drove the ring into his flesh. "We're in this together."

Bael and Asmodeus were now taunting each other with slurs and various oaths.

Constantine turned to Bee, taking her other hand in his. He looked at her face, the softly flushed cheeks marked with a scattering of freckles, her eyes filled with concern. He looked beyond the obvious, and saw the shining brightness of her soul, the joy that her being seemed to exude in an aura of warmth. The stubbornness he first thought was an irritation was now a sign of her strength, her loyalty, and her dedication to righting wrongs. "If you had been born when I was, you would have been a warrior," he told her.

Her eyes widened slightly, and then she flicked a glance over his shoulder to where the demons and demon lords were squaring off. "Okay. Um. Maybe we should talk about the past another time? I think we're about to have a situation here, and I'm fairly certain that any result will not be good."

"No, it won't," he agreed. "Which is why I must ask you for your fealty."

She frowned and gave a little confused shake of the

head. "My fealty? Honestly, Constantine, I wouldn't be here if I didn't want to be—"

"Will you honor me and my sept above all overs?" he asked, urgency driving him forward.

"Your sept?" She gasped a little, her eyes now searching his. "You're asking me to be your mate? I thought I made it clear—"

"You *are* my mate. I see that now. We were wrong in assuming you weren't. But you must accept me now."

"Why?" She was smart enough not to continue to protest, a fact that made him smile a little.

"Because as a wyvern's mate, you will be immortal."

Her gaze went briefly to the demons. She watched them for a moment, then gave him a brief nod. "All right. So long as we both understand that I'm doing this simply because I don't particularly want to die right now, and when it's all over with, we're going to change back to normal mode."

"That can be discussed later," he agreed, although he had no intention of letting her go now that he knew that life would pale without her.

"Agreed." She took a deep breath. "In that case, I accept you as my wyvern, and will honor you and your sept above all others."

"As I will cherish and honor you beyond all who exist now, or will ever exist," he declared, and claimed a quick kiss before pulling one hand up and blowing a little fire over her left wrist.

"Ow!" She jerked her hand back, her gaze moving between him and the demons, who had now all pulled out swords as Bael and Asmodeus began shouting taunts. She rubbed her wrist, frowning when a tan mark resolved itself. "You branded me?"

"It is the mark of a wyvern's mate." He took a deep breath, the one all-consuming worry now eased. At least now he had given Bee a good chance to survive whatever happened next.

"It looks like a sheep," she said, giving it another quick glance.

He made a noncommittal gesture. "It was the only thing I could think of on the spur of the moment. We shall have to create our own sept, though. What do you think of indigo?"

"It's my favorite of all the Roy G Bivs," she replied.

"Excellent. We are in agreement. And now, let us deal with—"

A roar of fury erupted from Bael and, without thinking, Constantine moved in front of Bee to shield her from danger, taking a few steps forward with his sword held at the ready lest any of the demons think of attacking them rather than each other. The demons roared and lunged forward to attack their opposing faction. Asmodeus screamed orders and snatched up a sword from a fallen demon, slashing and hacking his way forward.

Bael stood still for a moment, but Constantine saw his fingers moving. As a son of the First Dragon, Bael had the ability to use arcane magic, powerful magic.

"Stand back," he said over his shoulder to Bee. "Brace yourself for another shock wave."

He really should have known his father better, he thought in hindsight a few minutes later. Bael may be many things, but a showman was not one of them, and he would not use a showy spell like an arcane blast when a simpler solution could be managed.

Bael finished weaving his spell and cast it over the

fighting demons before him. It froze them into place, including Asmodeus, who was engaged in taking down two of Bael's demons. Bael simply walked over to his nemesis, pulled out the crystal that resolved itself into the light sword, and lopped off Asmodeus's head.

Following that, he turned toward Constantine and Bee, and gave them a tight smile, his gaze moving beyond them for a moment. "And that is how you take control of Abaddon, should you ever wish to do so. Ah, but you eschewed that path, didn't you, in favor of ruling a dragon sept. How did that turn out?"

He heard a muffled gasp from Bee behind him, but couldn't turn to reassure her. Right now, Constantine was more concerned with how he could destroy the man who had given him life, the man who had taken from Constantine all that he had ever loved.

"I cannot let you proceed," Constantine said simply. He gestured vaguely with his sword to the still-frozen demons, and the pool of blood that drained from the now-lifeless Asmodeus. "What you do here is of no importance to me. If you would content yourself to ruling Abaddon, I would leave you in peace. But we both know you won't do that. Your hatred for the dragonkin is too strong, is it not?"

Bael shook his head, dissolving the mage sword back into its crystal form and tucking it away carefully before responding. "Would you not hate being cast out, to have your very nature stripped from you? Would you not wish to seek revenge for those who deprived you of everything that should have been yours?"

"You chose the dark power rather than your own kin," Constantine said, his eyes narrowed, his body braced for a sudden attack. "You wished to rule legions of demons rather than form your own sept, as all the other children of the First Dragon did. *You* chose demons over dragons— no one else. You have no one to blame but yourself if your father saw the depths of your soul and stripped your dragon nature from you."

Bael's eyes closed for a moment while he gave a soft chuckle. "Perhaps there is some truth in that, although really, what does it matter now? I have gained almost everything I need to take my rightful place as the ruler of the Otherworld. Abaddon"—he waved a hand that took in everything in the room—"is now mine. Asmodeus's ring is mine. The only thing I have left to acquire is being held by an irritating mage who thinks he has the ability to withstand my attacks. He is wrong."

"And when you have it all?" Constantine couldn't help but play devil's advocate, although he appreciated the irony of doing so in a place that most mortals thought of as hell. "What then?"

"Then, my son, the dragons will be no more. The First Dragon will see what he hath wrought, and he will weep tears of purest sorrow."

"Patricide?" Constantine gave a little shake of his head. "I know well the feeling, but in your case, it is foolish even to try. You can be killed—the First Dragon cannot."

"You do not think that the wholesale destruction of all his children, the generations of his descendants, wiped out instantaneously, will not destroy him?" Bael's face hardened. "It will destroy him as nothing else could."

Constantine judged the moment to attack to be a point where Bael would be distracted enough by visions of his own grandiosity into leaving himself open. With a "stay where you are" gesture behind his back at the thankfully silent Bee, he lunged forward, the tip of his sword carving a graceful arc through the air. He was just about to part Bael's head from his body when a noise behind him sent him spinning around.

At least twenty demons stood in silent formation, Bee held in their center, one of the demon's hands over her mouth. Her eyes were huge, pleading with him to save her. Or perhaps it was to finish Bael—knowing Bee as he did, he wouldn't be surprised if she had discounted her safety altogether and wanted him to destroy Bael at whatever the cost.

"So predictable," Bael said, taking Constantine's sword from his unresisting hand. "You were thus with the mortal who bore you, too. Do you remember? You sought to protect her in much the same manner, brashly assuming that I would be disarmed enough to allow you to harm me, when all along, I held her life in my hands. And now I hold the life of this mortal."

Bael stopped, frowned, and examined Bee more closely. "But not mortal anymore, I see. A mate? Well done, my son. Taking her life will be even more of a pleasure than taking your mother's."

Constantine snarled and leaped toward Bael, but Bee squawked, and Constantine knew without looking that she was being held as a hostage for his good behavior.

"What is this? Wisdom?" Bael's voice held a distinctly mocking tone as he strolled nonchalantly over to where Bee was being held by a knife-wielding demon. "Something I did not expect to find in you, I admit. You surprise me."

Constantine realized at that moment what Bael was

doing. He pulled back his fire, which had been threatening to escape, and struggled to present as calm a demeanor as the demon lord before him. It took a minute, but he was at last able to say evenly, "How did you know I have the ring?"

Bael smiled. It was unpleasant at best. "I have my spies. You will, naturally, give it to me for the life of your mate."

"Yes," he said without a moment's hesitation.

"Constantine! Don't—" Bee's words were cut off when one of the demons holding her lifted her off the ground by her throat.

Constantine glanced toward them, marking the two demons, but otherwise not letting any expression show. He pulled the ring off his finger and made a show of examining it. "Release my mate. Now."

Bael gestured toward the demons, who dropped Bee. She stumbled and fell to her knees. Constantine took the few steps to her side, and helped her to her feet. "Are you harmed?"

"Not really." She stopped, rubbing her throat and making a wry face at the croak that had come out. She proceeded at a whisper. "But don't do this. We can find a way around it."

"Give me the ring, and you and the woman may leave," Bael said, holding out his hand.

Constantine hesitated, then walked over to where his father stood. "My sword," he said, holding out his own hand.

Bael flipped the sword and presented it hilt first with a little bow. Constantine, without another word, spun around and lopped off the right arm of both demons who had strangled Bee. He wished he could kill them as quickly; he knew full well that they would regenerate their arms in time, but this small vengeance would have to suffice.

They screamed and would have attacked had Bael not silenced them with a command. Constantine turned back to Bael, dropped the ring into his palm, and with a hand at Bee's back, escorted her out of Abaddon.

Eighteen

"I can't believe you did that. I mean, now Bael has two powerful tools."

Constantine hushed me as soon as I spoke, nodding toward the woman driving the taxi we'd caught on the outskirts of Paris. I was so furious, I was tempted to damn the driver and make Constantine discuss the situation with me, but I took a deep breath, reminded myself that I'd taken an oath to hide the dealings of the Otherworld from mortals whenever possible, and sat back to seethe silently.

That lasted for about five minutes, at which point I asked the driver if she spoke English.

"But of course!" She smiled, her gap teeth giving her a quirky look. "I drive around many English, you know? But not so many actors, like you."

"Ah. Just so," I said under my breath, giving Constantine a sidelong look. He'd used the excuse of being a sword-bearing actor on the way to a reality TV shoot, but he wasn't looking out of the window as I expected. Instead, his gaze was directed inward.

Another five minutes slipped by before I asked him in Latin, "Why did you do it? The whole reason we went through the fealty ceremony was so that I wouldn't be vulnerable to Bael."

"Oooh, you speak the Latin, too?" the driver asked, watching us in the rearview mirror with a big smile. "It is not many people who speak it, is it not? Mostly it is written, but me, I have a penchant for languages."

Constantine sent me a warning look, but said nothing.

I fretted for another ten minutes, creating and discarding statements varying from details about why it was the sheerest folly ever to give a power ring to a ruthless man who already had more power than anyone liked, to an acknowledgment of just how wonderful I thought he was for sending all of the other dragons out of danger so he could deal with Bael alone.

And it was that last thought that led me to the realization that Constantine wasn't just a typical arrogant dragon, one who did whatever he wanted because of who and what he was. Constantine was . . . nice. The word resonated in my head, making me want to smile despite the desperate situation. He was not at all what I had pictured when I thought of the ideal man for me; he wasn't even technically alive, although his dragon fire kept him warm just as if he were.

He was thoughtful, and concerned about others, but it was more than those traits that captured my fancy. I couldn't decide if it was his quirky nature, or the way he shared both trials and joys with me, or if it was the fact that his eyes turned to molten gold when he looked at me. Possibly it was all of that and more, but I knew at that moment that I simply did not want to spend my life with any other man.

It didn't hurt that the sight of him striding into Asmodeus's ballroom with that big herking sword in hand was like something out of a *Highlander* movie—and it sent delighted chills down my arms just thinking about it.

"You're a hero," I said softly, causing him to send me another glance. I put my hand on his where it rested on his thigh. "*My* hero. And I'm very proud of you."

He set the sword aside, turned and pulled me against him, his mouth finding mine in way that made me sigh with happiness. His kisses were sweet and hot and spicy all at once, and I was about to demand he give me his fire when I realized that my fingers in his hair were alight. I tamped down so the driver wouldn't see (and I wouldn't set the taxi on fire), whimpering more than a little when Constantine broke off the kiss.

"Change of address," he told the driver, and gave her the street for the brothel.

"What—"

He kissed me again, shutting me up completely, but I wouldn't have complained even if I could have talked. I didn't even blush when the driver giggled and made a comment about lovers who couldn't wait. In fact, I ceased to be aware of anything but Constantine—the feel of him under my hands, so warm and strong and very, very different than me. His fire threatened to swamp us both, but I kept it down during the length of time it took to get to Constantine's rooms. It was a close thing, though.

He flung money at the cab driver, who laughed even

harder when we both raced into the brothel. I was so inflamed by both my passion and a need that I felt deep in Constantine, I didn't even stop to chide him about the fact that we should be meeting with the other dragons to give them the bad news and not racing to get between the sheets.

And a race it was, although at least I didn't have to worry about keeping Constantine's fire from sight in the brothel. As it was, we left a scorched trail behind us as we made our way to his room. He slammed the door shut and turned to me, but I was on him in an instant, pressing him against the door. "Dear goddess, I need you. Like, right now!"

"That is because you were taken from me," he murmured in between kisses. I kept moving, trying to get him out of his clothing as quickly as possible, so he ended up kissing my temple, my cheek, and my left ear before he growled, "Cease tormenting me and stand still so I can kiss you as right and proper."

I giggled. "Only a dragon could make kissing sound like it has rules."

"I am a wyvern. Everything I do is of a superior nature," he said, whipping my shirt off over my head before diving for my breasts. He nuzzled them, cupping my bra-clad breasts in his hands before blowing a line of fire between them.

"Right, that did it!" I yanked my bra off over my head without even bothering to unhook it, all but ripped his jeans off, and dug my fingers into his butt cheeks in order to pull him closer to me. We stumbled over to the bed, both of us trying to get the last few items of clothing off while at the same time touching, licking, and kissing all exposed body parts.

We fell onto the bed with Constantine on the bottom, clunking our heads together painfully.

"Ow," I said as I sent my tongue on a foray into his mouth.

He twisted around me, pulling off his shoes, socks, and the jeans that had gathered at his ankles before assisting me with my undies. At last we were both naked, panting, and coated with a light sheen of fire.

I straddled his hips, looking down on him with bemusement. "I don't know what's going on, or why I'm so crazy wild to make love to you when we should be adulting and telling the others what happened, but I *am* crazy wild, and evidently so are you—honestly, Constantine, did you get bigger? I don't remember you that…*erect*…before—so I'm not going to waste time talking and asking questions, and instead will go wild all over your ass."

"Again with my ass," he said, trying to capture one of my nipples in his mouth. "I am beginning to think it is an obsession with you. You may admire my ass. You may touch it. You may even rake your fingernails across it, because that is pleasing, and does not make me uncomfortable. However, that is all. Please accept the fact that I do not desire any further action therein. And while you're at it, stop squirming so that I can love you the way I wish to."

"Arrogant wyvern," I said saucily, and took his penis in both hands, an act that had him freezing beneath me. "You are so in my power now."

"Yes, yes I am," he fervently agreed, his eyes oh, so hopeful.

I smiled a slow, wicked smile, and leaned down to take just the tip of him into my mouth. He moaned, clutched the sheets, and writhed around in absolute, utter ecstasy. Although I'd never much been one for oral sex, there was something about Constantine that made me ache to taste him. And where other men tasted like...well... men, Constantine tasted like he kissed, all spicy sweetness, like a red-hot candy that sent a burn throughout my body. I wanted him, desperately wanted him, not just in a purely sexual way, but I wanted him in my life. Every day. I wanted to wake up to see him lying on his stomach next to me, and I wanted to fall asleep each night in his arms. I wanted him when he was grumpy, or bossy, or making me laugh with some silliness. I just wanted him, and it was at that exact moment I decided that even if he wanted out of the temporary mate arrangement we'd agreed to, I was going to fight to remain by his side.

"I'm falling in love with you, you irritating, annoying, incredibly wonderful man," I told him, my voice quavering a little when I admitted the truth, but if there was one motto that held true, it was not to live my life in fear. It was the reason I'd become a Charmer. "And if you think you're going to get rid of me once the situation with your father is over, you'd just better think again."

He stopped writhing, lifting his head up to glare at me. "You're stopping?"

I pinched his hip. "Dammit, I just told you I loved you! Is that all you're going to say? You're supposed to react to my statement! Appropriately, I might add."

"You did not say you were in love with me; you said you were falling in love with me. There is an important difference. Tell me when you are fully in love with me, and then I will react appropriately."

"Argh!" I yelled.

"Are you not going to finish?" he asked, looking pointedly at his penis, now waving at me quite happily.

I wrapped both hands around the base of it, and made the meanest eyes I could at him. "If you ever want to see this penis again, you'll tell me you love me."

"I love you."

"You can't say it like that—I want you to say it like you *mean* it!" I slapped my hands on his belly. His wonderful, smooth, sexy belly. "Seriously, Constantine? Is this all I mean to you—sex? Steamy, red-hot sex?"

He sighed then, the true sigh of a martyr, and pulled me upward so that his mouth could tease mine. "Do you think that I would take a mate if she didn't hold my heart?"

"We did the mate thing because you were trying to make me immortal," I protested, a lovely warm glow spreading inside me despite my protest.

"And do you think I could not have removed you from Bael's presence if all I wished to do was protect you from harm?" He shook his head. "A wyvern by himself is strong, but one with a mate at his side is stronger. And while some may think that love makes for weakness, I have always believed that it makes us stronger. Together, we can face anything."

"Oh, Constantine," I said, melting all over him. I kissed the corners of his mouth. "That was lovely. And I wholeheartedly agree—we are stronger together."

He smiled, his eyes downright molten with desire. I sat up, looking down at this man of mine, a man who was so much more than just a drool-worthy body. He was thoughtful, he was caring...and he was mine.

"So are you going to go back to what you were doing?"

he asked with a nod toward his groin, a crooked smile on his lips.

"Demanding, bossy...tsk." I slid downward, taking him in my hands again, allowing my fingers to do some exploring. "If I knew what I'd be letting myself in for..."

"You'd still have accepted me," he said, gasping as I hit a sensitive spot. And just as I was bending down to swirl my tongue around that very spot, he moved, flipping us around so fast, I wasn't aware I was on my belly until he spread my legs and positioned himself.

"Constantine!" I squealed when he thrust inside. I swear the sensation of him deep inside me made my eyes cross, and it took several seconds before I could speak again. "I wanted to be...oh, gods, yes, that is sooo good...I wanted to be on top this time."

"Later. First I must claim you as a dragon does his mate."

"Really, you mean—hoobah!" I don't know what Constantine did to kick into high gear, but whatever it was, it had my wholehearted approval. And best of all, he unleashed something in me that had me bucking beneath him, wanting nothing more than to touch him, and hold him, and even bite him. And when he bathed my back with fire, it pushed me over the edge, causing my entire body to arch like a bowstring. Muscles I didn't even know I had clenched with ecstasy, sending Constantine into his own version of paradise.

He collapsed down onto me, and time as I knew it just kind of drifted past us, leaving us in an eddy of sated happiness, not bothering to disturb us until my brain started working again. I tried moving my arms and legs, not absolutely certain they'd still work, but happily, Constantine hadn't sexed me right out of functionality.

"Christos," he swore, rolling off me.

"You can say that again." I scooted over until I was draped partly on top of him. "That was—man alive, Constantine! I've never heard of anyone being loved to death, but I'll be damned if that didn't come close to it."

"It was nice, wasn't it?" He looked smug as sin, but given the pleasure he'd just fired between us, I figured he was due it. "That is the way of dragons. Now that we are mated, I can teach you many things."

I lifted one of his hands. At the end of each finger was a long, curved, ivory-colored claw. "This is about as dragony as I like you. I hate to discriminate against your dragon form, but your human form is sexy enough for me. And speaking of that, did you notice that we had a perfectly lovely time without any of your toys?"

He grinned and gently dragged one of the claws down my spine, making me shiver in response. "I did notice. And I have nothing against enjoying you and you alone, but you must admit that variety is nice as well."

"Hmm," I said, swirling my tongue around a slightly salty nipple. "Perhaps. You may have to work at convincing me on that subject, though."

"Happily," he said. "I will add that to my list of things I wish to show you."

We lay in silence for a few minutes, me trying to gather my still somewhat scattered wits and lazily drawing patterns on Constantine's chest.

"What are we going to tell the others?" I asked at last.

I think he had been about to drift off into sleep, because he jerked beneath me. "About the ring?"

"Yes." I sat up, looking down on him and wondering

how much he had changed my life. "They're not going to be happy with us."

"Do you believe they would have thought it would turn out any other way than it did?"

I frowned. "Are you saying you knew how this was going to turn out? You knew that Bael was going to lop off Asmodeus's head—which, incidentally, will give me nightmares for years—and that his men would sneak up behind us and hold me hostage?"

"No. But I knew it would not be easy defeating Bael, and we were going into his presence with a ring that he very much coveted. I knew that such an outcome would be possible if I was not very lucky."

"And you weren't," I said sadly, feeling responsible for the situation for some insane reason.

"On the contrary, I am very lucky. I have found a mate despite having lost the only woman I thought I desired. I was wrong."

I leaned down to kiss his nose. "I was wrong about dragons, too, so we're even. But what are we going to do now?"

He tugged me down onto his chest again. "It will take immense power to defeat Bael as he is now."

"We don't have immense power," I pointed out.

"No, not even joined can we take him down. We are going to need help."

"The other dragons?"

He was silent for a long time before his arm tightened around me. "Something like that."

And annoyingly, that was all he'd say on the matter. I tried to get him to spill what he was planning, but he just said he had to think things through, and he'd tell me when he came to a decision.

"Overbearing, cavalier dragon," I said with a snort as I marched into the bathroom to take a shower. "So much for having a mate to share things with!"

"I will share my thoughts with you when I can get them in proper order," he said, putting his hands behind his head and staring up at the ceiling.

I looked back at him lying on the bed, so sexy that we'd left scorch marks on the sheets, and told myself I was crazy to tie myself to a dragon.

Sometimes, crazy is a very good thing.

Nineteen

It was almost night when Constantine greeted the red-headed man who opened the door. I couldn't remember if he was Pal or Istvan, but whoever he was, he bowed when Constantine said, "We have come for Gary."

"It is good to see you alive," was all the redhead said before standing back and gesturing for us to enter Aisling's house. "There was no trouble?"

"Oh, there was plenty of trouble. There was a hell of a lot of trouble. There was trouble coming out of our ears." I took a deep breath and entered the hall.

"It went as I expected," Constantine said, taking my hand. "Are the others still here?"

"Yes. In the sitting room." Pal or Istvan—I really should figure out which one was which—gestured toward the double doors.

One of them opened before we could reach it. Gary barreled out on his truck, now denuded of knives. "Connie!

Bee! I thought you'd never get back. Jim says that dragons have a thing about needing personal time with their mates when they get stolen, so I'm not going to feel hurt because you're wearing different clothes, although that means you must have at the very least stopped to get Bee's luggage instead of coming here to reassure me that you're alive and well, and in fact, judging by the looks on your faces, you probably blew the grounsils first before you came to fetch me."

I shook my head briefly. "We what now?"

"Blew the grounsils." Gary pursed his lips, and turned his truck to reenter the sitting room. "You know, polishing the porpoise."

"Feeding the kitty," Jim said with a nod and a wink at Gary when we followed the latter into the room. "Filling the cream donut. Stuffing the worm into—"

"And that is enough out of you, demon. Silence until I tell you that you can speak again," Aisling said, glaring at her demon.

I looked at Constantine.

One side of his mouth quirked. "I will explain to him how it is with a wyvern and his mate. He will learn not to have hurt feelings when we go off to fill the cream donut."

I pinched his arm.

"What happened? Are you two all right?" Aisling greeted us with worried looks. "Did you get rid of Bael?" She turned back to Drake, who was approaching us from the other side of the room. "I told you we should have stayed! I'm a Guardian. I could have helped them deal with Bael."

"They have not said they needed your help," Drake pointed out while at the same time giving us both piercing looks.

"Is everything all right?" Ysolde asked, joining them. She, too, looked worried.

"No," Constantine said in his usual frank manner. "Asmodeus is dead. Bael has his ring. I was unable to kill him on my own. He is too powerful, and we will need to seek the assistance of the First Dragon to rid ourselves of him. Bee is now my mate, but that is a good thing. We have decided to form our own sept and are thinking of indigo as a color. I also thought of naming ourselves the spirit drag-ons, but since Bee is not a spirit, it would not be appropri-ate. We will make Gary an honorary indigo dragon."

"Wooties!" Gary shouted, driving a triumphant circle around Constantine's feet. "I'll be the best dragon you ever had!"

"A mate?" Aisling looked startled, then happy. "How exciting, a new mate. But..."

"We thought you decided you weren't a mate," Ysolde finished for her. "What changed your mind?"

"It was me," Constantine said, not even trying to look humble. "She couldn't resist me. And my ass—she par-ticularly likes that."

"You big bullfrog," I said, elbowing him in the side. "Don't make me regret agreeing to be your mate the very same day I accept the job."

He grinned at me, and my innards all seemed to melt in a happy puddle.

"A new sept." Kostya frowned, sliding a glance at his brother. "That will have to be voted upon by the others before it can be accepted, but I do not like the idea of a sept led by a spirit."

"Pfft," I said, irritated by his reaction. How dare Kostya try to rain on Constantine's parade? "He's as solid

as you are. The only difference is that he's not alive anymore. So what's the problem with him heading up his own
sept? You guys don't have a law that says he has to be
alive, do you?"

"Bee," Constantine said sternly. "You do not have to
champion me to the weyr. Not that I don't appreciate the
fact that you want to—I do, very much so. But it is not
necessary. Besides, if there is any chastising to be done, I
wish to have the fun of doing it."

"Consider us chastised, then," Drake said, taking Aisling's arm and helping her to a chair. I thought it was a bit
funny the way he treated her like she was made of glass,
since she was, from everything I'd heard, one badass lady,
but I gathered dragons were an overprotective bunch, and
that was how they responded to pregnant women.

I slid a look sideways at Constantine.

He raised an eyebrow in response.

"You're dead."

"I am."

"Can you...uh...is all of you dead?"

He raised the other eyebrow.

I sighed and said softly, "Can you make babies if you're
a spirit? Don't look at me as if I'm crazy—I've never met a
spirit before. I know there's lots of things you can do, like
eat, and other things you need to do, like shave and brush
your teeth, but I didn't know if you had...you know...
sperm."

His gaze turned into liquid gold. "With a mortal? No.
But you are my mate. That fact may well transcend mortal
realities. We shall have to find out together whether or not
we can have children."

I leaned in close to him and said softly, "Well, if it

turns out I can get pregnant and you treat me like I can't sit down by myself when I clearly can, I will punch you in the gooch."

"I will remember that should the day arise."

"You do that."

"This is not a formal sarkany," Drake said when he had Aisling seated to his satisfaction. He gestured toward the other couches and chairs. "But it is evident by what Constantine has said that we have much to discuss. Perhaps we can have a recap of what happened after we left?"

Constantine gave it to them, almost word-for-word. Kostya muttered something under his breath about just handing over the ring without a protest, but Aoife shot him a squinty-eyed look that left him silent.

"So your plan is to ask for intervention of the First Dragon?" Drake asked, glancing at Baltic. As usual, the latter wore an expression that gave nothing away. "I am not convinced that is the right path. If the dragonkin band together—"

"He will destroy us," Constantine said tiredly. "You do not realize just how powerful he is now. He destroyed Asmodeus with one swing of the mage sword. That leaves him in control of Abaddon as well as much of the Otherworld."

"Just because he says he's the Venediger doesn't mean he really is, right?" Aoife asked.

The others shook their heads. "Claiming the position by defeating the prior occupant and stating the intention to hold the position is valid. Unfortunately, until we can remove him from the position, he is in effect the Venediger," Drake said.

"And that's bad because . . . ?" Aoife looked confused.

"It means Bael will be able to rule the Otherworld in Europe," Kostya answered her.

"Well, that's just Jim Dandy fine," I said, sighing and leaning into Constantine. We were seated on a loveseat, and despite the grim situation, I felt a certain amount of happiness just having him so close to me. "Nothing like having a deranged serial-killer demon lord ruling over you. We are in so much trouble."

"Looks like we'll have to get your father in," Aisling told Baltic. The latter made a face.

To my surprise, Ysolde made one as well. "He's *such* a pain in the patootie." She must have noticed everyone looking at her because she added with a little apologetic gesture, "Sorry, didn't realize I said that in my out-loud voice."

"How do you summon the First Dragon?" I asked Constantine, a bit nervous because I'd never been in the presence of a demigod. "Are you going to do it right now? Should I leave?"

"We will need the dragon heart," he answered.

The other dragons instantly looked away.

"Is it an actual heart?" I asked, trying not to look appalled.

"No. The dragon heart is made of shards. Those are what the First Dragon used to create the original four septs. Each wyvern holds a shard. The one I held is now in the possession of the silver wyvern." He frowned and glanced around the room. "Why is Gabriel not here?"

"It takes a while to get from Australia to France," Aisling told him. "Gabriel, being a dragon, hates portals, and May said they had some sept business to wrap up, so they'll be here tomorrow."

"You all have shards. If we bring them together, it will be enough to summon the First Dragon."

To a man, the three wyverns pursed their lips and looked unwilling to help. It took a solid half hour of arguing, wheedling, and downright demands by the women involved (myself included) to get them to agree to it.

I figured the ceremony of bringing the First Dragon to us would be something that took place late at night, in a secluded wood, or some other such dramatic setting. As it was, all that happened was Drake left to go to another room, returning with a wooden box. Kostya reached a hand into his inner pocket and withdrew a leather pouch. And Baltic gestured at Ysolde, who pulled on a chain around her neck, tugging up a small glass vial that hung next to a silver pendant.

"You had them with you all along?" I asked, all shades of incredulous. "You made us go through all that, and you guys had them on you? What the hell, people? What the serious hell?"

"Abaddon," Gary corrected, receiving a paws-up from Jim.

I gave him a look that had him backing his truck away from me.

Constantine took the shards from each of the wyverns, held them in his hands, and said simply, "Father of all dragons who ever was, who are, and who will be, we summon you."

The air in front of Constantine shimmered a little, like it was made of water, then did an odd ripple that resolved itself into the shape of a man.

I say *man*, but really, it wasn't a man. Oh, he looked perfectly normal. He had two arms, and legs, and hands and eyes, and everything that a normal man has...but there was something about his eyes that wasn't quite normal. For one, the color of his irises was kind of an old gold that appeared to be splattered with red and black and silver. His pupils were slightly elongated, not quite like a cat's, but not round like they should be. And then there was the air of something...*other*...that surrounded him.

Even the look of surprise on his face when he saw Constantine was slightly off.

"Constantine. Was I mistaken in thinking you died some five centuries ago?"

"No. I was resurrected by Ysolde." Constantine gestured behind the First Dragon, who kept his eyes firmly on his grandson.

"Ah, you are a spirit." His gaze shifted to me for a few moments. I felt myself blushing, although I couldn't think of why I'd do such a thing. "And you have a mate. How interesting."

Not *good*, or *yay for you*, just *interesting*. I started to think that the First Dragon was a bit of a jerk.

"Ysolde is here?" The First Dragon turned around slowly, smiling at Ysolde, who summoned up a welcoming smile of her own. "My child, you look as charming as ever. Baltic is here, too, I see."

"Yes," Baltic said ungraciously. He looked sour and annoyed as hell to see his demigod parent. I wanted to hug him at that moment. "I'm here. For the record, I was against Constantine calling you."

"It's nice to see you, too," the First Dragon said with a little quirk to his lips that had my irritation easing a smidgen. He glanced around at the others. Drake and Kostya both made low bows to him, murmuring something about it being an honor to see him.

"Why have you summoned me?" the First Dragon asked.

"It's Kashi," Constantine said abruptly.

The expression on the First Dragon's face went from mild amusement to absolutely nothing. In fact, it felt like everything in the world was holding its breath, waiting for a reaction.

"That name has no meaning," the First Dragon said slowly, turning back to face us.

"Bael, then. He has tried to destroy the dragonkin for the last two years, but only recently was released from where he'd been held in the Akasha. And now he is gathering power, more power than he ever had before, and he intends on wiping us out."

The First Dragon's eyelids drooped.

Constantine took a deep breath. "I tried to eliminate him in the past and failed. And now he is too strong, and will grow stronger with each passing day. We need your help in destroying him."

"What call does a demon lord have on me?" the First Dragon asked in a very neutral voice.

"He is your son," Baltic said.

"He is not." The First Dragon's gaze slid to Baltic for a few moments. "Do not think because you are a favored child that I will involve myself in your business. I did so in the past because I wished to see your line continue. Nothing more."

"Should I point out that you haven't even asked how Alduin is doing?" Ysolde asked with a touch of asperity.

The corners of his mouth twitched. "Do you truly believe that I am unaware of him? And of you?"

Ysolde flapped her hands around vaguely. "Touché. He's well, by the way. As we all are, all the dragons, now that the curse that your *other son* placed on us has been lifted by Constantine and Bee."

"Baltic," the First Dragon said wearily. "Your mate—"

"I know," Baltic interrupted, holding up his hand. "She never has displayed reverence for that which deserves it, but that does not lessen her charms."

"I love you, too," Ysolde told him, kissing his cheek. "Even if your dad is a pain in the—" She stopped and smiled brightly at the First Dragon.

The First Dragon came close to rolling his eyes, I swear he did, but evidently demigods have a standard to maintain, and he managed to simply lift a hand in a graceful gesture of refusal. "This fight you speak of is not mine." His gaze dropped onto Constantine. "Nor is it yours alone, Constantine of Norka. It is not the fight of the dragonkin—you have work to do, yes, but others must do what you cannot. Only one who is mortal-born can defeat a demon lord. So it is, and so it has always been."

"Who?" I couldn't help but ask, driven to it by frustration. The man was a friggin' god, for cripes sake! Why wouldn't he just step in and stomp his former son to smithereens? "What mortal? And how is he or she supposed to defeat Bael to begin with? Constantine's tried, and if he couldn't do it, I don't understand how a mortal is supposed to do it."

"And that will be your failing if you do not correct it," the First Dragon told me. He started to fade, just like he was made up of millions of tiny light particles that began to go out. "Seek a warrior, one who can undo that which gives Bael strength. Only then will you restore the weyr."

"What on earth does that mean?" I asked, wanting to shake the annoying man, but he continued to fade, his odd, inhuman eyes on Constantine the last thing visible before they just blinked out of existence.

"What an annoying, deliberately obtuse man," Ysolde said, biting the ends off of the words. "Now I remember why we never get in contact with him. *'And that will be your failing if you do not correct it.'* Seriously, Bee, he used to say the same sorts of cryptic things to me, and it drove me nuts! I was forever trying to figure them out, and to this day, I still don't know what half of the things he told me really mean."

"I think I irritated him," I said somewhat apologetically. I was new to the dragon world, after all. "I should have been a bit more polite, but after all we've gone through..." I took a deep breath and stopped from saying more.

"We have work to do," Constantine said slowly, clearly mulling over the First Dragon's comments. "A warrior who can undo that which gives Bael strength. A mage, do you think?" he asked Baltic.

The latter shook his head after a moment's thought. "Bael considers himself a mage of sorts. And he was born a black dragon."

"As were we all," Kostya said with a wry twist of his lips.

"Really? I thought you were a green dragon?" I asked Drake.

"I am. But my father was a black dragon. My green dragon ancestors claimed me as their own, however."

"It's a long story," Aisling said, giving her husband an odd look. "Drake's a special sort of dragon. They call them reeves, and I have a whole lot to say about that because it means he can take another mate if I die, but he knows full well if he even *thought* of it, I'd haunt him to the end of his days and make his life a living hell."

He kissed her hand, and murmured something in her ear that had her giggling. "So what do we do now?" Aoife asked.

Everyone looked at Constantine. Slowly, as if he was still thinking it all through, he answered, "Bael's source of power is the items he will use to make new tools—the light sword and Asmodeus's ring. To unmake them, we'd need an alchemist. But those don't exist anymore."

I froze, watching Constantine.

"They do, I think," Drake said, turning to Aisling. "I heard there were two still in existence. Did not Dr. Kostich say that to you at one time?"

"Not me, but to May."

"Dr. Kostich?" Constantine asked. "The archmage?"

"Yes, he rules the Otherworld. He's a big pain, but that's a long story," Aisling told him. "All I remember hearing was something about his quintessence, and why it was so valuable, and that it had taken a Welsh alchemist years and years to make. And May asked why he didn't get more alchemists making them, and he said there were only two that he knew of. Alchemists, that is."

"I thought alchemists were like..." Aoife waved her hand around vaguely. "Like old-time chemists. Didn't they try to turn lead into gold and all that jazz?"

"That's the mortal version," Aisling told her. "They were half mystics, half chemists who didn't know what they were doing. The Otherworld version is different. They can unmake magic."

"How do you unmake magic?" Aoife asked, shaking her head a little.

Aisling shrugged. "The same way that Bee unmakes curses. You just...you know...break it down to tiny little bits. Alchemists used to be popular because they could take a simple bit of magic like a spell, and break it down into base matter that was used to form super powerful things like Dr. Kostich's quintessence."

"And a quintessence is...?"

"A priceless bit of magic material that can do just about anything," Ysolde told her. "It can bring something back to life. It can wipe out a continent. It can create matter from nothing. It's literally priceless, and one of the reasons there are only a couple of alchemists around anymore. Most of them died because unscrupulous people would hold them hostage, forcing them to make quintessence by threatening to kill people they loved."

"And if we need one of those guys to unmake Bael's tools-in-progress..." Aisling gave a little shudder. "We're up shit creek, we really are."

My heart dropped at that. Panic hit me then, panic and a strong desire to protect my little family, now grown larger to include Constantine and Gary. I bit my lip, suddenly overwhelmed with the desire to be away from it all, and alone with Constantine. The happenings of the day were just too much for me.

Constantine must have sensed something, because he pulled me closer, whispering in my ear that we would soon be done, and then we could leave. "I will allow you to have your way with me this time," he added, his voice rubbing against me like silk on my naked flesh. "You may even use my faux-fur–lined handcuffs if you like."

"Deal," I said. "And perhaps I might even try those nipple teasers on you."

"We are leaving now. We're done!" Constantine said abruptly.

"We are?" Drake looked a bit confused. "But we still have things to discuss. How will we find an alchemist?"

"Who is the mortal warrior we need to take down Bael?" Ysolde added. "We need to talk about that, too."

"We can't just leave Bael out in the world, running amok," Kostya agreed. "We have to find the mortal that the First Dragon spoke of, the only one who can destroy Bael. We have to find an alchemist to unmake the magic tools."

I leaned into Constantine, drawing strength from him, but more, drawing a bone-deep satisfaction. It was like our souls fit together perfectly, one complementing the other. Separately, we held power unto ourselves, but together... I smiled up at him. I'd do just about anything to guarantee a future with my ghost dragon. Reluctantly, I admitted to myself that there was no other way but to admit the truth about my brother. "I think I have the answer to all the problems you've mentioned, Kostya."

"You do?" Aoife looked surprised. I braced myself against the hurt that I knew I was about to inflict.

"Yes. We have a brother, Aoife and I. His name is Rowan. He's a social anthropologist, working in Brazil this year." Everyone was watching me now, but it was Constantine's eyes that I met; his lovely dark amber eyes always seemed to pull me in and bathe me in a warm glow of happiness. "He's also one of the two alchemists alive. And he's mortal. You know him by a different name, though."

The impact of that statement took a few seconds to sink in, but Constantine got it instantly. "Dragon Breaker," he said.

The other dragons gasped.

I nodded, praying that Rowan would understand when he found out I was the one who turned their eyes to him. "But it's not like what you think."

"Think?" Drake snorted. "We all know what the Dragon Breaker did. He killed four innocent dragons. The First Dragon bound danegeld to him for that crime, and told him he must repay the dragonkin for what he took from us, and yet the debt has not been repaid."

"It's not like that," I started to say, but the dragons all began talking at once, arguing about whether or not they should involve someone as heinous as the infamous Dragon Breaker in the plan.

Everyone but Constantine. To my surprise, he smiled, leaning down to bite my lower lip, sliding his tongue along it to take away the sting. "Do not despair. Your brother's actions have nothing to do with you."

"He's not guilty of killing those dragons. You have to believe me. Honestly, I think he did the wrong thing by going into hiding, but it was his choice. I just hope he forgives me when he finds out I'm the one who told you all about him."

Constantine struggled for a moment, clearly wanting to believe me, but finding it difficult. "If he helps destroy Bael's power, then I will be satisfied."

I leaned into him, wishing there was another way. "Just don't let the past bias you against him. He's a nice man, and I know he'll help us once I explain the situation."

"For your sake, it will be so."

"Thank you." I pressed a kiss to his lips, feeling his fire roar to life.

His smile broadened. "Definitely I will let you use the nipple clamps on me tonight. And afterward, I will get on my knees and thank the gods and goddesses for sending you into my life."

"Such a drama llama," I said with a little laugh, and kissed him as I had wanted to ever since I met him.

The others were talking excitedly, asking a hundred questions, and getting no answers as Constantine and I left the room, arm in arm, with Gary following behind.

"Remind me to introduce you to Ramona," Constantine said as we walked out of the front door.

"Who's that?" I asked, wondering if I should be outraged. "You know that I'm not into threesomes, don't you?"

"Ramona's his blow-up sheep," Gary said, pulling a little spinning wheelie on the sidewalk. "He keeps her in a special bag stuck under the bed. I thought someone at the brothel had left it there by mistake, but Connie said it was his."

"Really, Constantine?" I asked as we followed Gary. "A blow-up sheep?"

"I was lonely," he said, trying to look innocent, and failing. Dear goddess, how I loved him. "I didn't know you. I didn't know I would ever find you. I needed comfort, and Ramona was there."

"A *blow-up sheep*," I repeated.

"She's quite comely. She has stockings and everything," he countered, his mouth twitching.

"Do you seriously think I'm going to want to invite a blow-up sheep to romp with us when we're filling the cream donut?"

"I would," Gary said, and zoomed ahead. "Oooh, taxi. I'll grab him, shall I?"

I sighed with a mixture of happiness and resignation. "That poor mortal driver."

"We'll tell him Gary is a movie special effects prop that we're trying out. Now, about tonight...how do you feel about warming lotions? Feathers? Where do you stand on the subject of vibratory devices?"

We strolled on, happy as a spirit dragon, his mate, and a disembodied head could be.

A foe to all of dragonkin, an alchemist known as the Dragon Breaker is about to undergo the transformation of a lifetime. But his love for a beautiful woman may change him even more…

Please see the next page for a preview of

Dragon Soul.

One

"I'm sorry for waking you. Would this happen to be your vibrating butterfly?"

The man I was crouched next to squinted at me even though the lighting on the plane had been turned down so as to be conducive to sleep. His face scrunched up even more when I gingerly held up a bright pink object wrapped in a crinkly plastic package, and his voice, when he spoke, was thick with sleep. "What? Who are you?"

"I'm so sorry I woke you," I apologized again, shifting a little when my calf muscle began to complain about the fact that I had spent the last twenty minutes squatting my way up the first-class aisle on the flight from Los Angeles to Munich. "My friend—really, she's more my charge than my friend—appears to have mysteriously acquired this object from someone on this side of the plane, and I wondered if it was you."

His eyes focused on the sex toy. "The hell? Do you think I'd use something like that? I'm a man!"

"Oh! That's mine, George," his seatmate said with a little giggle. She flashed him an embarrassed little smile, and said in a rush, "I thought we could try it out once we got to the hotel. Second honeymoon and all."

I assumed the last part was aimed at me, and I duly dropped the toy into her outstretched hand with a murmured apology and a loud plastic rustle that seemed overly loud in the hushed cabin.

"Although I don't know how it fell out of my luggage…" She glanced upward at the overhead bin as if expecting to see her belongings hanging out of the opened door.

I gave her a wan smile and stood, gratefully stretching my cramped muscles. "My client must have mistaken your bag for hers. Sorry to disturb you both."

The husband grumbled in a low tone to his wife, but I didn't wait around to hear how she was going to explain her plans for their stay in Germany—I had an elderly lady to watch, and as the last few hours of the flight had shown, I had to watch her like a hawk.

I hurried to the galley area between the first-class section and coach, and slipped in with a couple of flight attendants busy with beverages for the few folks who were still awake. Next to them, seated on a small pull-down emergency seat, sat a tiny old woman, her hair a mass of white curls and her brown face bearing a myriad of wrinkles and crisscrossed lines. She bore an air of fragility and profound age that made one think she was crumpling in on herself, but I hadn't been with her for half an hour before I realized just how false that impression was. "Here I am, back again. Have you enjoyed your visit with the flight attendants?"

The old lady, clutching a can of Coke and gleefully stuffing crackers into her mouth, shot me a look out of eyes the color of sun-bleached jeans. "I told them you took away my pretty pink shiny, but that I forgave you because you're taking me to my beau."

I smiled the smile of a martyr—even if my martyrdom was short-lived, I already felt very much at home with it—and said gently, "That sexual device was not yours, even if it was a nice shade of pink. I'm glad you've forgiven me for giving it back to its rightful owner, although I didn't know you were meeting a gentleman friend in Cairo. Your grandson…er…drat, I've forgotten his name. All he said was that you were going on a cruise."

"I have been kept from him for a very long time," she said, confusingly scattering pronouns along with a few cracker crumbs. "But you will take me to him. And you will find me more shinies."

I spread my smile to the nearest attendant, who earlier had taken pity on me and offered to babysit while I returned the pilfered object. It was the second item I'd had to return since I picked up my charge at an L.A. hotel—the first had been a watch that I had seen Mrs. P pluck from some unwary traveler's bag. "Thanks so much for your help."

"Oh, it was no problem, Sophea," Adrienne the flight attendant said in a chirpy voice that perfectly suited her manner. "We enjoyed having Mrs. Papadom…Mrs. Papadonal…"

"Mrs. Papadopolous," I offered. "She likes to be called Mrs. P, though."

"Yes! Such a difficult name." A look of horror flashed over her face when she realized what she'd said, and she hastily added, "But an interesting one! Very interesting. I like names like that."

"It's not my name," Mrs. P said, letting me assist her to her feet. "It never *was* my name. He gave me the name. He thought it was amusing."

"I'm sure Mr. Papadopolous had an excellent sense of humor," I said soothingly, giving Adrienne a little knowing look. She'd been on my side ever since I explained how Mrs. P had used my visit to the toilet to blithely rifle through the bags of fellow sleeping passengers. I herded my charge toward the last row of seats, saying softly, "Now, would you like to watch another movie, or do you want to have a little rest? I think a nap is an excellent idea. We still have another five hours before we land in Germany, and you don't want to be tired when we get there, do you?"

Mrs. P turned her pale blue eyes to me. "I like gold. You must like gold, too. Isn't it pretty when it glistens in the sunlight?"

"Uh ... pardon?"

She gave me a beatific smile. "I knew your husband when he was a youngling dragon, still learning to control his fire."

"Dragon?" I gawked at her, not sure I heard the word correctly.

"Yes. He has much better manners than you. He would never treat me as if I have no wits left to call my own."

I stared at her for a few seconds, unsure of how to take that. "I didn't ... I apologize if I seemed rude, Mrs. P, but my husband was most definitely not a dragon. And for the record, I'm a widow."

She said nothing, just pursed her lips a little, then slid me a gently disappointed look.

"As in, my husband died almost three years ago. And yes, he had lovely manners, but he's not around anymore, and in fact, when I met him, it was the first time he'd been to the U.S. He spent most of his time in Asia running a family business. Let's get you back into your seat. Hello again, Claudia."

The last sentence was spoken when we approached the woman across the aisle from our seats, a pleasant woman in her mid-forties who was on her way to visit family in Germany. She had been very chatty during the earlier part of the trip, taking an interest in my plight when I hurriedly explained to her that Mrs. P was an elderly lady in need of watching. When we stopped at our row, she was holding a book on her lap.

"Ah, you have found the owner of the pink sex toy?" she asked in a voice that was very slightly German. She tipped her head in question and I got Mrs. P settled in her chair.

"Yes, thankfully. It was owned by a lady on the other side." Wise to the ways of Mrs. P, I made sure to buckle her in before relaxing my guard.

"I will watch a movie," Mrs. P graciously allowed. I got her headphones plugged in, and flipped through her movie choices, stopping when she said, "That one. No, the one with the male dancer. Did I tell you that I was a president's hoochikoo girl?"

"Yes, you mentioned that when I picked you up at your hotel."

"I was quite the dancer in those days, you know. I received many shinies for my dancing, many pretties that I kept hidden. Men used to ogle me when I danced, and afterward, they gave me things." She cackled quietly to herself. "It was a long time ago, a very long time ago, but I remember it well. I remember each of the shinies given to me, although I don't remember all of the men. A few I do remember, but they were the ones who gave me the best pretty things. I won't tell you the president's name, because I never was one to kiss and tell, but one time, he wanted me to pretend that he was a walrus—he had a very big mustache—and that I was a little native girl, and so we got naked while he took a tub of lard—"

"I'm sure you were an awesome dancer," I interrupted, trying to expunge the sudden mental image she had generated, "but as I think I mentioned in L.A., for you to have been that particular president's...uh...companion would mean that you are a very old lady indeed."

Still chortling at her reminiscences, she patted my knee with a gnarled hand. "Appearances can be deceiving. You remember that, and you'll survive just fine."

Survive? I didn't realize that was in question. I gave her another suspicious glance, but she was settled back happily watching her movie. Mrs. P had a way of inserting an unexpected word into a sentence that made me feel uncomfortable. And then there was her mention of knowing my late husband...

"She is quite the character, isn't she?" my seatmate said with a benign smile directed past me toward Mrs. P.

"Hmm? Oh, yes, she surely is that."

"And you said you are going to Egypt together?"

"Cairo," I agreed. "My husband's cousin...uh...man, I really can't think of his name...he asked me if I'd escort Mrs. P to her Nile River cruise since he couldn't take her, and she's a bit frail and could use a helping hand."

"Oh, that sounds so very exotic," Claudia said with a

little sigh. "I can only imagine how wonderful a cruise up the Nile would be."

"Down it, actually." I made an apologetic gesture. "The Nile flows north, so the ship sails downriver."

"How fascinating," she said politely, then added, "Will your husband be joining you there?"

I leaned forward and pulled my own book from the bag under my seat, using the time to put a placid expression on my face. "My husband passed away a few years ago."

"Oh, I'm so sorry," she said, her expression contrite. "I really put my foot in it, did I not? Please forgive me."

"There's nothing to forgive. Jian...my husband...we weren't married very long." Her face was filled with sympathy, so I did something I seldom did—I unburdened. "In fact, he died less than an hour after we were married. We didn't even get a wedding night together. It was...it was so horrible."

"You poor thing. How terribly tragic." She leaned across the aisle to give my arm a sympathetic pat. "Do you mind if I ask what happened? If you do not wish to talk about it—"

I glanced over to make sure Mrs. P was still settled, and was relieved to see her eyes closed. "I don't mind at all, but there's not too much to it. I met him while I was working as a tour guide in Chinatown. The one in San Francisco."

"How very interesting. I don't think I've ever met a tour guide."

"I'm not one anymore. I really got the job because I look Asian—well, I suppose I *am* Asian, or at least partly so, according to the orphanage where I was left as a baby—and the owner of the tour company said tourists liked authenticity." I shrugged, but I wasn't certain if I was dismissing the eight months I spent showing tourists around, or the fact that I didn't know my own parents' ethnicities. "One day, I bumped into a handsome man on the sidewalk in front of one of the shops we take the tourists to, and four days later, we were getting married at the courthouse. Unfortunately, there was a drunk driver outside, and as we were crossing the street to the parking lot…" I swallowed back the harsh memories. "Jian knocked me out of the way so I wasn't hurt, but he…he wasn't so lucky."

"How very tragic," she repeated. "I'm so sorry for your loss."

"Thank you," I said, swamped with remembered guilt. "If he hadn't taken the time to push me out of the way…"

Her hand moved again, as if she wanted to give me another reassuring pat, but stopped herself this time. "You can't think like that. What ifs will always plague you if you let them. I'm sure your husband did what he thought was best."

"Yes," I agreed sadly, struggling with the secret fact that although I'd fallen hard for Jian, we had been together such a short time that I wasn't sure anymore if I was grieving for his loss, or for losing our potential life together. "It's been a hard couple of years. He wasn't American, you see, and I had no idea who his family were in China, and no way to contact them. I tried to go through the Chinese embassy, but they just said they had no record of him. I even hired a private detective, but he drew a blank as well, saying that Jian must have come into the country illegally."

"Oh, my. That doesn't sound…" She bit off the rest of her comment, no doubt aware it was less than polite.

"No, it wasn't good. There I was, newly widowed to a man I barely knew, with no idea of who his family was, or how to find them. I had quit my job to marry him, and the owner of the tour company was so pissed, he refused to take me back. Then things just kind of went to hell in a handbasket when the police were asking who Jian was, and why I had married him so quickly, and on and on."

"You really have been through it," Claudia said, stretching out and giving me another sympathetic arm-pat.

I shook off the old but familiar memories. "I have, but I feel like it's time to put that behind me. I'm taking this job as an omen that things are going to turn around for me." I gave her what I thought of as my brave smile. "And even if I don't get to actually go on the Nile cruise, I will get to see Cairo. I'll have a day there before I have to fly back home."

To what? A little voice in my head asked. *Back to the couch that your best friend lets you sleep on because you don't have a job, or money, or any sort of a life?*

I ignored the voice. I'd had long experience doing so after Jian's death.

"I'm sure that will be a lot of fun," Claudia agreed, and picked up her book.

I stared at mine for a while, not really seeing the words, but too tired to care. Memories of the events of the last ten hours flitted through my brain. Meeting Mrs. P at the hotel. Realizing right away that she had more character in her little pinky than most people have in their entire bodies, which was quickly followed by the awareness that her pinky—as well as her other nine fingers—was extremely sticky. And then there were the tales of her wild youth, with which she regaled me during the ride to the airport, and which I had a feeling were told in an attempt to shock me.

The drone of the engines and white noise of the air circulating through the plane lulled me into a half-sleep. I must have dozed off because one moment I was mentally wandering in a bleak landscape made up of a pointless life, and the next I realized that Claudia was gone, and a strange man was leaning across me with one hand stretched out toward the sleeping Mrs. P.

"Hey!" I said on a gasp, instinctively jerking backward against my seat. "What are you doing?"

The man's head turned, his dark eyes narrowing on me. There was something about his face that wasn't... right. It was his eyes, I think. The pupils in them were elongated, like a cat's. That and there was a sense of doom about him that had part of my mind screaming warnings.

"You have caused us enough trouble," the man hissed, his voice pitched so low that only I could hear it. "Do not interfere again."

That's when I saw a glint of metal in his hand. I didn't pause to think about how the man had managed to get a knife on board the plane; I simply reacted to a threat to a relatively nice—if somewhat confused—old lady who was in my charge.

"Terrorist!" I squawked, simultaneously pulling up my knees and using them along with my hands to shove the man into the seat in front of us. "Help! Air Marshal! Someone help!"

He hissed again, not a normal sucking in of air, but an animalistic hiss, and jerked away. At least that's what I thought he did, but I realized there was a second man beyond him, one who had evidently grabbed Hissy

Narrow Pupils by the back of his jacket and pulled him off us.

I checked Mrs. P quickly to make sure she hadn't been harmed, but her eyes were closed, her mouth opened a smidgen as she gently snored, and one earbud dangled free of her ear. Anger roared to life in me, sending me lurching to my feet to where the two men were standing.

"That man tried to stab my old lady!" I snarled, jabbing a finger toward the hissing man. He stood with his back to the dividing curtain, his head down as if he was about to charge, but the other man had a fistful of his jacket. "Are you an air marshal? I hope you arrest him, because he was clearly about to attack an innocent passenger."

The second man turned his head slightly, just enough that he could look at me. He was a few inches taller than me, had short, curly dark auburn hair, and gray-green eyes framed with the blackest eyelashes I've ever seen. It's like someone had dipped them in coal. "I don't think that's very likely, do you?"

"What do you mean it's not likely? I saw it!"

The green-eyed stranger considered the other man for a moment before turning back to me. "Why would he wait to kill her on a plane when he could have done so at any time?"

"What is going on here?" Adrienne pushed aside the curtain, accompanied by two male flight attendants. "Who was yelling? Is something the matter with Mrs. P?"

"No, but only because I woke up in time to catch this man trying to stab her. And then the air marshal here heard me and grabbed him."

"Stab?" Adrienne asked. One of the other flight attendants said, "Air marshal?"

"Yeah, him." I nodded toward my green-eyed savior. "And yes, stabbed. As in, with a knife. You can see it in his hand." I gestured to where a bit of metal glinted in the man's hand. He lifted his head at that, and shot me a look with so much malevolence, I swear there was a faint red glow to his dark irises.

Handsome Green Eyes released his hold on the jacket and took a step back, shaking his head a little. "I'm afraid the lady is confused. I'm not an air marshal."

"No, he's not. He's a passenger," Adrienne said with a little frown.

"Well, whoever you are, you stopped that man from stabbing my little old lady," I told him before adding to Adrienne, "I hope you guys have some restraints on the plane for nutballs."

"I have no knife," Mr. Hissy said, holding out his hand.

I stared in confusion at the curved metal bracelet that sat on his palm. The silver crescent, which was designed to resemble a twisted braid, glittered even in the dim lighting of the plane. It was very pretty, but not in the least bit deadly.

"Wait . . . that's not what you had in your hand . . . I could have sworn it was a knife . . ." I frowned, trying to make sense of it all. Had I seen a knife, or did I just assume the man was attacking Mrs. P?

Adrienne turned to the green-eyed man. "Did you see a weapon, sir?"

"No." His gaze flickered toward me for a moment, then away again. "I heard the lady complain about this man assaulting her, and was about to ask if I could be of assistance when he retreated."

"I thought it was a knife—" I stopped myself and made

a wry face. "I guess I just saw a bit of metal and assumed that's what it was. I apologize for accusing you of trying to attack Mrs. P. Although... why were you trying to put a bracelet on her?"

"The lady dropped it, and I was simply returning it to her," Mr. Hissy said smoothly, then handed me the bracelet before he made a little bow to the flight attendants. "Since you are acting as the lady's guardian, I will give it to you to return to her. Now, if I may return to my seat...?"

"I do apologize for the confusion and any inconvenience you may have suffered..." Adrienne's subdued voice drifted off as she and one of the flight attendants escorted the man back to his seat, located several rows forward.

"He looked like he was attacking her," I explained to the remaining flight attendant and the handsome man. "He was leaning across me to get to her. What would you have thought if that had been you?"

"I would have asked the gentleman," the flight attendant said gently, then with a little purse of his lips, returned to the coach section of the plane.

I turned to the remaining man, about to thank him for the assistance that it turned out I didn't need, but simply watched in silent amazement as he plucked the bracelet from my hand, saying with an unreadable look, "I'll take that. I'm sure there's some sort of nasty binding spell on it, and we wouldn't want any accidents, would we?"

He walked away without another word, leaving me staring in disbelief. Binding spell? I opened and closed my mouth a couple of times, tempted to accost him, but decided I'd better not. Perhaps I'd misheard him, or perhaps he was not quite all there…either way, since I didn't have the slightest belief in the strange narrow-pupiled man's story that he was returning Mrs. P's bracelet—one that she hadn't been wearing—I decided that I'd just let it go and forget about the whole episode.

I didn't, of course, and when Claudia returned from her visit to the toilet, I told her in a near whisper of the happenings. She agreed that it was most startling to be woken up in such a manner, but didn't seem to think anything odd was going on.

"You said you were certain the bracelet didn't belong to Mrs. Papadopolous, so does it matter if the other man took it? Perhaps it was his to begin with, and the other man was mistaken in attributing it to your employer."

"But then why didn't he say that? And what was that business with a binding spell?"

"You must have misheard him." She pulled out her book again. "Perhaps he was trying to save you from any further embarrassment."

That shut me up on the subject, and pretty much for the rest of the trip. I sat vigilant for the remaining hours of the flight, too embarrassed about raising a fuss over nothing to relax, and yet at the same time, oddly suspicious. What was that man doing leaning over me? Why had Mr. Handsome walked off with the bracelet without so much as a "do you mind?" And was it just paranoia to wonder if seatmate Claudia had disappeared into the bathroom at the ideal moment for an attempted attack on Mrs. P?

Too far, my mental sage warned. *You'll start seeing conspiracies everywhere if you go down that path.*

Fortunately for my peace of mind—what was left of it—Mrs. P slept the rest of the way to Munich.

You just have to get her through a change of planes, and then onto a ship in Cairo, my sage pointed out. *How hard could that be? Do that one little thing, and you'll pocket a cool two grand, which will give you a start to fighting your way out of a dreary future, frustrating talks with the unemployment office, and an all-around loveless existence.*

Unbidden, my gaze traveled along the rows of seats until it settled on the head crowned with short auburn curls.

My so-called savior was dressed casually in clothing that wasn't in the least bit flashy, but still gave off that subtle whiff of money. A navy blue blazer covered up a shirt in a lighter shade of blue, which was tucked into a pair of black chinos. Sharply creased chinos. This was a man who exuded quiet self-confidence and absolute comfort in his own skin.

Even the fact that he wore lace-up dark gray, somewhat-scarred boots rather than shoes didn't ruin that impression. I was musing on what sort of man he was, that he was so with it and together, yet marched around an airport wearing a pair of boots that would be more comfortable striding across a moor, when he must have felt my unabashed scrutiny, because his head turned and he glanced back at me.

Our gazes met in a way that left me breathless. My first impression of him had been one of chilly disinterest, but as I held his gaze, something kindled in the depths of those stormy green eyes, a brief flash of amusement that had me feeling strangely warm. One side of his mouth twitched, and he tipped his head a fraction of an inch in acknowledgement of...what? Awareness that I was clearly staring at him? Or perhaps it had something to do with our interaction with the nasty hissy man?

He turned back to the book he held, leaving me feeling oddly bereft.

The blush I had been working on faded as I stared at the back of his head, admitting that it was just too bad I wasn't going to see Mr. Bracelet Thief again. Those cool gray-green eyes combined with an air of mystery left my mind wandering down all sorts of paths, and not all of them were PG.

Book one of the Dragon Fall series

YOU FLIRT WITH FIRE. . .

For Aoife Dakar, seeing is believing - and she's seen
some extraordinary things. It's too bad no one else
believes her claim that a supernatural murder occurred
at an outdoor fair. Returning to the scene for proof,
Aoife encounters a wise-cracking demon dog. . .and a
gloriously naked man who can shift into a dragon and
kiss like a god. Now thrust into a fantastical world
that's both exhilarating and terrifying, Aoife is about to
learn just how hot a dragon's fire burns.

WHEN YOU DATE A DRAGON

Kostya has no time for a human woman with endless
questions, no matter how gorgeous or tempting she is.
He must break the curse that has splintered the dragon
clans before more of his kind die. But his powerful
attraction to Aoife runs much deeper than the physical -
and there may be more to her than even his sharp dragon
eyes can see. To survive the coming battle for the fate of
his race, he needs a mate of true heart and soul. . .

Available from Hodder in ebook and paperback

ISBN: 978 1 473 61112 2

Book one of the Silver Dragons series

The heat is on . . .

Despite her unique ability to protect herself by
hiding in the shadows, May's on the run for breaking
Otherworld law. And she's also in hiding from her
demon boss, Magoth, who is absolutely determined
to seduce her.

But then May meets Gabriel. The most gorgeously,
broodingly, handsome piece of trouble you can
imagine. Sparks fly – quite literally – when she
discovers he's actually a shapeshifting dragon.
And the passion that burns between them makes it
look like he could be the one to take her out
of the shadows for good.

That is, until Magoth orders May to steal one of
Gabriel's treasures. And she really does have to decide
if she's up to playing with fire . . .

Available from Hodder in ebook and paperback

ISBN: 978 0 340 99302 6

Book two of the Silver Dragons series

The sparks are flying . . .

Being held hostage by a demon lord is getting considerably chilly, especially when May Northcott's heart still burns for Gabriel Tauhou, the flaming-hot leader of the silver dragons.

Destined to be together and yet pulled apart . . . will there ever be a way to overcome what separates them without disaster?

Thankfully Gabriel has a plan to rescue his beloved mate. But it's risky – and would also force May to become a pawn in a very dangerous game involving hell, fire and all of humanity, in order to secure her freedom.

She insists she'd do anything to be with Gabriel. But if the deal falls through and things get too hot, will she be able to withstand the blaze? Or will her life go up in smoke?

Available from Hodder in ebook and paperback

ISBN: 978 0 340 99301 9

Book three of the Silver Dragons series

May Northcott is at the end of her tether. Her demon
boss has moved in and is making life hell. Her
scorching hot dragon lover seems to think everything
can be solved with a fiery kiss. And worse still, she's
being shadowed by her ditsy twin sister – a naiad
who simply can't seem to stay out of trouble.

The arrival of a nearly-dead man on May's doorstep
could be the final spark that sets light to their
tinder-box world. And with dragon war imminent, it's
looking increasingly like it will be up to May (and her
watery shadow) to stop it before the fire consumes
them all, and their lives end up in smoke . . .

Available from Hodder in ebook and paperback

ISBN: 978 0 340 99300 2